"You are badly in need of money. I have a great deal of it."

Catherine felt the color flooding her face gain. "I hope I am not so mercenary."

"No, I don't perceive you as mercenary—the word I would use would be *desperate*." He waited patiently for a reply.

Catherine struggled with warring emotions. He was right—her situation *was* desperate. Still, she balked at being forced into anything, let alone a marriage she didn't want to a man she hardly knew and had no hope of understanding. She took refuge in anger, a much stronger and more comfortable emotion than desperation.

"And you wish to take advantage of my predicament?"

Caldbeck's expression never changed. "I simply propose a mutually beneficial arrangement."

"And what do *you* hope to gain?"

"Your beauty, your energy, your superb elegance. You...warm me..."

Patricia Frances Rowell lives in the woods of northern Louisiana with her husband, Johnny, in a home they built themselves. There they enjoy visits from their collective seven children, numerous children-in-law and eight grandchildren, as well as making friends with the local wildlife. You are invited to visit her website at http://patriciafrancesrowell.com

**Mills & Boon® Historical Romance™
is delighted to welcome new author
Patricia Frances Rowell**

A PERILOUS ATTRACTION

Patricia Frances Rowell

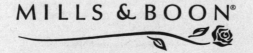

MILLS & BOON®

First published in Great Britain 2004
Harlequin Mills & Boon Limited,
Eton House, 18-24 Paradise Road, Richmond, Surrey TW9 1SR

© Patricia Frances Rowell 2002

ISBN 0 263 83978-8

Set in Times Roman 10½ on 12 pt.
04-0904-79170

Printed and bound in Spain
by Litografia Rosés S.A., Barcelona

For Judy Elise Rhodes,
my friend in this world and all others.
And for my chosen sister, Sue Harvey Harrison.
No one has encouraged me more.
And—always—for my hero, Johnny.

Prologue

Yorkshire, England, November 1783

The boy stood unmoving, one hand clutching his father's, the other held rigidly in a fist at his side. The rain beat down on the umbrella his father held above them, while the sound of sodden clods of dirt striking the casket mingled with the vicar's words.

"But thanks be to God who giveth us the victory...."

The boy gritted his teeth, willing his lip not to tremble. He would *not* cry. He felt proud to be allowed to stand with the men of the funeral party. If they considered him old enough, he certainly did not want to disgrace himself with tears. Yet a very small, childish part of him wanted to turn and flee—back to the house. Back to hide his face in the skirts of the women waiting there, and to sob the pain away.

"In the midst of life we are in death. Of whom may we seek succor...?"

The child dared a glance up into his father's face. It might as well have been carved in stone. He saw no tears.

No sign betrayed the man's thoughts or feelings, but his hand tightened encouragingly around his young son's.

"Therefore, my beloved brethren, be ye steadfast, immovable...."

The boy took a long breath and drew himself up in emulation, schooling his own face to stern control. His father was strong. He would be strong. Men didn't cry.

The vicar finished the reading and stepped forward to murmur a few private words. Then the boy's father turned and led him away from the grave of the woman who had been the anchor of both their lives.

Chapter One

London, England, October 1810

"You did what?" Catherine leaned her clenched fists on her uncle's desk and scowled at him across it, bristling with outrage.

He winced. "There is no need to shout. I am not deaf."

"I can only wish that *I* were! I cannot believe I heard you correctly."

"Of course you heard me. I said I have accepted an offer from Lord Caldbeck for your hand in marriage."

Catherine straightened up and stared at him in disbelief. "But, Uncle Ambrose, why? Aside from the fact that I have no wish to marry at all, I hardly know the man. I've danced with him a few times, but he has never shown any partiality for me. I've never even heard that he was hanging out for a wife."

"Caldbeck is well known for hiding his thoughts. One never knows what he intends. The man's an enigma."

"An automaton, rather." Catherine spun away from the desk, snatched her modish hat from her head and sailed it across the room into a chair. She felt her hair spring forth in its flaming halo, and ran her hands over it in a vain attempt to restrain it.

"Lord Caldbeck might as well be made of wood. He never smiles, he never laughs, he never…" Having paced the width of the library, she whirled, savagely kicking the train of her velvet riding dress out of her way, and again bore down on the desk. "What can you have been thinking? You have no right…."

Ambrose Maury's face began to show a tinge of red as he came to his own defense. "On the contrary. As your guardian it is my duty to speak for you. It's a damn good match. Caldbeck is as rich as Croesus. He made a very advantageous offer. I accepted it. It's that simple."

Catherine, who knew her uncle well, stopped her pacing midway across the room and turned to look at him, eyes narrowed shrewdly. "Exactly what sort of offer?"

Maury fidgeted a bit, blotting perspiration from his bald pate with his handkerchief. "Now, Catherine, you must understand certain things."

"What things? What sort of offer?"

"I've had a bit of bad luck investing in the Funds of late."

"Ah. And Lord Caldbeck is offering a handsome settlement. I begin to understand. But *you* must understand that I will not marry—I can't! *I won't!* Within six months I come into control of my fortune, and I shall no longer be dependent on your hospitality. Can't you wait until then to get me off your hands?"

"Catherine, I can't wait six months—not even six days."

"Are you run completely off your legs, then?"

"I don't know why you insist on using these cant phrases, young lady, but yes. You could say that. In fact,

I haven't a feather to fly with. Caldbeck will settle all my debts, forgive my mortgages and give me enough to emigrate to America.''

"America! I have no more wish to live in America than to marry Lord Caldbeck. Surely, as my trustee, you can arrange for me to receive enough from my inheritance for me to set up a small establishment here for the next half year.''

Ambrose leaned back in his chair and folded his plump hands across his ample midsection. Just a hint of malice glinted in his eyes. "What you do not understand, Catherine, is that you no longer *have* an inheritance.''

Catherine stood for a moment dumbfounded. Then she spoke very carefully. "Do you mean to tell me that you have lost, not only your own fortune, but mine, gambling on the Funds?''

Her uncle nodded. "On the Funds and some other…er, unfortunate investments.''

"But…how…? You were supposed to hold that money for me—in trust—until I am five-and-twenty. How could you…?''

"Come now. Don't be missish. You know I had the authority to invest it.''

"Yes, but not to gamble with it!''

"I used it better than you would—throwing it away on those damn brats at the foundling hospital.''

"You have bankrupted us both?''

"That's the long and the short of it. You may make your own decision, of course, about what to do, but I strongly recommend that you accept Caldbeck.''

"You…you scoundrel! You have the nerve to sit there and tell me… I'll have you before the magistrate!''

"Little good it will do you. If I could replace the

money, I wouldn't be emigrating to some backwater in America.''

Longing to slap the smug expression off her uncle's face, Catherine fought for control. ''You cannot make me do it!''

Scowling, Ambrose stood and stepped around the desk. ''Now see here, young lady. Caldbeck has already bought up my mortgages and is prepared to pay my creditors. He will do so on the understanding that you will wed him.''

''You sold me!''

''Oh, have done with your dramatics! He is expecting that you will do as we agreed. It is going to be damned awkward for me if you don't.''

''You should have thought of that before you created this situation.''

Maury lifted his hand in a threatening gesture, then let it fall to his side. ''Let me make your situation abundantly clear. This house no longer belongs to me. As of today you have no home, no money and no source of income.''

Catherine stopped pacing and stood for a second as still as a statue. ''You can't be serious.''

''I'm bloody serious. And let me tell you something else, Catherine Maury, I don't give a damn what you do! Your aunt and I are both ready to wash our hands of you—*and* your bloody brats, *and* your temper, *and* your high-handed manner. Not marry indeed. You should have been wed and had a brace of children by now, but no! You must play savior to every sooty sweep's boy, every street urchin and little thief who crosses your path. Much fortune you would have had soon, in any event, between your extravagance and your philanthropies. You may accept Caldbeck or go live on the street with your protégés. I don't care, but you are not going with us!''

Catherine stared at him for the space of three breaths, then, grabbing her hat from the chair, turned with a great swish of skirts and marched out of the room.

Out of sight of her uncle, Catherine abandoned dignity and fled up the stairs to her bedchamber. Slamming the door, she turned the key in the lock, threw her hat at the bed and resumed her pacing, her thoughts boiling.

My God, this can't be happening! Her uncle's announcement refused to become reality in her mind. No home? This house had been a refuge for half her life— not a comfortable one, perhaps, but a home. No money? She had been counting heavily on quarter day, as she had already all but depleted her allowance for the current quarter. There had been the clothes for the boys in the new home and the new beds for the foundling hospital and the expense of the reception for the contributors.

And, of course, there had been the new hunter.

She brightened a bit. Her horses! The hunter alone would bring enough to lease a house for a year. She could sell her horses, but…what if Uncle Ambrose had already sold them? Or more probably, lost them? She had no doubt that many of his *investments* took place at the card table.

At that thought rage consumed her once again, and the kick she gave her train as she turned almost undid her. Her foot tangled in the fabric, and only sheerest luck stopped her from falling headlong onto the carpet. Too much! It really *was* too much.

She seized the edge of her jacket and yanked, all but pulling the buttons off. She struggled out of it and flung it at the wardrobe. Her boots followed, and she tore at the fastenings of the treacherous dress. It came to rest under the bed.

Thus liberated, Catherine resumed her prowling, trying to relieve her frustration. Greedy! A sofa cushion bounced off the wall. Grasping! The small footstool clattered as it fell on its side near the window. Stupid man! A book tumbled off the table she struck with her fist. Sucking her bruised knuckle, she looked about for something else on which to take out her fury.

She caught the barest glimpse of her maid's head as Sally peeked around the dressing room door. The sight of her mistress stamping around her bedchamber in her shift evidently dismayed the abigail, for she quickly withdrew her head and closed the door. Catherine paused.

What would become of Sally? The question sobered her. Catherine suddenly realized that she was not the only victim of this disaster. All the servants would suffer. How could she prevent it? *No home, no money, no income.* Nothing with which to pay the loyal girl, no place for them to live. Fear began to replace anger. Her unseeing gaze fixed on the scene outside the glass, Catherine pulled the footstool to the window and sat down.

She must think. What was she to do? Income represented the greatest problem. Even if she could wrest her horses from Uncle Ambrose's grasp, the money would not last long enough to give her the independence she'd so eagerly anticipated.

At least, whatever she decided, she would be free of her venal uncle and his lachrymose wife. What a relief that would be! They had never wanted her in their home. The control of her fortune was the only reason they had accepted the guardianship of a twelve-year-old girl at all. At least Papa had been shrewd enough to link the two in his will. But apparently even he had not realized to what depths his brother would sink.

Catherine sighed and rested her elbows on the window ledge, chin on hand. She had friends who would take her in, but having been an unwelcome addition to one household, she did not relish the idea of repeating that experience. Could she possibly find gainful employment? For a gently bred young woman it would prove almost impossible. So…what?

A tentative tap sounded at her door, followed by the voice of her uncle's footman. "Miss Catherine, are you 'in'?"

"Not now." In no frame of mind for visitors, she turned on the stool to face the door. "I do not wish to be disturbed."

"The Earl of Caldbeck is below stairs, miss. He requests a few minutes of your time."

"I said *no!* Tell him I cannot see him now." Hearing the retreating footsteps of the servant, Catherine returned to staring out the window. Caldbeck himself—the last person she wished to see at that moment. Heaven help her, what *could* she do? Her thoughts simply would not come to order.

Reluctantly she considered Lord Caldbeck. She found nothing objectionable in his person—quite the opposite, in fact. Tall and elegantly slender, but with shoulders whose width owed nothing to his tailor, he might be very attractive were he not so cold. She could do worse.

But she had been determined for so long to avoid marriage. For one thing, Catherine had learned the hard way not to trust anyone but herself to take care of her, and a husband, by law, would have so much power, so much control over her.

Giving up her longed-for independence would be a bitter pill to swallow, but it was already lost. Her money was gone. Swallow she must. But the other thing, the bigger thing... So much more important; the loss of the decision so much harder to accept.

And so tempting to accept.

Children. Marriage meant children, and nothing stirred her heart as a child did. It fell within her reach at this moment to allow herself her dearest, most secret wish— a family of her own, a home of her own, children on which she could lavish the love and attention she had lacked since she was twelve years old.

But children were so appallingly vulnerable!

Catherine sighed. She could not take the risk. She'd long ago made up her mind to that, though it tore her very soul. Now, if she accepted Caldbeck, that wonderful, terrifying possibility again became a reality. But if something happened to her... If her children were left alone in the world as she had been, as the waifs she befriended were... The very thought brought tears to her eyes.

She dashed them away. She must think. Could she possibly live with someone like the reticent earl? Her emotions were always evident and vigorous. Surely a man so reserved would stifle her, try to restrain her, want her to be a docile and efficient wife. Could she change her nature enough ever to be that? Very unlikely—not for anyone. They would both be mad with aggravation within six months!

A half-smile touched her lips. Caldbeck obviously did not know what he had bargained for. What a shock he would get if she did accept him. He might find this a marriage of *inconvenience*. It would serve him right, thinking he could buy her.

At that moment a firmer knock rattled the door panels. Annoyed, she glared at the door.

"I told you, I am not to be disturbed."

"It is I, Caldbeck. I would like to speak with you."

Catherine sat silent for a startled moment. Good heavens, the man stood at her door! How dare he? What in the world could she say to him? She couldn't talk now. She needed more time. Time to think…

"I do not wish to talk now. Come back tomorrow." As soon as she spoke the words, Catherine realized that she might not be in that house tomorrow. She no longer lived here. Already she heard the sounds of packing and the preparations to close the mansion. She began to feel a bit panicky.

"I believe it would be of benefit for us to talk now." The voice on the other side of the door was flat, without inflection. Catherine heard not a smidgen of persuasion in it. How could he sound so…so unfeeling at a time like this? Had the man no sensibility at all?

"Of benefit to whom? You are trying to buy me. Go away!" She turned her back and resumed staring at the street.

An instant later, with a thunderous crash, the door flew open.

Catherine leapt to her feet. Strangling on a scream, she spun to face this new menace. She beheld Lord Caldbeck, his tall frame filling the doorway. As she watched with frightened eyes, one hand pressed against her mouth, he straightened his dove-gray coat and tugged his snowy shirtsleeves into position.

Catherine stood frozen in place, for once in her life speechless. Her tongue stuck to the roof of her dry mouth, and her heart pounded in her ears. Caldbeck pushed the door shut, and after a cursory inspection of the broken latch, nudged a dainty boudoir chair in front of it to hold it closed.

He then turned to her and bowed politely.

"Miss Maury."

Catherine nodded silently as he crossed the room to stand a few feet from her. She looked up into an impassive face dominated by ice-gray eyes. The mouth did not smile. The once raven-black hair brushed severely back from the face was now so liberally streaked with gray that it shone the color of gunmetal. Catherine swallowed, trying in vain to think of something to say.

Running footsteps in the hall mingled with alarmed voices.

"Miss Catherine, are you all right?"

"What the devil is going on here?" Her uncle shoved past the footman, pushing the chair out of the way to stick his head into the room. "Oh. Caldbeck. I see you found my niece. Did you make that confounded racket?"

Lord Caldbeck nodded wordlessly at the door. Maury examined the broken wood and scowled. "I told you she would be unreasonable, but couldn't you find some way of gaining admittance without destroying my door?"

Caldbeck sent him a level stare. "I believe the door is now my property."

Maury flushed. "Yes, of course." Then, with a sneer, "Very well, we shall cease disturbing your visit with your bride." His glance took in the clothes scattered around the room. "You certainly have not wasted any time."

He jerked his head at the footman, and they both departed, the servant covering a grin with one hand. Caldbeck replaced the small chair holding the door and returned to Catherine.

Catherine felt the wave of heat creeping up from her breasts to the roots of her hair. Great heavens! She stood before his lordship in nothing but her shift!

How could she have forgotten that rather significant fact? What must Lord Caldbeck be seeing, with the light from the window behind her shining through the sheer linen? And what must he be thinking of her? Catherine started to cover herself with her hands, realized the futility of that measure, and was about to turn her back to Caldbeck when his voice arrested her.

"It doesn't matter. His opinion is no longer important."

The blush deepened. Catherine, knowing her milk-white complexion, inwardly cursed it. Her face must be absolutely crimson! And she could not fathom the least clue to *his* thoughts. Even though he had kicked the door in, neither his face nor his voice betrayed any sign of ardor or anger. His eyes gleamed as cool and gray as ever. Stabbed again by fear, she wanted to turn and run, but her pride would not let her.

She decided instead to muster what dignity she might.

Catherine lifted her chin and drew herself up, her face a haughty mask. "Well, my lord? What is it that you are so eager to discuss?"

"The conditions of our marriage."

"I thought that you and my uncle had already made those arrangements." Catherine's voice dripped acid. "That the two of you had completed the terms of sale."

Caldbeck raised one eyebrow a hair's breadth. "I am sorry to hear that you view the contract in that light."

He watched silently as Catherine stalked past him to the other end of the room, then stalked back, anger gradually replacing fear.

"How else am I to view it? How my uncle thought he could force me into it, I can't imagine. I fear you have spent your money for nothing, my lord."

"Indeed?" Caldbeck's expression held nothing but the smallest amount of polite inquiry.

Catherine considered herself the equal of any man in a verbal battle, but she found Caldbeck's icy reserve to be just the least little bit daunting. He did not rise to the hook of her barbed words. Hunting for a new tack, she cleared her throat. "It is obvious, my lord, that I can't marry you. I hardly know you, but surely you must see, as I do, that we are utter opposites."

Caldbeck nodded in agreement.

"You are aware of that?"

"Of course."

"But...but surely we would drive one another into Bedlam within a twelve-month!"

"I believe the results of our marriage may not be quite so unpleasant as all that."

His tone was as even as ever, and Catherine studied his expression once again for some clue to his feelings. Finding none, she sighed in exasperation. "My lord, this is madness in itself. We would not suit."

"On the contrary, Miss Maury, I believe we shall deal together very well."

"You can't mean that. How could two such different people possibly live together?"

"Very happily. We each have that which the other needs."

Catherine felt intrigued in spite of herself. "What in the world could that be?"

"I think we can agree that, at the moment, you are badly in need of a means of support. Your uncle—" somehow, without having altered his tone of voice whatsoever, Caldbeck imbued the word with disdain "—has placed you in a highly untenable position. You need money. I have a great deal of it."

Catherine felt the color flooding her face again. "I hope I am not so mercenary."

"No, I don't perceive you as mercenary—the word I would use would be *desperate*." He waited patiently for a reply.

Catherine struggled with warring emotions. He had the right of it, of course. Her situation *was* desperate. Still, she balked at being forced into anything, let alone a marriage she didn't want to a man she hardly knew and had no hope of understanding. Nor any hope of his accepting her. She took refuge in anger, a much stronger and more comfortable emotion than desperation.

"And you wish to take advantage of my predicament!"

Caldbeck's expression never changed. "I simply propose a mutually beneficial arrangement."

"And what do *you* hope to gain?"

"Your beauty, your energy, your superb elegance. You…warm me." Even as he searched for the words, his countenance remained composed, his voice without emotion. "I also admire your ability to consider the plight of those less fortunate than yourself. It is a very rare trait in our time. I need someone to assist me with my responsibilities to society."

For years, Catherine had heard nothing but disbelief, irritation or amusement on the subject of her charities. Astonished, she could only stammer, "You—you do?"

"I do, and I am prepared to offer you some assistance. My seat is situated in Yorkshire. Countless children are in unfortunate circumstances in the cities of that area— in the mines, the woolen mills, the foundries. The district provides endless scope for your talents and my funds."

Catherine narrowed her eyes in thought. "Yes, I have heard many horrifying tales of children in the mines and

mills. But what of my work here? I have only just suc-
ceeded in organizing a board of contributors for the
foundling hospital, and I am still trying to do so for the
new boys' home.''

''I have no objection to an occasional trip to London,
although I prefer to live on my estates so that I may
oversee them myself. But one can place only so much
dependence on others.''

''Yes, that is certainly true. It is one of the reasons I
desire to remain in London.'' And unwed.

''I understand that, but I believe that you may accom-
plish a great deal of the groundwork for your London
projects through the post, if you plan your visits to best
advantage. In time you will be able to shift your attention
to Yorkshire.''

Catherine turned and once more looked without seeing
at the scene outside the window. Caldbeck waited calmly
for a response. His offer indeed tempted her. He had the
power to help her causes in so many ways, if only he
would. It would be a relief to have a supporter. The
money was important, of course, but... She turned back
abruptly.

''Would you speak in the House of Lords on the laws
governing child labor?''

Caldbeck paused, considering. Catherine tapped her
foot impatiently.

At last, he nodded. ''Yes, from time to time, if you
provide me with the information. I rarely speak in Par-
liament, but I shall do so now and then. I do not wish to
involve all my time with your projects. I have business
of my own. That is one reason I need you.''

Catherine again directed her gaze toward the window.
Could she believe his promise, or was he just trying to
convince her to accept him? How long would it be before

he lost interest in her, and his own business took precedence over hers? She could not know until too late. She still did not entirely understand his wish to make her his wife.

You warm me. Could anyone warm this human icicle? Beauty? Elegance? Perhaps he simply wanted a tall, well-dressed woman at his side as an ornament, one he could enjoy in his detached way, who would perform the duties of his countess. Perhaps he would make no demands on her in the marriage bed. That might be an advantage. She would not have to fear for her children. But...*was* that entirely an advantage?

Catherine felt the color rising again in her face and kept it carefully turned to the window. A woman of strong feelings, she had been aware for some time in this conversation that Caldbeck's presence created sensations in her that she had rather avoid. She must make this decision with a cool head, not in response to unruly prompting from her lower body. Though what in that unmoving visage inspired passion, she was sure she didn't know. Just because he had broad shoulders and well-muscled legs...

Her next thought stopped her. What a miserable existence it would be to live with a man who aroused these desires if he had no inclination to explore them with her! Catherine had been aware for years of a burning curiosity to understand the intimacy of the bedchamber, but except for a few discreet kisses, she remained in ignorance. She understood too well the penalties for pursuing the subject in her unwed state to risk them. Her impetuosity did not extend that far. She shuddered to think of having a child under *those* circumstances.

Besides, she would be compromising her integrity to use another person in that way only to satisfy her curiosity. And she would *not* allow herself to be used thus. Did she, in effect, contemplate that very thing in this proposal of a loveless marriage?

She pivoted and again gave her attention to Caldbeck. "My lord, I appreciate the value of what you are offering. However, let us have some plain speaking. Only vaguely do I comprehend what you want from me in return."

He paused for so long that Catherine wondered if he intended to continue. At last he answered.

"I desire you."

"Oh."

That answered *that* question.

"Did you think that I might not want you in my bed?"

Catherine cursed the hot blood again creeping up her neck, but she held her ground. "I didn't know… It is very difficult to… Never mind, the bargain is now clear."

And was it a bargain she was willing to make? His wealth for her body? She didn't like the sound of that! Yet many marriages were based on no more. And Catherine was a realist. Her situation would oblige her to wed *someone* sooner or later. When she considered the good that marrying Lord Caldbeck might allow her to do… Would he uphold his part of the bargain? She could not be sure, but his very rigidity indicated that he would keep his word. And she must admit he wasn't asking for something she felt unwilling to give in return.

And she had no idea what else she might do.

"Very well, my lord. I fear that we are engaging in folly of monumental proportions, but my decision is made. I accept your proposal."

Chapter Two

Lord Caldbeck waited so long to reply that Catherine feared he had suddenly changed his mind.

"I am relieved."

Catherine shook her head in disbelief. If his lordship had been laboring under any anxiety whatsoever, it certainly was not apparent.

"When do you wish to have the ceremony performed? I…I may not be able to stay here much longer." She gestured toward the door, through which the thump of boxes and trunks being moved about was audible.

"As soon as possible. I already have a special license. Perhaps you need to do some shopping. Have you a white dress?"

Catherine looked at him blankly. "A white dress?"

"To be married in. I would like to see my bride in white." He paused and then inquired neutrally, "I assume it is appropriate?"

Catherine's face positively flamed. "Of course, it is appropriate! Do you think…?"

Caldbeck held up a restraining hand. "Like you, I believe in the need for plain speaking. It is one thing I believe we have in common. Have you a dress?"

"Yes." Catherine hated herself for stammering. How did this man manage to put her out of countenance so easily? And without ever raising his voice? "Yes, I have a white ensemble that will be suitable. It is quite new, in fact. When…?"

"This afternoon. At four o'clock. I have made the arrangements with the chapel. If you have anyone whom you wish to be present, give me their names at once, and I shall have my secretary send cards. I have already taken the liberty of inviting a few of the people I know to be your friends to join us for dinner at my London house."

So soon! Irate again, Catherine put her fists on her hips. "Wait just a minute! You have *already* invited *my* friends to a wedding dinner? How could you be so sure I would accept your bargain?"

Caldbeck lifted her chin on one finger and looked intently into her outraged face. "You had very little choice, Kate. You were not bred to toil…and that would be a dreadful waste. I thought you would want to have your friends with you, and that you would wish to say goodbye. We shall be returning to Yorkshire very soon."

This time Catherine could not fail to hear a certain gentleness in his tone. Perhaps he understood more of her feelings at this unsettling moment than she did. In her need to reach a decision she had not let herself feel the pain of losing her comfortable life, all her hope of independence, of leaving everything and everyone she knew. At the unexpected sympathy a lump formed in her throat. She nodded without speaking.

"Good. You will stay at my home, of course. You'd best have your maid pack your belongings, and I shall send my footmen to transport them."

Lips compressed, Catherine nodded again, blinking back tears. Caldbeck extended a hand. She placed hers

in it, and he carried it to his lips. Then, as if thinking
better of it, instead of kissing her fingers, he pulled her
to him. Catherine felt the warmth of his big hand on her
back through her shift. Before she had fully taken in that
sensation, the roughness of his coat pressed against her
breasts. She felt the light scrape of a carefully shaved
cheek as he lifted her face with his free hand and covered
her mouth with his.

The warmth of his kiss flowed through Catherine from
her lips to her knees. Without thinking, she leaned into
the embrace. His arms tightened around her, pulling her
up against a bulge between his legs. Catherine had never
been kissed in her shift. Heavens, she could feel so much
of him! She was aware of the bulge as never before.
Apparently the Earl of Caldbeck was not devoid of *all*
feeling.

The fabric of his breeches and the smooth leather of
his tall boot brushed against the skin of her legs as he
slipped a foot between hers. Catherine sighed and her
legs went weak. The hand on her back pressed her closer,
supporting her against him. Just as her senses began to
reel, he released her and stepped back. She stumbled, and
Caldbeck quickly steadied her.

He touched her face with one finger. "That's better. I
do not wish to have a red-eyed bride."

Catherine hunted once again for traces of laughter—or
perhaps displeasure—but as usual, found none. She drew
in a deep breath.

Caldbeck turned and started for the door. "I shall call
for you at half after three."

Somewhat before half after three, Catherine sat at her
dressing table, attired in the new white dress and pelisse.
A good thing that white became her! Even though it was

associated with young debutantes, she liked the dramatic effect it created with her vivid coloring. Satisfied by the reflection that looked back at her from the dressing mirror, she fingered the pearl necklace, which had been delivered to her an hour earlier. Lord Caldbeck was nothing if not efficient.

She reached up to alter slightly the tilt of the tiny hat that Sally was fastening to the fiery mass of ringlets piled at her crown. Tipping her head, Catherine watched the play of sunlight from the window across her gleaming locks. She always marveled at the way the sun brought out the deep colors, turning them almost purple in the shadows.

Red hair was far from fashionable, but Catherine liked hers, nonetheless. It suited her. She dabbed a tiny bit of powder over the all but indiscernible freckles across her nose. Freckles were another matter. She really should wear nothing but wide-brimmed hats, she told herself for the thousandth time.

While Sally rummaged in the wardrobe for gloves and reticule, Catherine had time—unfortunately—to reflect on her situation. In less than a day she had gone from being a wealthy young woman, looking forward to the independent control of her own fortune, to being a pauper. Now, a few hours later, she faced becoming the bride of a man with a face of stone. She shivered.

His bride! She would spend tonight in his house. Her stomach sank. Now that her curiosity was about to be satisfied, she found herself pulling back. Tonight she would lie in the bed of a total stranger. She would be completely at his mercy, and she had no idea of his true nature or of what to expect from him. Catherine considered herself a bold woman, but even if he had not broken the door, those glacial eyes held enough menace to strike terror to a heart braver yet than hers.

For a moment panic gripped her. She jumped up from the vanity stool and strode around the room. She couldn't go through with it! She couldn't. She started at the sound of her maid's voice.

"Miss Catherine? Come and sit down, do, Miss Catherine. I need to put your gloves on you. See? I've picked the stitches loose on the ring finger so you can tuck it under. And you've a strand of hair come loose."

Catherine sighed and, returning to the dresser, sat and extended her hand. While Sally coaxed the tight kid gloves into place, Catherine took several deep breaths and strove for calm. It would not be so bad. Surely it would not. He was a handsome man, and the kiss they had shared… Oh, dear! This line of thought didn't help. She was turning red again.

"Are you warm, miss? To me the room is just a thought too cool." Sally began to fan her with the pierced ivory fan from her reticule.

"No, no." Catherine pushed the fan away. "I'm fine."

At that moment they heard the crunch of carriage wheels in the street. Sally hurried to the window. "I think that's him, Miss Catherine," she reported. "Oh! Would you look at that carriage! All silver-gray like, and with the finest dapple grays. Alike to a hair, they are!"

Catherine, none too fond of the idea of being caught peeking out the window at her bridegroom, peered over Sally's shoulder. The shield and wolf's head coat-of-arms on the door of the carriage undoubtedly identified it as the property of the Earl of Caldbeck. As the earl emerged and made his way up the steps, the hall clock chimed half after three.

"Well," Sally observed, "at least he's punctual."

Of course he was punctual. What else would he be? Catherine stepped a little closer to the window and looked down into Caldbeck's upturned face. Drat! She dodged back. And what else would he do but catch her peeping! Perhaps she should let him cool his heels awhile. Always begin as you mean to go on.

But even that bit of rebellion was to be denied her. A tap at the door and the footman's voice announced that the Earl of Caldbeck awaited her downstairs. Sally slipped the cord of Catherine's reticule over her hand and hustled her to the door.

"You best be going, miss. You can't keep the vicar standing. Oh, wait. Let me pin up that curl. There, now. You're done."

Catherine allowed herself to be led to the door—and her waiting fate.

No guests waited in the quiet dark of the chapel when they arrived, save two. A well-dressed gentleman Caldbeck presented as his friend, Adam Barbon, Viscount Litton. The earl introduced the stylish, dark-haired woman—more handsome than beautiful—to Catherine as his sister, Helen, Lady Lonsdale. They made an attractive pair, he with his fair hair and laughing brown eyes, she with shining black curls and black-fringed eyes as blue as Catherine's own. Startled, Catherine stumbled over her response as she clasped the other woman's hand.

Caldbeck had a sister! How little she knew of him, indeed.

She was just wondering whether her marriage would take place with only her bridegroom's associates present, when Mary Elizabeth flew into the chapel. Catherine hastened to meet her.

"Oh, Liza, I feared my note had not found you at

home.'' Catherine gratefully embraced her dearest friend. ''I am so glad to have you here!''

''I *was* out. You can't imagine the hurry I have been in to be here by four.'' As usual, Mary Elizabeth's short, plump figure looked a bit rumpled. ''I am positively out of breath. Oh, that plume on your hat is perfect, just perfect. You are getting married! I can't believe… And without a word to anyone. How could you? And to Lord Caldbeck! I couldn't believe my eyes when we received his invitation to dinner tonight. I told George—oh! George? Are you…? Well, of course you are. We came together….''

''How do you do? I am Caldbeck.'' The gray-clad earl took advantage of Liza's indrawn breath to cut through the monologue and extend a hand to her escort.

''Oh. This is my husband, George,'' Mary Elizabeth finished, quite unnecessarily.

''George Hampton, your most obedient servant, sir.'' The trim younger man bowed and shook Caldbeck's hand.

Hampton then took his wife firmly by the arm and led her to where Caldbeck made the balance of the introductions. Those having been completed, Caldbeck gravely presented to Catherine a magnificent bouquet of white roses and lilies, with ribbons trailing to the floor. Their intoxicating scent flowed over her as she took them in her arms. Murmuring her thanks, she looked up into unreadable gray eyes.

The waiting vicar, balding and well padded, cleared his throat for attention and directed the party to assemble before him. Suddenly Catherine stood at Caldbeck's side. The vicar was reading the service.

''Dearly beloved, we are gathered here in the sight of God and these witnesses to join together….''

To join together! Oh, heaven, what was she doing here? She was marrying this man—this man who, until this morning....

Children. Oh, God! Children!

"Who giveth this woman in marriage?"

A resounding silence ensued. Catherine had not even invited her uncle to be present, let alone to give her away. She heartily hoped that the tearful, if insincere, farewell that her aunt had bestowed upon her would be the last she ever saw of either of them. Nonetheless, a major contretemps loomed.

She looked helplessly at the vicar, who was peering over his glasses at her. Stepping gallantly into the breach, George Hampton took her arm and announced, "I do."

He placed Catherine's shaking hand into the earl's outstretched one, and Caldbeck's fingers immediately closed warmly around hers. The vicar resumed his reading.

"If any man knows any reason that these two should not be joined, let him speak now or forever hold his peace." The churchman looked sternly around the all but empty room.

Me! I do! The words echoed through Catherine's mind, but apparently she had not said them aloud, for the vicar was again speaking.

"Do you, Charles Eric Joseph Randolph, take this woman, Sarah Catherine Maury, to be your lawfully wedded wife, to have and to hold...."

Charles. His name is Charles Randolph. How could she not have known that? Did no one ever call him Charles? His strong voice answered.

"I do."

"Do you, Sarah Catherine..." Now or never. Once the words of the vow passed her lips, she could never take them back. Children. Her children. Silence seemed to stretch into eternity. Then she heard a whispered, ''I do.''

Was that she? Had she spoken those words? She must have, for the vicar was saying something about a ring. Catherine looked in confusion at the flowers in the crook of her left arm. Then she smelled Liza's perfume, and the flowers disappeared. Caldbeck fitted a heavy band of gold onto her trembling finger. The vicar was praying.

She looked up at him as he placed a hand behind her head, her eyes questioning. He carefully drew her toward him. She felt his mouth warm on hers for a moment—then it was gone. Catherine took a deep breath and turned to Liza, who was dabbing at her eyes with her handkerchief and trying simultaneously to return the bouquet. The men were congratulating Caldbeck. Helen's hand was soft on hers, and her voice warm.

''Welcome to the family.''

Family. A husband. Children. God help them.

Once again Catherine sat at a dressing table while Sally fussed with her hair. This, however, was a completely different table in a completely different room in a completely different house. A very grand house. Sally was ecstatic.

''Did you never see such a place, Miss Catherine? And to think, you are mistress of it now!'' She tugged the brush through Catherine's springy curls. Catherine had removed the pelisse to reveal the elegantly simple silk dress beneath. The fabric skimmed low above her firm breasts—much too low, her aunt had insisted when Catherine bought the dress—and clung to her small waist and full hips. Satin slippers replaced the kid half-boots, and Sally replaced her hat with flowers from the bouquet.

''It sounds as though there are ever so many people

here.'' Sally readjusted a hairpin. ''Must be half of Lunnun.''

Catherine had been wondering about that herself. His lordship had said that he'd invited a ''few'' of her friends. The windows of her new room opened onto the garden, so they were unable to see the carriages as they arrived, but certainly the hubbub rising from below required a great many voices.

The entrance of the earl himself followed a brief knock at the door. He yet wore gray, but now it was gray satin. He bowed and held out one hand, his eyes scanning her face. ''Are you ready? Our guests are eager to meet the new Lady Caldbeck.''

Catherine nodded and got shakily to her feet. What ailed her? She loved parties. Why did her knees threaten to buckle? She was to make a dramatic entrance on the arm of her new husband. She loved being the center of attention. Why, tonight, did she want to bolt?

With great determination, she pasted a smile on her lips and laid her hand on Caldbeck's arm. He covered it with his own briefly, then led her out of the room. They descended the marble stairs slowly, pausing at the first landing. The crowd at the foot of the staircase ceased their murmuring, and every head turned in their direction.

A cheer went up, and applause echoed against the tall ceilings. Catherine blossomed at the sound, and her smile became real. These *were* her friends. She glimpsed nearly everyone she knew in the assembled throng—and many, many more faces to boot. How had Caldbeck done this? And why? There was clearly more to Charles Randolph, Earl of Caldbeck, than met the eye.

The evening proved long, but exciting. Helen, elegant in lavender silk, assumed the duties of hostess so that Catherine had nothing to do but enjoy the attention. Surrounded by friends and well-wishers, Catherine found her misgivings beginning to fade. She pushed her anxiety to the back of her mind, talking and laughing with friends at dinner and afterward presiding over the dancing. She also made the acquaintance of several people whom she had long wished to approach as supporters for her charities. Already her alliance with Lord Caldbeck was bearing fruit.

Her uneasiness returned somewhat when Caldbeck led her onto the floor and took her in his arms for the first waltz. He was a superb dancer, however, and the pleasure of skimming over the floor with him soon overcame the strangeness. Catherine was acutely aware of the sureness of the hand on her back, of the power of the legs brushing against hers, the ease with which he moved her about the room. She had danced with him before. Why had she never noticed his strength?

Later, though she was claimed by other partners, her attention remained on Caldbeck. He played the perfect host, chatting easily—if solemnly—with his guests, but now and again she could feel his glacial gaze on her. Each time, rather than feeling a chill, a sensation of warmth washed over her. And each time she missed a step of the dance.

How different he seemed in his own home than he had at other social engagements. At those he seemed out of place—invariably serious in the midst of the flirting and laughter. Even his expert dancing had never captured her attention. Had he been watching her then as he did now? A little shiver trailed down her back.

Here he appeared confident and relaxed, comfortably conversing with men that she knew to be among the most powerful in the kingdom. He must wield considerable influence to be able to gather those men at his invitation.

Was the purpose of this party to display his prize to them? At that thought Catherine bridled. She did not fancy figuring as the spoils of war!

Still, it was becoming clear to her that, in her sudden fall from affluence, it might be said that she had landed in a pile of feather beds. It remained to be seen what bruises she might yet sustain. In spite of his courtesy, she felt a tiny prick of fear when he pursued her with those frosty eyes.

At last, in the small hours of the morning, the company departed, leaving Catherine, Caldbeck and Helen bidding the last lingerer farewell. Helen excused herself, and her carriage bore her away to her own London home. Catherine glanced uncertainly at her new husband.

Before they reached whatever came next, she recognized something she needed to do. As often happened to her, her agitation had run away with her tongue this morning. She must put her pride aside and recognize the unfair things she had said to Caldbeck. She cleared her throat.

''My lord, there is something I must say to you.''

Caldbeck tipped his head a fraction of an inch in inquiry.

''I...I am sorry for what I said earlier today. About your buying me, I mean. You have, in fact, rescued me, and you have gone to a great deal of trouble to provide me with a real wedding celebration and lovely flowers and these beautiful pearls.'' She touched the strand at her throat. ''You did not have to do that under the circumstances. I...it.... You were very kind. How in the world did you manage it?''

Caldbeck did not quite shrug. He simply opened one hand, palm up. ''Most of the arrangements were Helen's doing. She is an excellent hostess. I have known for some time in what case your uncle stood and have been making plans.''

Catherine shook her head, eyes wide in amazement. ''You have been planning…. And you never even *asked* me?''

Caldbeck nodded. ''I should have, perhaps. However, I thought it highly likely that you would refuse my suit if not given a compelling reason to accept it. I did not want you to develop a resistance to the notion.''

Some of Catherine's annoyance returned. ''And you had the effrontery—'' She stopped abruptly, her eyes narrowed in thought. ''But this doesn't make sense. If you knew that I would soon be in a desperate situation, you had no need to contract with my uncle. Knowing I would be destitute, you might have just as easily given me the same argument that you did this morning. I would have had no more options. Why did you go to such expense?''

''The arrangement with your uncle made the idea of marriage to me appear a fait accompli. Besides, if Maury remained in England, he would forever be an embarrassment to you and an annoyance to us both.''

Catherine digested this information in silence, then asked, ''Did you suggest that he emigrate to America?''

''I insisted on it.''

Catherine's mind swam with revelations about this man that she had wed. ''Well…I must offer my thanks for that. However, I must also say that I resent your arranging for my capitulation without ever considering my feelings! What if I had wished to marry someone else?''

''You would have said so.''

''You might have at least talked to me.''

''I did talk to you—this morning. Or, rather, yesterday.'' He looked at her with mild interest.

''Yes…well… Still, if you knew about Uncle Ambrose, why did you wait so long and rush me into it this way?''

''I have always found timing to be of the essence in accomplishing one's goals.''

Catherine heaved a frustrated sigh. Apparently, his lordship was a very cool gambler. And, damn him, he had an answer for everything—and all the efficiency and sensibility of a machine!

Suddenly Catherine felt very tired. It had been a grueling twenty-four hours. She had suddenly lost all control of her life—her home, her money, her dream of independence. And, she realized with a stab of alarm, the hardest part yet loomed. She would soon lose control of even her body. She felt the blood flooding into her face.

Caldbeck brushed the back of his hand across her cheek. ''Do not be anxious, Kate. You are exhausted, and while I could not give you the time you wanted to become accustomed to the idea of marriage to me before, I now can. I shall not press you tonight to fulfill your part of our bargain. We have a great deal to do tomorrow, and I then wish to be on the road to Yorkshire the next day. I shall welcome you to Wulfdale as my bride.''

Relief and disappointment fought for ascendancy in Catherine's breast. It seemed she was to remain in ignorance for a few more days. Yet she could not but be glad for the reprieve. Perhaps she would be better prepared to accept this man as her husband after being in his company for the time it would take to travel to Yorkshire.

She smiled up at him. ''You are very considerate, my lord. I *am* very weary. However, I do keep my word. If you want—''

''No, Kate. Even though I am eager to consummate our agreement, I shall wait.''

Eager? Caldbeck sounded as cool and polite as if they had been discussing a trip to the theater.

The next morning Catherine, an early riser, surprised his lordship at the breakfast table. He rose and helped her seat herself across the table from his own place, drawing out her chair.

"You are abroad early. It is my experience of ladies that they rarely appear before noon."

My experience of ladies? What experience? Catherine racked her brain for some gossip that she might have heard concerning Lord Caldbeck's mistress—or lack thereof. Nothing came to mind. Could it be possible, at his age, that he did not have one? And come to think of it… "Excuse me, my lord. May I know how old you are?"

It could not be said that Caldbeck appeared startled, but he lifted his gaze from his breakfast and looked at her. "I am five-and-thirty. Why do you ask?"

Catherine flushed. "No real reason. I have just been realizing how little I know about you. Your hair…" She stopped, fearing to offend him. He, of course, showed no sign of offense, or of anything else.

"Yes. The men of my family gray very early." The earl returned his attention to his beef and eggs. Catherine studied her new husband. Five-and-thirty. Yes, in spite of his hair, he did not look old. A few marks of maturity could be seen. Just the slightest receding at the temples, perhaps, revealed by the austere style. How did he keep his hair so smoothly brushed back without the pomade so many men used?

Only a few lines marred his face—a handsome face of angular planes, narrow with a straight nose and a decisive jaw. The firm lips did not frown, but neither did they smile, remaining consistently uncommunicative. But warm. Warm lips. Catherine flushed a bit at the memory.

The object of her scrutiny had a few more bites of his beef, flicked a crumb from his dove gray coat and changed the subject. ''I would like for you to be present today for a meeting with my man of business. We must finalize the arrangements for your jointure.''

''My jointure! Good heavens, this is the first I have thought of that. Surely my uncle did not—''

''No. Maury did not think of that, either.''

Did she hear a hint of sarcasm in his voice—of contempt, perhaps? Catherine could not be sure. ''Then why...?''

''Because, along with your beautiful person, I have accepted a responsibility. I must see you are provided for in the event of my demise. Would you like to have your uncle's house as a part of the settlement? We have no way of knowing at this moment who my heir might be in future years. You should have a place of your own.''

His heir! Catherine swallowed her bite of eggs abruptly. Another issue that had not been discussed. She put her fear firmly aside and considered his question for a moment. She had never been happy in that house. ''No. I am not fond of the place.'' A roguish expression lit her face. ''Besides, it has a broken door.''

Her husband looked at her quickly, and one eyebrow twitched. ''So it does.''

''However, since you already own it...''

''No. I shall sell it and buy something you prefer. We shall meet with Guildford at two. Until then I have other errands. Meantime, you should be preparing to get an early start in the morning.''

Rising from the table, he started for the door, then turned back. ''If you need to do any shopping in London,

I have had your allowance deposited to your account. Good day.''

Catherine watched his departing back thoughtfully. Perhaps she had not made such a bad bargain, after all. Her new mate might not be as exciting as she could wish, he might be just a bit intimidating, and he was definitely controlling her, but he also had a number of sterling qualities. At the present they were behaving as strangers— courteous, distant, uninvolved—as if they were both taking care to be on their best behavior. How long would that last? And what would replace it?

She still simmered over his high-handed arrangements to constrain her to accept him. He had not exactly tricked her into marriage, but he had certainly maneuvered her, and she resented it. She knew that in time she would erupt. How would he react? The small spark of fear flared for moment, but considering his restrained manner, Catherine did not believe he would hurt her in anger. Perhaps he would not react at all.

A depressing thought.

At least she would not have to worry about her security.

Stifle her he might, but abandon her he would not.

It was upon him again. The restlessness, the guilt, the disgust. The peaceful Yorkshire Dales held no peace for *him,* gazing at the soft moon, no solace. He jabbed the horse's sides impatiently, cursing when the animal reared before pounding down the slope into the valley. It was of no use. He could not outrun the torment. Soon he must act. Soon.

Chapter Three

Catherine's vivid carriage ensemble splashed emerald against the silver-gray of the traveling coach, contrasting brightly with the few glowing curls revealed by her bonnet. Caldbeck, as usual in immaculate dove-gray, handed her up while she yet called instructions to Sally. Her maid, nodding her understanding, climbed into the coach she would share with his lordship's valet, Hardraw. Gray-liveried footmen found their places, and the postilions set the powerful team of matched grays in motion.

Catherine, excited to be starting on the longest journey she had ever made, yet felt sad to be leaving London. She had lived in Town all her life, as did all her friends. When might she see Liza again? Yorkshire was much too far away from London for a casual visit. It might be months or even years.

How she would miss her! Liza's veneer of outward silliness covered a shrewd mind and a kind heart. She had been Catherine's confidante for all the lonely years since Catherine had lost her parents. And lucky Liza had a husband who adored her!

Catherine, one cheek resting against the window, watched the passing scene as they swept through the busy streets. In spite of herself the warmth of a tear trickled down her face. She surreptitiously blotted it away with her scrap of a lace handkerchief. A second tear followed the first, and soon the handkerchief became a soggy mess. Catherine dropped it into her reticule, sniffing as quietly as she could manage. A flicker of white from the far side of the coach caught her eye. Turning ever so slightly toward it, she discovered a large, white square of linen being offered to her.

Catherine took it, choking out her thanks. As she blew her nose, she felt the warmth of a large hand on her knee. Caldbeck said nothing, but did not move his hand until they had left London behind. At last her sobs grew silent, her eyes were again dry and her nose ceased running. He then began to point out items of interest along the road, calling her attention to the rich colors of fall and the beauty of the countryside.

"And the roads, so far, are better than I had hoped. I'm afraid that the farther north we get, the worse they will become. We've had a very wet summer followed by a dry autumn. The ruts will be hardened into stone."

"How long do you expect us to be on the road?"

Caldbeck shifted to lean comfortably against the velvet upholstery in his corner, facing her. Catherine followed his example in her own corner.

"Ordinarily four days. If we encounter very bad roads, it will take another day, and if you like, we might take a day of rest near the Peak District. It is quite a pleasing sight at this time of year."

A pleasing sight. Catherine smiled to herself. His lordship was hardly given to hyperbole. Thinking back, she remembered that the strongest word she had ever heard him use was "beautiful." At the time she had thought it only a gentlemanly compliment, but she begin to hear a different significance.

"You seem to have a great appreciation of beautiful sights."

Caldbeck considered a moment. "Yes. I have."

Silence fell. So much for that conversational gambit. Catherine tried again. "Is Wulfdale very lovely?"

"I consider it so."

She waited a moment, then sighed. "Tell me about it."

After a thoughtful minute, Caldbeck nodded. "The house is very old and has been enlarged in many stages, some of them more attractive than others. It began in the twelfth century as a pele tower. Then a hall was added, and it continued to grow from there. The Tudor portions are a veritable maze, but the recent sections are more tasteful. The Georgian front was finished in 1750, and is quite impressive. I think you will like it."

Well, thought Catherine, that's some progress. "Are there gardens?"

"Yes. Several, in fact."

Did she hear a bit more warmth in his voice? Catherine pricked her ears, but could not be sure.

"We have a knot garden, and one for roses, but my favorites are the natural garden and the woodland. You should find them very pretty in their autumn foliage."

Sudden perception dawned on Catherine. *He wants me to like the place. He should, after trapping me into this marriage!* In spite of the annoying reflection, the thought touched her.

"I'm sure I shall like it very much." She smiled. "And tell me…does Wulfdale have a ghost?"

"A ghost?"

"Yes, of course. A house that old must surely have at least one ghost?"

His lordship appeared to consider. "Nothing much. Unless you count the headless bride. She is very seldom seen."

Catherine, who loved ghost stories, clapped her hands over her mouth in delight. "The…the what?"

"Headless bride. But she carries her head, of course, with her veil draped over her arm."

"Oh." Catherine felt a little thrill slide down her backbone. "And how…?"

Caldbeck viewed her levelly. "How did she lose her head?"

Catherine nodded.

"She displeased her husband, the first earl."

His frigid voice blew over her like a winter storm, quenching her enjoyment of the story. For a moment Catherine sat silent with horror. What did that frozen countenance hide? She looked more closely at her new husband. She could see no change in the chill eyes, but felt something…. She couldn't quite put her finger on it…. She spoke uncertainly, eyes narrowed.

"My lord, are you teasing me?"

Caldbeck's silvery eyes regarded her without expression.

"I?" asked his lordship.

Taking stock of her new husband, Catherine decided that she *did* know more about him than she had when she married him. But not much.

He was quite ruthless. She still felt very cautious with him. He had not hesitated to kick her door in, and the way he had orchestrated her acceptance of his proposal was as masterful as it was infuriating. Catherine still chafed at having been so manipulated. Nonetheless, her faults did not include repining. Having agreed, she would do what she could to make the best of the situation.

Her curiosity regarding the marriage bed increased in direct proportion to the time spent with him in the close confines of the carriage. A subtle scent surrounded him, warm, almost smoky, mixed with wool and starch. It stirred her senses. She found herself casting furtive glances across the width of the carriage. Caldbeck sat as coolly as ever, one booted leg propped on the opposite seat to buttress himself against the lurching of the coach.

As he had predicted, the roads had gotten steadily worse. Catherine rocked back and forth in the seat, clinging to the overhead strap and bouncing against the wall of the narrow space. By the fifth day, having slept— alone—in several inns, in varying degrees of discomfort, she felt decidedly buffeted and bruised. Her long legs would reach the far seat, and unladylike though it might be, she was on the verge of steadying herself as he did.

As though he read her mind, Caldbeck turned his gray gaze on her and held out one hand. "Come here, Kate."

Startled, Catherine looked at him in question. Surely he would not choose such a moment to make love to her!

"You are being unmercifully battered by this infernal jolting. Here… No, turn, so." Following his guiding hands, Catherine found herself leaning across his lap, her breasts against his chest, her feet drawn up onto the seat. One strong leg, knee bent, now braced her back, and an equally muscular arm gripped the strap and supported her head. "Is that better?"

She looked up shyly to answer and found penetrating eyes looking intently into hers. Her breathing faltered, and her loins flooded with warmth. Without taking his eyes from her face, Caldbeck untied her bonnet ribbons with his free hand and tossed the confection onto the opposite seat. Liberated, her bright hair flared into a nimbus around her face. His fingers threaded through the glowing cloud and lifted her head.

His eyes might be cold, but his lips were very warm. So was his tongue. He brushed it along her mouth, inviting her to open. After a moment's hesitation she did so and felt an intriguing tickle on the inner side of her lip. She gasped for breath, and his tongue slid farther into her. Catherine went suddenly weak.

At that inopportune instant the coach hit an especially deep pothole, jerking her face away from his. She lifted her eyes and found him gazing into them. She thought that, perhaps, he sighed.

"Try to sleep, Kate. I believe we should push on to Wulfdale tonight, and it will be quite late before we arrive."

So, protected by his strong body, she did.

It was indeed late when the carriage turned onto better-kept roads and made its way across Wulfdale's rolling hills to the lights of the looming gray-stone mansion. At the sound of wheels in the drive, the old house came to life. Footmen in gray livery hastened down the front steps, and grooms came running from the stables. Catherine shivered with fatigue and cold as Caldbeck lifted her off the coach steps into the chill night air.

With great dignity a portly, silver-haired man descended the steps and bowed. "My lord, welcome home. My lady." The butler's appraising glance rested on her only a moment before he bowed again. "It is a pleasure to welcome you to Wulfdale."

Before Catherine could answer, a plump woman hurried down the steps and curtseyed. "Welcome! Welcome, my lord! We were sure you would be here by tonight.

You have brought us a bride at last! Do come in, my lady.'' The housekeeper extended an inviting hand. ''You must be perishing of weariness.''

Caldbeck nodded at the couple. ''Allow me to present to you Hawes and Mrs. Hawes, Lady Caldbeck. I'm sure Mrs. Hawes will see to your comfort immediately. I must confer with Hawes for a time, but I shall show you around your new home tomorrow.''

''Right you are, my lord.'' Mrs. Hawes guided Catherine up the steps. ''It's very happy we are to have you here, my lady.''

The housekeeper led her into a hall of grand and impressive proportions and up two pair of graceful, curving stairs to the second floor. They crossed an elegant salon to the door of a huge bedchamber decorated in feminine fabrics and soft greens. A Dresden clock graced the mantelpiece, along with several dainty china ornaments. Catherine was torn between collapsing on the bed, half seen in the shadowy corner, or on the cushiony sofa before the cheerfully crackling fire.

The sofa was closer.

''Now, my lady, don't you worry about a thing. I shall help you this evening myself. I'm sure your young maid will be as done up as you are. She'll be shown right to her room.''

A twinge of guilt assaulted Catherine. She had hardly spared a thought for Sally. The girl must indeed be exhausted.

''Good, here's Betty with the tray. There's cheese and biscuits and some mulled wine. I knew you would be chilled. Just let me help you off with your pelisse and pretty bonnet. Now... You have a little taste of wine while I see to getting your dressing case and trunk up here.''

Mrs. Hawes bustled out of the room, and Catherine took a grateful sip of the mulled wine, too tired to do more than nibble at the cheese. But she found the wine sweet and strong and warm. She had almost dozed off when the housekeeper returned with footmen carrying her baggage.

As soon as the men had been shooed out of the room, Mrs. Hawes set about laying out Catherine's nightgown and brushes, and before she knew it, Catherine found herself tucked up in the big curtained bed, drowsily watching the flicker of the fire through the drapes. It seemed that her husband, once again, would not join her, but that was just as well. She was too tired to have even a shred of curiosity left.

Catherine awoke shortly before noon the next morning, as Sally pulled back the bed curtains. The welcome smell of hot chocolate wafted to her from the bed table.

"Good morning, miss…oh!" Sally giggled. "I mean, my lady. Have you had a look at this house? Did you see your very own drawing room? Grand, miss, very grand! I believe his lordship's room is through the dressing rooms. That door leads to his, and that one to yours." She waved a vague hand and turned to open the window curtains. "And a fine day it is, too. Chilly a bit, but fine."

Catherine sat forward while Sally arranged her pillows. "I must have slept half the day."

"Very nearly, mi— my lady. And I slept till a sinful hour myself. So kind as Mrs. Hawes is, she told them to let me rest. I wouldn't have waked you yet, but his lordship is to take you around the place himself. I know you'll want to look your best." Sally giggled again.

Catherine viewed her henchwoman through a half-open eye. Speculation must be running riot among the staff. Sally could not help but know that she and his lordship had not yet shared a bed, and if any member of a household knew something, *everyone* knew it. Catherine groaned to herself. Heaven help her the morning after they did take that step!

By two o'clock she had breakfasted and—dressed in a deep purple morning dress, her fiery hair subdued with many pins and a pair of gold combs—set forth to find his lordship. After asking directions twice, she discovered him in his library. He came quickly to his feet as she stepped through the door.

"Good day. I hope you slept well?"

"Yes, thank you. Sally let me sleep an unconscionably long time. I hope I haven't kept you waiting too long."

"No. I wanted you to rest. I did not arise at my usual hour myself. Are you ready to meet your staff?" He offered her his arm.

They spent the next two hours in a tour of the reception rooms and introductions to every member of the staff, from Caldbeck's secretary to the bootboy. Catherine found it astonishing that Caldbeck knew them all. Her head swam with names and faces. Without a guide, she might never find her way from the formal dining room to her bedchamber.

Caldbeck's secretary, Richard Middleton, was the younger son of the local vicar. A slender young man with a shy expression, he greeted Catherine gravely, welcomed her to Wulfdale and quickly returned to his duties.

Caldbeck did not take her through every part of the mansion. "I'm sure you will find the older sections interesting, but you will likely enjoy exploring them at your leisure."

Catherine looked sideways at him. "Is that where I shall find the headless bride?"

"Of course."

"Then perhaps you'd best escort me."

Caldbeck paused for a minute before answering. "That might be best," he finally agreed.

Catherine eyed him suspiciously, but he made no further rejoinder.

They toured the gardens until the late-afternoon nip in the air sent them back inside.

"We dine at seven o'clock here. I trust that is acceptable to you?" Caldbeck paused at the foot of the stairs, but did not wait for an answer. "You have time enough for a nap."

Catherine smiled, but shook her head. "I slept all morning. Besides, I am not accustomed to sleeping in the afternoon."

"Nevertheless, it is advisable that you do so today."

Catherine lifted her chin rebelliously. She was just opening her mouth to explain to him that she was *not* a child, when she looked into a countenance so chilling, the words froze in her throat. "Oh…oh, very well. I shall at least go to my room for a while."

Taking no notice of her pique, Caldbeck lifted her hand to his lips, his eyes on hers. "Until later, then."

After stalking around her room for fifteen minutes, muttering about men who thought they could order one about as soon as one married them, Catherine began to ask herself why this particular man insisted so firmly that she nap. The answer to that followed so closely on the heels of the question that she stopped dead still in the middle of the room, eyes wide.

A fierce tingling in her stomach dropped suddenly into her pelvis, creating a most disturbing sensation.

Tonight she would know.

Tomorrow she would be curious no longer.

Good heavens!

Catherine tried to lie down for a few minutes, but her agitation would not let her rest. Reading proved to be out of the question. She stared unseeing at the pages of a usually thrilling romance until, in annoyance, she tossed the book onto a table. When Sally appeared to help her dress for dinner, she heaved a sigh of relief.

Joining Caldbeck in the family dining room, Catherine tasted not one morsel of the food that passed her lips. The chef had completely wasted his skill on her. Caldbeck made polite conversation, as though she were no more than a casual acquaintance, but Catherine responded with monosyllables. Richard, the secretary, did his best to hold up his end, but excused himself and fled as soon as they finished the meal.

As the party included no other gentlemen with whom Caldbeck might drink his port, and no ladies with whom Catherine might drink tea, they each retired very early to their respective bedchambers. Catherine arrived at hers to discover a tray with brandy and glasses on a table near the sofa and a pitcher of mulled wine on the hob. She took a deep breath and tried to rub the knot out of her stomach.

She stared into the middle distance, her mind a blank, while Sally brushed her brilliant curls and pulled them up to the crown of her head, tying them with a satin ribbon. She didn't question Sally's choice of gown and negligee, but slipped her arms into the soft, creamy silk without comment.

The smooth fabric molded over her breasts and skimmed down her body, causing her to shiver. She was adjusting the lace edging the robe when a tap sounded on the door to the adjoining room. Sally quickly straightened the dressing table and looked inquiringly at Catherine.

"That will be all, Sally. You may go." As Sally departed, and Catherine turned toward the door, a second knock sounded. Caldbeck stepped in, and the sight of him took Catherine's breath away. He had removed his coat, his cravat and his shoes. His breeches clung to muscular legs, and the top few buttons of his shirt were unfastened, revealing the strong column of his neck. Sleeves turned back at the cuff showed sculptured forearms. As usual, he bowed.

"Will you take a glass of wine with me, Kate?"

Catherine nodded silently, suddenly acutely aware of the revealing neckline of her gown and diaphanous robe. The telltale warmth flooded her face and breasts, and she quickly turned and walked to the sofa. The clinging fabric whispered around her legs and generous hips, and she could all but feel Caldbeck's gaze on her bottom as he followed.

Catherine sat, and after pouring the warm wine for her and brandy for himself, Caldbeck sat beside her. She kept her eyes on her glass and searched in vain for something to say. Caldbeck showed no sign of unease. He sipped his brandy comfortably and studied the fire. Catherine leaned into the sofa cushions and took a long swallow of the hot wine. The comforting heat seeped through her, spreading into her limbs. After several more swallows had warmed her, Caldbeck turned to look at her.

"Tomorrow, if you like, we shall ride, and I shall show you some of the estate."

"Oh, yes. I love to ride. But…what happened to my horses?" She had had no time to think about them, but held little hope that they had survived her uncle's fall from grace.

"I redeemed them. They arrived this morning. That is a very fine chestnut hunter."

"Indeed she is." Catherine always warmed to a discussion of her horses. "I have not tried her in the field yet. I'll ride her tomorrow." The wine and the fire began to have their effect. She relaxed a little more and leaned toward him. "And thank you so much for thinking of my horses. So much has happened."

"Yes, we have been much too occupied. I have had no opportunity to give you this." He reached for a small, velvet box on the wine tray and handed it to her. Catherine set her glass down and took it. Slipping the ribbon from it, she removed the lid and stared in wonder at the contents.

"Oh, how beautiful!" She lifted out a delicate necklace of deep blue sapphires set in gold. Catherine looked into Caldbeck's face. "I—I don't know what to say. You are too generous. You have already given me the lovely pearls." She rocked her hand so that the jewels caught the light of the fire. "It's gorgeous!"

"Pearls are for a bride. These are for my wife." Leaning forward, Caldbeck took the necklace from her. He circled her with his arms and deftly fastened the necklace. Resting his hands on her shoulders, he gazed at her for several breaths. "Yes," he said finally, "they are just the color of your eyes." He stroked her slim shoulders, pushing the silk of the negligee off onto her arms. "And breathtaking against your exquisite skin." He drew her toward him.

Catherine could not see that his lordship's breath had been taken, but *hers* certainly had. She opened her mouth for air just as his came over it. His hands tightened on her arms as he flicked his tongue over her lips. Without taking his mouth from hers, he shifted and pulled her across his lap, thrusting his tongue into her and pressing her body against the growing bulge at his groin.

The room lurched for Catherine. Sensation poured through her lower body as never before. All of it mingled with the feel of his hand pushing her negligee off her arms, and slipping her gown down to reveal one high, firm breast. He took his mouth from hers to gaze intently as his fingers circled the nipple.

"Ah." As the rosy crest tightened, he leaned down to cover it with his mouth. His tongue made lazy circles, and Catherine moaned, arching upward. Caldbeck's hand slid down her, across her stomach to the joining of her legs, and applied a gentle pressure. Her head dropped back, and instinctively she lifted her hips against his hand. All at once he stood, scooping her into his arms and carrying her to the bed. Her robe fell unnoticed to the floor.

Caldbeck set her upright long enough for the gown to follow, and then lifted her onto the bed. Still breathless, she watched as he stripped off his clothes. His erection sprang outward from the thick, night-black curls spreading across his groin. The same dark hair covered his broad chest in a black veil and ran in a V down his stomach. His warm, male scent washed over her.

He lay down beside her, propping his head on his hand so that he could see the length of her body. He touched the sapphires briefly, tasting the skin around them with small kisses. He began to lightly stroke her breasts, her belly and the inside of her thighs, brushing them with his fingertips.

Catherine had never felt anything like this. Every muscle in her body tightened. Heat and sensation throbbed at the apex of her legs. She sighed and stretched her arms over her head against the pillow.

"So beautiful. So much fire." Caldbeck trailed his tongue over her breasts and kissed one taut nipple. Catherine's whole body quivered. His mouth moved over her, to her waist, her navel.

Now his hand was doing something between her legs, while his lips tantalized her nipple. Darkness closed in around the edges of her vision, and her world narrowed to the touch of his hand, the warmth of his mouth and the rush of feeling they were creating. Desire grew in her until she thought she must explode.

Suddenly, she *did* explode.

The world went dark. Myriad tiny lights sparkled across her vision, and every inch of her skin tingled and throbbed. She could hear her own voice gasping and crying out as the flood of sensation engulfed her. She writhed in his arms.

His weight came down on her, and he joined his body with hers while she yet fought for breath. She was dimly aware of pain and pressure and the rhythm of his movements. The world still whirled around her as she heard his hoarse cry, felt his powerful hips pumping his seed into her. Gradually he quieted, and with him, the world settled back into its accustomed place.

Withdrawing, Caldbeck rolled to one side, taking her with him so that her head rested on his shoulder, and his arms clasped her tightly against him. Catherine lay relaxed and drowsy, listening as his breathing and heartbeat slowed.

After several minutes he asked, "Are you in pain?"

Catherine shook her head. She ached and stung a little, but not enough to disturb her lassitude. "No," she answered, "not to signify."

"Did you find the experience satisfactory?"

Catherine pulled back enough to smile at him. "Well, my lord, I have nothing against which to judge it, but I should say that I found it entirely satisfactory." His eyes did not change, but his lips softened a little, and for a moment she thought he would smile.

Then he pressed her close again. "Your passion is quite as wonderful as I imagined."

Catherine waited for more words—an endearment, perhaps?—but none were forthcoming. She sighed. At least, thus far, the earl seemed pleased with his bargain. She was foolish to wish for more.

Another woman. Now his lordship had brought one into the dale. He had seen her. The earl had lifted her out of the carriage, his hands on her body. Her body! A shudder convulsed him. The hateful warmth spread across his loins, and he struck at it with his fist, wailing his anguish. Pain burst over him, but the heat was not cast out. She glowed in his memory. Burned like a flame against the black sky. Like a demon, screaming in his soul. He could endure the evil no longer! It was claiming him. He must drive it out! Out of all of them!

Chapter Four

Catherine wakened in the curtained bed to the sound of hot water cans scraping against the hearth, and the refreshing smell of lavender. Apparently Sally was preparing a bath for her. That was strange. Catherine hadn't ordered one. She rolled over and winced, every part of her stiff and aching. Little wonder! She had spent several hours, with very short periods of rest, either twisting and moaning in ecstasy under his lordship's expert hands and mouth, or caught up in the rhythm of his hard body against hers. A small, delicious shiver of remembrance took her. However icy his features and manner, the frost clearly did not extend to his blood!

She was no longer curious.

She sat up and cautiously peeked under the covers. Oh, yes. A largish red smear definitely stained the bedding. She groaned silently. Now there was no doubt at all that the whole staff would shortly be apprised of the change in status of their lord's and lady's relationship. How could she look Sally in the eye?

And what had happened to her nightgown?

She found it lying across the foot of the bed. Caldbeck must have placed it there when he arose, leaving her to sleep on. She gathered up his empty pillow and buried her face in it. Yes, she could still smell the smoky, masculine fragrance. It sent another shiver through her.

She pulled the gown over her head and slipped her feet out of the covers. Sally turned as she heard the rustle of the drapes, and hurried to help Catherine pull them back. The maid was all cheery nonchalance.

"Good morning, my lady. Hardraw gave me your message to prepare your bath."

Hardraw? Oh, yes, Caldbeck's valet. That explained the bath—the earl's instructions, no doubt. A twinge of annoyance swept through Catherine. What did he think he was doing, ordering her bath? She pushed the irritation aside and decided not to look a gift horse in the mouth. She needed that bath.

"I hope you slept well, miss. It's another lovely day."

Sally bustled about pouring hot water into the copper tub. When the temperature satisfied her, she motioned to Catherine, who stepped into it. Ahh! She slid down until the hot water lapped at her chin.

"Mrs. Hawes suggested I steep the lavender first. So refreshing it is." Sally handed her a face cloth.

Catherine resisted making an unladylike grimace. Another person minding her business. She replied with noncommittal murmurs until the warm water and soothing herbs had soaked away her discomfort.

An hour later, feeling quite renewed, Catherine made her way to the breakfast parlor and found her husband— yes, truly her husband now—finishing his breakfast. He stood as she entered the room.

"Good morning. I trust you rested well?" Caldbeck's cool gaze took in the flush that Catherine could feel burning in her face.

"Uh...yes." She decided to be gracious. "Thank you for ordering the bath. You are very considerate."

"The mark of a gentleman." His eyes never flickered, but this time Catherine was sure she detected the slightest change in his voice. Was he teasing her? It seemed so unlikely, yet...

"I see you are attired for riding. Are you certain you still wish to do so this morning?"

Catherine could feel her face positively flaming. "I believe I do. I...I do not ride astride."

"A fortunate circumstance."

Catherine cast him a suspicious glance. There it was again—that minute change of tone. He *was* teasing her.

Wasn't he?

"Indeed." She put a touch of ice into her own voice.

His lordship, of course, did not react to it. "Then when you have eaten, let us be on our way."

They rode in the crisp fall air across the rolling dales, Catherine's new hunter and Caldbeck's dapple gray cantering along companionably. The hills, crowned here and there with autumn woods and dotted with white sheep, rose green against an indigo sky. Small watercourses raced down from the heights, cutting into the soil and plunging over outcrops of stone in diminutive waterfalls. A hint of wood smoke prickled their nostrils.

Catherine flung a quick look at her husband. He sat ramrod straight in the saddle, his shoulders square, his muscular thighs expertly guiding his mount. The superfine of his coat fit smoothly across his back, and his hat rested at what could only be called a dashing angle. How could she ever have missed that bold physical aspect of him? Now she could see nothing else.

Her happy mood expanded to encompass the whole landscape. To her, all the colors glowed with unusual brightness, and the breeze blew soft and caressing. "Oh! This is so beautiful." Catherine's gesture took in a complete circle. "Is Yorkshire always so lovely?"

"The Dales are well known for their beauty," his lordship replied with his usual moderation.

Today his tone did not dampen Catherine's spirits. "I have always loved visiting in the country, though I wanted more opportunity to do it. My uncle always lived in London."

"I much prefer the country." Caldbeck drew rein. "I especially wish to show you an old manor house on a piece of land I am thinking of buying—known as the old Buck Manor. It might make just the headquarters for your children's relief work. It has plenty of room to house orphans, also. Like Wulfdale, it has some very old sections, plus some newer ones, and a home farm."

"Oh! That would be wonderful. I would love to see it." Catherine restrained herself with difficulty from bouncing excitedly in her saddle. "A farm would be perfect. Children need chores to teach them responsibility— but not all the time, mind you. They need some time to play. In some of the institutions for homeless children the conditions are so strict as to be abusive. Even in the foundling hospitals so many of the babies die. I don't want mine to be like that. I want them to have a *home*."

Caldbeck nodded his head to the west, and they cantered off in that direction. "And were you assigned chores, Kate, as a child?"

Catherine wrinkled her nose. "Oh, yes. Or, at least, while my parents were living. My aunt and uncle never bothered. They let me do pretty much as I wished, as long as I stayed out of their way. But when I was little, I had to sort and wind all Mama's embroidery silks and yarn, and to walk her little dog and read to my grandmother when I grew older. I never minded reading to Grandmama, though. She was such a dear.'' Her face clouded a little. ''I missed her very much when she died.''

''You have a tender heart.''

''Do you think so?'' Catherine pursed her lips thoughtfully. ''I never thought of myself that way, nor has anyone else, apparently. Everyone talks only of my terrible temper.''

The earl glanced at her again. ''So I have been told.''

She rolled her eyes skyward. ''You are very calm about it now. I wonder how you will feel when you encounter it.''

''An interesting speculation, indeed.'' Caldbeck reined in his mount and pointed down into a little valley. ''There is the house, and just beyond it is the byre. Shall we inspect it now?''

''Certainly!'' Catherine nudged her horse, and Caldbeck followed her down the hill.

The house was, in fact, quite large. Four wings enclosed an old courtyard, and numerous chimneys made their way to the roof to stand out against the blue of the sky. The mildewed gray stones needed mortar in places, and shrubbery grew over the few windows that were visible.

''Why are most of the windows filled in with stone? Did they do it for defense?'' Catherine turned to her husband.

''More likely because of the window tax. It should be no great task to uncover them.'' Caldbeck evaluated the structure with narrowed eyes. ''The house is defensible, however. The windows were probably added long after the house was built.''

Squinting dubiously, Catherine urged her chestnut

through the portal into the courtyard. Following her in, Caldbeck dismounted and lifted her from the sidesaddle. As Catherine scanned the yard, a shudder ran down her spine. She stopped in her tracks. "My lord, do you feel that someone is watching us?"

"No." Caldbeck looked around. "And I don't see anyone."

Catherine's gaze followed his around the enclosure. "I...it's odd. Probably I am just being fanciful."

He looked down at her and took her arm. "You do have a lively imagination, Kate, but also a strong intuition, I should think. But there does not seem to be anyone here."

Catherine nodded, gratified by his seriousness. Her uncle had always declared her notions to be foolish past permission. Together they entered the largest door opening onto the yard. The hall smelled musty, but not damp. As they wandered from room to room through lopsided doors and up and down odd little staircases, Catherine's enthusiasm for the house increased.

"This is a delightful place! One never knows what lies beyond the next door. Children will love it."

"Very well, then. If you like it, I shall complete the sale."

"You believe it can be restored?"

Caldbeck examined the plaster near him. "Yes, it's sound enough. We can begin with the newer portions and leave the very old ones to the end." He pushed open a door and stopped in the doorway. "That must certainly be removed. It's a wonder the place has not burned to the ground."

Catherine squeezed past him to look and giggled. Hay filled the room. "Oh, my. Someone has used it as a hay barn.'' She kicked at a pile of hay. ''But not recently, I think.''

''No, the hay is old.'' Caldbeck came up behind her and circled her waist with his arms. ''It is dry, however.''

He bent to kiss the back of her neck. A tiny quiver ran through Catherine. The familiar melting sensation started in her stomach as he touched his tongue to her ear. His hands slipped, one upward and one downward, cupping her breast and stroking her belly. Catherine relaxed against him.

Just as Caldbeck turned her toward him, they heard a rustle in the hay, and something darted across Catherine's foot. She shrieked. Caldbeck tightened his hold and swung her quickly away from the pile of hay.

''There are rats!'' She shrunk back against him.

Caldbeck ushered her toward the door. This time she was certain he sighed. ''Yes,'' he agreed, ''there are rats.''

Riding homeward, Catherine discoursed on her plans for the orphanage. Her husband listened indulgently, occasionally offering a comment or suggestion. She rattled on about tutors and a matron and a manager for the farm. She describe her vision for the interior. She debated what livestock would be suitable and how the children should be dressed. ''And we shall call it the Buck Orphan Asylum.''

''I believe,'' his lordship interjected, ''that the Lady Caldbeck Home for Orphans would be more appropriate.''

''Do you think so? I would love that!'' Catherine launched anew into her vision for her charges.

At last the earl threw up an arresting hand. ''Enough. I can see that you are going to bankrupt me in a twelve-month.''

Catherine looked quickly to see if he were in earnest. Of course, she could not tell. Annoyed by that fact, she looked at him archly. "Worrying about your investment, my lord?"

"Not yet."

"Very good, then. I shall race you back to the stable."

Without further warning she kicked her mount and tore away at a gallop. She could hear the thunder of hooves behind her as the gray responded to her challenge. Laughing, she leaned into the wind and urged the hunter on. The stable could be seen across a gentle hill, and she made for it, easily clearing several dry-stone walls as she came to them.

Her mare came from fine stock, but the earl's stallion was both larger and stronger. Inexorably the gray head began to pull alongside her. As she coaxed the chestnut to greater speed, she realized that it was Caldbeck's superior knowledge of the terrain that was going to bring about her certain defeat. He was veering off to the right.

Seeking the reason, Catherine spied, hidden in a fold of the land, a small watercourse with a low stone wall on the other side. She would have to turn to the right, also, and that would throw her far behind her husband. She considered her options.

If she followed the earl and avoided the barrier, she would never catch the faster horse. The ravine, however, extended too far for an easy jump, and the wall on the other side might conceal a yet unseen hazard. It was a dangerous obstacle. Apparently, Caldbeck did not want to make the attempt, and he knew the land. Or perhaps he thought that she could not manage it and thus led her away.

Suddenly Catherine fervently wanted to win.

She did not want to lose to this icy, enigmatic man

who had taken control of her life. She eyed the ravine, gauged the narrowest spot and put the hunter straight at it.

The hunter was a good horse. With a mighty lunge she sailed over the ravine and cleared the wall, her hind hoof just clipping the stones. As the chestnut landed on the rough ground, her speed carried her too far forward, and she broke stride to regain her balance. The change of rhythm, added to the momentum of the leap, jarred Catherine's knee free of the saddle, and she parted company with her mount.

She fell hard. The breath knocked out of her, she sat up gasping like a landed fish, her skirts around her waist. She vaguely heard pounding hooves coming toward her. Caldbeck had come around the end of the ravine and had his horse at a dead run. He pulled in a few feet from her, vaulted out of the saddle before his mount had stopped moving, and ran to where she sat.

"Kate! Are you hurt?" For once she could actually hear urgency in his voice.

"N-no. I'm fine. I think." She became able to breathe again. "'No fence you can't get over with a fall'," she quoted, trying to grin carelessly. She looked up into her husband's face. He did not wear a comforting expression, and she hastily looked elsewhere. The small tingle of fear returned as he looked coldly down at her. The fall had shaken her worse than she wanted to admit, and she didn't feel up to bravado.

Caldbeck pulled her to her feet and picked up her hat. He then silently examined her horse and led it back to where she stood. He did not give her the reins, but stood watching her for a moment. Finally, he spoke. Quietly.

"If you ever overface your horse like that again, I assure you that it will be the last time you ever see her."

Even spoken softly, the words hit Catherine in the face like a freezing wind.

"How—how dare you!" She grabbed angrily for the reins. Caldbeck calmly moved them out of her reach.

"I mean it, Kate. You will not endanger yourself and your mount in that way again." He handed her the reins and, putting his firm hands on her waist, tossed her up. She turned the chestnut and rode to the stables in haughty silence.

The knowledge that she was absolutely in the wrong did nothing to ameliorate Catherine's anger. On the contrary. Just because she had acted imprudently, perhaps— well, perhaps rashly even…and, yes, *possibly* irresponsibly—he had *no* right to threaten her. Take her horse away, indeed! Treating her like a child! Just because she had agreed to marry him did not make him her lord and master. Never mind the law.

Never mind that he was right.

She plunked down in the chair and attacked the implements on her desk. Arrogant bore! Scolding her! A half-written letter she ripped into pieces, scattering them on the floor. Ordering her bath! Who did he think he was? She threw the pens into the pigeonhole and shoved the wax jack against the wall with a resounding thump. Telling her when to nap! Did he think her an infant? Nobly forbearing to throw the inkwell, she got up and stamped around the room.

She would *not* let him get away with such high-handed treatment. He would regret it. She wasn't afraid of him. A little unnerved perhaps…on occasion. Just because he was tall and strong and smelled so like a man that she… He had no right! None at all. She did not wish to speak to him. She would not eat with him. He could have his dinner in solitary grandeur tonight. Every night! Sally could bring her a tray.

At that thought, Catherine went back to the desk and gathered up the torn bits of paper. No use making extra work for Sally just because she was in a dudgeon with her husband. She tossed the scraps into the fire and glared at the figurine of a china shepherdess that adorned the mantel. The shepherdess smirked back. Catherine did not care for that figure.

"Don't you laugh at me! You are a very ugly shepherdess. Mind your manners, or I shall pitch *you* into the fire."

Somewhat pacified by the making of this dire threat, Catherine sat down on the couch with a sigh, arms crossed over her breasts. Why did the man have to be so exasperating and still so damnably attractive?

So his lovely bride was in a snit, was she? Not coming down to dinner, eh? Her message to that effect had been distinctly chilly in tone. Charles basked in the inner amusement as he tied a fresh cravat.

What did she expect him to do now? Whatever it was, it was highly unlikely that he would do it. But if he was any judge of character, her indignation would not last long. He looked forward to a long life filled with her volatility and the inevitable reconciliations. Not that this little tempest qualified as a full-blown temper tantrum. The first real display of the infamous temper was still to be anticipated.

He could hardly wait.

But perhaps he should not have spoken so harshly. He had no intention of trying to rule her with an iron hand. Her impetuosity and her courage, her caring and her passion had attracted him to her in the first place. His words had threatened her. His actions had already forced her under his control. In fact, he had virtually kidnapped her. Perhaps he should be ashamed of himself. He wasn't. Not the smallest bit. Charles told himself he appreciated her as few men could.

But he couldn't let her risk herself that way. She or that hunter she was so proud of might easily have been killed. Charles shuddered afresh at the memory of Catherine sprawled on the ground, struggling to breathe. The thought of losing her and the beautiful fire he had wakened in her the night before filled him with a cold, bleak emptiness. A too-familiar emptiness.

He must take better care of her. It was his responsibility.

He saw Her fall. Saw Her skirts fly up. Her white legs. White legs! He moaned softly. Evil! Evil, evil. It was consuming him. Eating him from within and from without. It must be scourged, cleansed.

The power was growing within him. He felt it, tasted it, tried its strength. He flung his arms wide and lifted his face to the night sky, a cry wrenched from the depths of his being. Soon! Soon.

Chapter Five

By morning Catherine's mood had significantly improved. As always, her anger flared brightly, but briefly, and she was ready to admit her error. Considering whether she should apologize to Caldbeck, she entered the breakfast parlor only to find that he had already finished and gone out. A certain disappointment stirred within her, followed by a definite sense of relief. She concluded that, if one must eat crow, it is far better not to do so for breakfast.

Hawes informed her, as he brought in a fresh supply of scones, that his lordship had ridden out to one of his estates, which lay some distance from Wulfdale. "He asked me to express his regret that he will be very late getting home. He may not see you until tomorrow."

Bleakness settled over Catherine as she picked at her breakfast. It seemed that his lordship might be even angrier than she had supposed. She had been herself so infuriated when he had rung his peal over her that she had hardly noticed his manner. Not that she would have been able to tell what it meant, anyway. Sighing, she turned her mind to what to do with herself for the whole day.

The idea of exploring the old section of the house presented itself, only to be rejected. It would seem very flat without Caldbeck's company. The thought startled her. When she had first met him in London, she had found him dull—handsome, perhaps, but dull. When had that changed?

And where had he really gone? A sick sensation gripped her. What if he *did* have a mistress? He must have a great deal of experience in lovemaking to be able to arouse the feelings that had overwhelmed her. But with whom?

Had Catherine so disgusted him with her childish temper that he had returned to a former love? Must she share him with some shadowy figure, everyone else knowing, but keeping it from her?

How humiliating!

She bit her lip and choked back tears. Loneliness washed over her. What had she done? Had she already ruined her chance for happiness? Had she ever had a chance of happiness in this senseless marriage at all? She pushed away her plate and fled up the stairs to her bedchamber.

Catherine did not spend a pleasant day. She had treated herself to a good cry and felt a little better afterward, but the emptiness in her persisted. She had not felt so isolated and lonely since her father died. Writing a long letter to Liza only made her wish all the more for the depth of love that Liza and George Hampton shared—the kind of love that Catherine had seen between her parents. She had not recognized it as a child, but now… Staring out her window at the hills that had seemed so magically beautiful the day before failed to cheer her. The overcast sky drizzled rain, the dim light fading the colors.

Eating her own dinner in solitary grandeur, Catherine found that she did not like it at all. How could she have been so foolish as to have kept to her room like a sulky child last night? She retired to her bedchamber and was brooding as Sally brushed her springy hair for bed.

When a knock sounded at her door, she almost jumped off the dresser stool in her surprise, causing Sally to drop the brush.

"Oh! Oh, I'm sorry, Sally. That must be his lordship. You may go." Then, turning toward the door, she called, "Come in."

Caldbeck came through the door and paused by the dressing table as Sally hastily took herself off. Her manner stiff with constraint, Catherine indicated the sofa, where wine and brandy sat on the side table.

"Will you have some refreshments, my lord?"

"Thank you." The earl strolled to the table and poured for each of them, handing Catherine her glass as she sat on the sofa. He sat beside her, perfectly at ease. "Are you recovered from your fall?"

"Yes. A few bruises only." Catherine sat silent for a moment, playing with the tie of her wrapper, her eyes downcast. At last she took a deep breath and plunged in.

"I...I feel...I should...I should apologize to you, my lord." There! She had said it. "I showed very poor judgment in putting my horse at that ravine yesterday. I might have injured her badly—strained a hock, or even broken a leg."

He did not speak, and she peeped up at his face. She could read nothing in it, so she gathered her courage and went on. "And then for me to have been in such a temper... No wonder you did not visit me yesterday evening, and took yourself off today!"

Caldbeck reached out and lifted her face, obliging her

to look at him. "You think that is the reason I did not come last night? That I feared your temper?" Catherine thought that hint of something might be back in his voice, but if so, it disappeared as she searched for it. His expression remained cold. "You do not know me very well, Kate."

"That is quite true, my lord. As you know."

"Yes, quite true. I also regret the way I spoke to you yesterday. I was the more angry for also being frightened. You might have broken your neck."

"You? You were frightened? I never guessed."

"Just because I do not give outward evidence of my emotions, Kate, does not mean that I have none. You will come to know me better." He took possession of her hand. "I had business that I had been putting off. Since it was raining, today seemed an opportune time to take care of it. Had I seen you this morning, I would have explained."

He lifted her hand and kissed the palm, letting his tongue touch it. "But neither did I stay away last night out of anger. I did not come because I subjected you to some very hard use the night before. I thought you might need some time to recover."

The heat crept up from Catherine's breast to her face. She dropped her gaze. "Oh."

Much later, Catherine looked up into her husband's face as he lay beside her in the cave of the big curtained bed. "I need to say something else, my lord. I haven't yet thanked you for buying the manor house for me and my orphans."

Caldbeck stroked the glowing halo of her hair where it swirled across the pillow. "I feel quite adequately thanked."

Catherine giggled. "I'm glad, but I wanted to tell you."

"There is one thing you might do to thank me, Kate." The earl appeared to consider.

Catherine sat up. "Of course, my lord. What is it?"

"Call me Charles."

The next morning Catherine had the novel experience of being wakened with a kiss—and with a few other things as well. How strange to share a bed with a husband, and how strange to discover ardor in him on awakening. Her uncle had kept the whole household trembling from his temper until he had breakfasted.

Charles left her at last, and she rang for Sally. After her bath, Catherine went in search of her breakfast. As usual, his lordship had preceded her and sat sipping coffee and reading a newspaper. He came around the table to her place, and not only held her chair, but kissed her cheek as she sat. Startled, Catherine touched the spot on her cheek and smiled up at him.

He returned to his chair and put the newspaper aside. "I wish that I might ride with you again today, but I have to attend to some more very tedious business. It is always thus when I have been in London for a period. It will not take me as long as it did yesterday, however. I shall be here to have dinner with you, perhaps earlier."

Catherine face must have fallen, because he hastened to add, "I fear residence at Wulfdale is very flat for you at the moment, but that will improve when you have made some friends in the area. I would like for you to start planning a reception for our neighbors so that you may meet one another. Are you agreeable?"

"Why, yes. I think that would be a wonderful idea. I love parties. Richard can help me with the guest list."

She smiled at him. "Yes, that should keep me busy for a while."

Charles nodded. "And in the next few days, we should be able to start work at the orphanage."

Catherine brightened. "Wonderful! I shall be extremely busy then. Perhaps I shall compose some letters today regarding my London projects and have that done before I am overwhelmed. And, if you have no objection, I may ride over to the manor and look at it again." She paused ruefully. "If I can find it."

"Of course, if you wish. I have assigned James Benjamin as your groom. He will show you the way." He stood and bowed. "I would prefer that he accompany you when I cannot. We cannot have my bride getting lost amongst the dales."

True to her word, Catherine dived into her correspondence with renewed vigor. By early afternoon she had prepared several letters and felt the need to get out into the sunshine. The weather had again become glorious, and she set out on her expedition with a high heart.

She discovered James Benjamin to be a stocky young man with a pleasant face and a friendly manner. When he brought her mount to the door, she discovered that he had saddled not her hunter, but her bay hack. Still feeling a little guilty that she should have taxed the mare's strength so, she made no comment.

As they rode into the courtyard of the old house, Catherine again felt the hair on the back of her neck rise and tickle. She looked around, scanning the windows with anxious eyes.

"What, m'lady?" James Benjamin followed her gaze. "You see somewhat amiss?"

"No…" Catherine didn't want to sound foolish. "I

just have a strange feeling. I had it before when we came here—as though someone were looking at me.''

James Benjamin sharpened his attention and glanced around the walls and roof. ''Maybe it's only an owl close by the flue.''

Catherine cast her own eyes around the chimneys. ''I don't see any owl.''

James Benjamin shrugged. ''I wouldn't be surprised at any fleysome thing tonight—not in an old place like this.''

Catherine jerked her head around to look hard at the groom.

''What do you mean—'fleysome' thing?''

''Boggarts. Tonight's All Hallows.'' He grinned. ''I don't care to be out after dark. I might meet Old Padfoot.''

''Old Padfoot?''

''Aye—a great black hound, he is. Them that sees him are sure to be in the graveyard soon.''

''Oh, pooh!'' Catherine realized she was being teased again. ''Next you will be telling me about the headless bride.''

''Nay then!'' The young man laughed. ''I've heard naught of a headless bride.''

''His lordship told me about her.'' Catherine decided that two could play the game. ''She inhabits the older part of Wulfdale. Carries her head and veil in her hand.''

The groom looked a little less cocky. ''If his lordship tells something, I'd believe it.''

''Would you, indeed?'' Catherine raised one eyebrow. It pleased her that she had shaken her escort a bit, but instead of feeling reassured, she began to shift uncomfortably in her saddle. For heaven's sake! They were frightening each other with their nonsense! She decided she didn't want to go inside the hulking building, after all.

"Well, it will soon be dark, and if we are to avoid Old Padfoot, we best be going."

"Aye." James Benjamin glanced back over his shoulder.

As they turned their horses for home, Catherine resisted looking back. She didn't want to give her mischievous companion the satisfaction. Yet she still felt uneasy. What had his lordship—no, she must remember to call him Charles. What had he said of her—that she had a lively imagination? Perhaps too lively. But he had also commented on her intuition, and her intuition told her that there was something strange about that courtyard.

At dinner that evening Catherine regaled Charles and Richard with the story of the trip to the manor. "That rascal James Benjamin thought he could frighten me with stories. By the way, what in the world is a boggart?"

Charles looked up from his leg of lamb. "A boggart? A boggart is a ghost."

"I thought it must be—because of this being All Souls Eve. I got a bit of my own back, however, by telling him about your headless bride." She chuckled at the recollection. "He said if you told the story, he believed it."

"It is pleasing to know that one has the confidence of one's employees." His lordship did not look particularly pleased—nor displeased, for that matter. "But perhaps I should speak to him about frightening his mistress."

"Oh, no! I was not really frightened, and he is not impertinent. I believe we shall go on very well."

"Good. I chose him because he is both reliable and intelligent. I want to be sure of your safety."

"Thank you. You take very good care of me." *He*

does, Catherine thought. *Perhaps too well. As though I...* Not wishing to pursue that line of thought at the moment, she returned to the original subject. "He also told me about Old Padfoot—a harbinger of death, I collect?"

"So the old people say. Did he tell you about the cock crowing at midnight?"

Catherine accepted a serving of mint jelly from the footman. "I've heard that before—another sign of impending death."

"Surely James Benjamin did not omit the screaming skull?" Charles looked up quickly as the footman jumped, rattling the serving spoon against the dish. "What's the matter, John David?"

"Uh...naught, my lord."

Charles regarded him a moment longer. "Come now, John, out with it."

"It's nothing, my lord. Just...well, all the talk of fley-boggarts... And on All Hallows... And the skull..." John David shivered as unobtrusively as he could manage while holding a dish of mint jelly.

Charles leaned back in his chair and scrutinized his henchman. "I take it that you won't be going down to the village inn this evening?"

John David shook his head emphatically. "Nay, my lord. I'll keep to my bed tonight."

"A wise precaution, no doubt."

"Just a minute," Catherine interrupted, "what is this about a screaming skull?"

"It resides at Burton Agnes Hall. Supposedly it once belonged to a daughter of the house—at the time of Queen Elizabeth. It refuses to leave, and sets up the most intolerable screeching if anyone attempts to remove it."

Catherine narrowed her eyes at her husband doubtfully and glanced inquiringly at his secretary.

Richard smiled shyly. "Aye, my lady. They do say that."

"Oh. I thought that surely it belonged to the headless bride." She favored his lordship with a suspicious stare.

He returned his attention to his dinner. John David took his mint jelly and made good his escape.

"Well, Kate—" Charles took Catherine's arm as they left the dining room "—would you like to brave the uncanny influences of the night and join me in a walk? The moon is full."

She looked at him saucily. "All Souls *and* a full moon? I thought we were to cower in our bed until morning."

"I would have no objection to that."

Catherine stumbled over nothing, and Charles steadied her. She felt the heat creeping up her face. "I meant... You know what I meant!"

"Alas, yes. You would prefer the walk, then?"

Flustered, Catherine continued to stammer. "I didn't say—I didn't say that, either!"

"A difficult decision. Let us compromise, then. We will walk now and cower in our bed later." Caldbeck's expression remained completely serious.

A gurgle of laughter escaped Catherine. "My lord! You are the most complete hand! You *are* teasing me. And I never even suspected that until we... Never mind, let me fetch my cloak. It is getting chilly."

A few minutes later found them strolling away from the mansion toward the gardens. The full moon rode high in the sky, covered from time to time with scraps of ragged cloud being blown by an increasing wind. Their cloaks—her emerald velvet and his gray—alternately clung to them or billowed out behind, according to the whim of the capricious gusts. In the rose garden a few hardy blooms bobbed wildly at the end of their stalks.

Charles cast a practiced glance at the scudding clouds. "It appears to be blowing up some weather. More rain would be welcome. It has been much too dry."

Catherine sighed. "I'm sure the rain is needed, but I hate to see the lovely fall weather go."

"It won't be gone for good yet, and it will be followed by some lovely winter weather." He dropped his long arm across her shoulders and pulled her closer. "In a month or a little more, we may have snow. The Dales are quite dazzling in the snow."

Catherine snuggled a bit nearer to the warmth of his body.

"I'm sure they are. I enjoy snow, too."

"You seem to enjoy most things." Charles looked down at her inquiringly.

"I do! Life holds so many interesting things. It would be a great waste not to appreciate them."

"Indeed."

They wound their way around the rose garden and took the path that led through the natural garden and into the woodland. The leaves, so colorful in the daytime, looked black in the moonlight, and great drifts of them blew off the branches to go flying across the silver moon. The stripped limbs stood out in stark relief against the lighter sky.

Charles seemed to have no trouble following the dark path. Catherine breathed in the crisp air, savoring the chill and the gloom. Their footfalls crunched on the hard earth, and in the bushes a rustle revealed the flight of some small creature. The beat of wings sounded somewhere above them, and she slowed, looking up, searching for their owner. Charles paused with her, and then, when she saw nothing, they continued along the path.

After a few more minutes of walking, they reached a small hill and, at the top, a circle of trees. Charles stopped, and Catherine looked around, enthralled.

"Oh! How beautiful! Just look at how the moonlight casts shadows on the ground—all twisted and eerie. A perfect setting for All Hallows." Catherine lifted her arms above her head and twirled around the clearing, her cloak streaming behind her. She laughed in delight. "I feel like an ancient priestess. Do you think this might once have been a sacred grove?"

She ceased her gyrations and came back to Charles's side, shivering in a particularly sharp puff of wind. He pulled her close and wrapped his own cloak around both of them. The heat of his body enveloped Catherine.

"My old tutor thought it must have been," he answered. "This has been one of my favorite places since I was a boy. I thought you would like it."

Perception dawned on Catherine. *He is sharing something with me that is special to him.* What a surprising man her husband was proving to be. She slipped her arms around his waist and tipped her head back to look into his face. She found it as stony as always, the flickering shadows imbuing it with a strange otherworldliness. The moon reflected weird lights in the clear, silver eyes, the eyes of a pagan priest intent on some unearthly ritual. A delicious thrill slid down her backbone. An owl cried out softly somewhere in the trees.

"It *is* a frightening night." Catherine shivered again and huddled closer. She giggled. "Thank you for bringing me here. I am enjoying myself immensely. They say that the border between this world and the spirit world fades on All Hallows. Here, I believe it."

"Visiting here with you increases my enjoyment a great deal." Charles glanced over her head at the trees and tightened his arms around her. "After my tutor taught me about the groves when I was a lad, I would slip out of the house and come here on All Hallows. I kept hoping to see a boggart, but I never did. Perhaps you may attract the spirit that avoided me." He brushed his lips across her forehead.

"I wonder what kind of rites the ancients performed here. Perhaps the ghost of one of their sacrifices will come forth if we wait long enough."

"Perhaps so, though I myself would prefer to believe that they conducted fertility rites." Charles bent his head to taste her lips. "Yes, I am almost certain that is the spirit I sense." He increased the intensity of the kiss, and Catherine sighed and ran her tongue around the edges of his mouth. He groaned and pressed her hard against himself. She melted into him. Slowly he began lowering them both to the earth.

At that moment an ungodly howl rent the air.

Catherine screamed. Charles spun around, eyes searching through the shadows. The howl sounded again—low at first and rising in pitch, ending in an agonizing wail.

"What is that?" Catherine found herself clutching at Charles's cloak.

He continued to search the darkness, but relaxed a bit and put his arm back around Catherine. "It is naught but a dog howling at the moon."

"Are you sure?"

"What else could it be?" Charles glanced down at her and pulled her close again.

"I am afraid to ask! It sounds almost human." The hideous howling again marred the night. Catherine trembled and retreated further inside Charles's cloak. He lifted her chin so that he could look into her face, studying her in the darkness, his voice quite without expression. "Padfoot?"

"Yes! How could you ever come here by yourself?"

"I never heard Padfoot before."

Catherine gave him an indignant look. "Are you laughing at me? No, of course you aren't. You never..." She shrugged. "Does hearing him count as an omen?"

"No. I believe one must see him. But you are getting chilled." Charles definitely sighed. "Are you ready to go back to the house?"

"I guess so, but I am going to keep my eyes shut so that I don't see him." The howl rang out again, and she quickly took Charles's arm. His hand closed over hers.

"I believe," said his lordship, "that it is time for us to cower in our bed."

Chapter Six

What an eerie night! Catherine thought as she dressed for breakfast the next morning. She'd been jolted awake around midnight by the sound of a cock crowing. She must tell Charles about that as soon as she saw him. She had barely arrived at the table when she launched into the story.

"Strange, hearing it that way when we had just been talking about it last night," she finished.

Charles glanced up from his coffee. "Perhaps you dreamed it."

"I might have. I heard it only once after I sat up—or thought I did. Perhaps our walk in the woods and hearing Old Padfoot made me dream of unnatural things." She reached impulsively across the table and squeezed his hand. "I loved seeing the grove in the moonlight. Do you really think the druids might have used it?"

"More likely it would have been the Viking settlers. They worshiped in groves and on islands. My family name, Randolph, is Anglo-Saxon."

"Is it really? I would have thought your ancestors were Norman. Your hair is dark, and so is Helen's."

"Apparently we resemble my mother."

"Probably. What does the name Randolph mean?"

"It is from *rand* and *wulf*—shield and wolf."

"So you have a shield and a wolf's head on your coat-of-arms. I had wondered…" She halted as the door opened to admit Hawes.

"Excuse me, my lord." The butler looked very grave. "I am sorry to disturb you, but I fear there has been a great tragedy."

Caldbeck instantly riveted his attention on Hawes. "Of what nature?"

"A fire, my lord. The Widow Askrigg's cottage. They found her body within."

"Oh, no!" Catherine clapped a hand over her mouth. "Did she have any children? Did they also die?"

"She has—had—children, my lady, a boy and a girl, but fortunately, they were not in the cottage last night."

"Oh, the poor dears!"

Caldbeck laid his napkin on the table. "I'll go at once. Has the magistrate been notified?"

"Yes, my lord. I sent one of the grooms 'round to Lord Arncliff as soon as I heard. One of her neighbors came to the kitchen just a little while past."

"I want to go with you." Catherine jumped up from her chair. "I want to see about the children."

After a moment's pause, Caldbeck nodded. "Very well."

It took Catherine but a few minutes to race back to her bedchamber for her riding dress while the grooms brought the horses around. Caldbeck tossed her up, and they rode without conversation to the still-smoking ruins of the widow's cottage. The wind, sharp now with the scent of burning, continued to blow a gale, and the clouds were increasing. The damp air pierced Catherine's jacket and made her shiver. A bleak scene indeed met their eyes as they arrived. The magistrate, a number of Wulfdale tenants and several landowners of the district gathered solemnly in the scorched cottage garden.

Caldbeck acknowledged greetings and looked around the group. "When did this happen?"

"In the night, me lord." A man in a farmer's smock stepped forward. "When I come out to feed the animals, I saw smoke, so after I had done, I thought I best go look." He swung his hand to indicate the still-smouldering building. "I found this."

"Has the body been removed?"

"Nay, me lord. Too hot. But you can see her. Nothing but bones left, any road."

Catherine craned her neck to see where the man pointed, but Caldbeck pulled his horse up between her and the cottage. Irritated, she tried to peer around him, but he remained stubbornly in her way. Confound the man! She did not need that much protection.

Then she remembered the cock.

"I heard a cock crowing last night. It must have seen the blaze and taken it for the dawn."

Several tenants shuffled their feet.

Charles surveyed them with his glacial gaze. "Did no one else hear it?"

After an embarrassed silence, one of the women spoke up. "Aye, my lord. I heard it, but…"

The rest of the crowd looked at their feet, the hills or the clouds.

"And, of course, no one dared get out of bed to go to the window." Did just a bit of annoyance sound in his lordship's voice?

His answer manifested in a general shaking of heads.

Catherine interrupted. "Are her children safe?"

The farmer nodded. "Aye, me lady. They stayed the night at her old dad's place—down the lane a piece."

"Has anyone carried the news to Mrs. Askrigg's father? No? Very well, we'll go there next." Charles looked at the stout, gray-haired magistrate. "Are you satisfied?"

"Aye, my lord. Pretty simple." Lord Arncliff shook his head sadly. "A shame. A good woman. Attractive, except... Well, it's a pity."

Leaving the magistrate, Charles and Catherine trotted down the lane to a small cottage. It looked a bit the worse for time, but the yard was neat enough. An old man, bent with rheumatism and deaf as the doorpost, answered Caldbeck's knock. A small girl of about six and a boy a little younger peeped from behind him. It very soon became evident that making the elderly fellow understand what had transpired would be no easy task.

Catherine could not bear the thought of having the knowledge of their mother's death shouted at the children. She placed a hand on Caldbeck's sleeve. "My lord, let me take the children for a walk. Then you may explain to their grandfather."

He nodded in agreement, and she beckoned to the children and sent them for their wraps. Eyes wide with questions, they followed her out, and Catherine led them down the lane and out of earshot. Now that the problem of informing them of their mother's death had fallen to her, what could she say? However did one tell children that they had become orphans?

She walked on in silence, memories of the terrible moment when she herself had learned of her father's death tumbling through her mind. Catherine could still feel the knifing anguish and the terror. Biting her lip, she considered her young charges. Their huge eyes dwarfed their little faces. They knew something terrible had happened. She must tell them.

Kneeling in the dust of the road, Catherine placed a hand on a shoulder of each and looked into their eyes. A flurry of wind swirled a clutch of dead leaves around them and blew their hair across their faces. She moved it aside gently.

"What are your names?"

The little girl answered. "I—I'm Jill, ma'am, and he's Jesse."

"I have something very bad to tell you, Jill and Jesse. Your mother has died. Do you understand?"

Jill nodded. "Like Pa?"

"Yes. I'm very sorry."

Tears began to trickle down both little faces. Catherine felt her own heart break. She gathered a child in each arm and pulled them to her. Her tears dampened the small heads as she laid her cheek against them. Neither child made a sound, but wept silently in her arms.

She still held them thus when Caldbeck rode back up the lane, leading her horse. She looked up, wiping dust from her streaked face. He dismounted and came to kneel on one knee beside the forlorn little group.

"I finally made the old man understand. He is quite distraught. You told the children?"

Unable to speak, Catherine nodded. Caldbeck laid an arm on her shoulders. "We will get one of the village women to come. The children's grandfather is clearly too infirm to care for them. Why did she leave them there?" He shook his head in disgust. "I believe you have the first candidates for your home, Kate. Someone will care for them temporarily, but few can afford to feed two more mouths. Their welfare will now depend upon me."

Together they stood, and Charles lifted the tiny boy

into his arms. Each taking a hand, they led Jill back toward the village.

The children's grief stayed with Catherine throughout the rest of the day. She could not put it out of her mind. The threatening rain had finally begun to fall, darkening the sky, and Catherine's spirits even further. That evening, as she and Charles shared their evening wine, he reached over and brushed her cheek with his fingertips.

"You look very solemn. Sad memories?"

Catherine nodded and sighed. "Yes. I'm afraid so. Those poor children. You can have no idea how frightening it is to learn that you are all alone in the world."

"No, I was a grown man when my father passed away. It is not the same. How old were you?"

"Twelve. Not as young as Jill and Jesse."

"No, but still a child."

Catherine managed a wan smile, but a tear slid down her cheek. "I didn't think so at the time, but…yes, I was a child."

Charles extended an arm, and Catherine snuggled into it. "Were you very unhappy with your uncle and aunt?" he asked.

"No, not unhappy exactly—well, perhaps." Catherine sniffed and tried to blink the tears away. "I never felt that I belonged there. They obviously didn't want me." She stopped and took a deep breath, controlling the sobs that threatened. "I imagine that is how my notorious temper came into being. At least, when I displayed it, they noticed me."

"Ah, yes. The infamous temper."

Catherine nodded, looking down at her lap, tears dripping onto her clasped hands.

''I'm sorry you were alone.'' Charles pulled her across his lap so that her head rested on his shoulder.

Catherine didn't realize how much fear and sorrow and loneliness she had sealed up inside herself—losing first her mother, then her father to illness, then enduring long, comfortless years with no one to care about her, no one to talk to.

No one to hold her when she cried.

She gave up all attempt at control. Sobs erupted a few at a time, increasing until the pain poured out of her in a torrent. She cried until she thought she had reached the depths of her being, and then she cried harder.

She realized that her husband was gently rocking her in his arms. Warm arms, strong arms. Rocking her like a child. Catherine tried to respond to that thought with resentment, but couldn't. She needed the comforting so much. How surprising to find it in the taciturn Earl of Caldbeck.

At last the storm passed. Exhausted, she relaxed into his embrace and quietly drifted off to sleep. She did not wake even when he carried her to the bed and lay down beside her, still holding her close.

Charles waited until Catherine had fallen into a deep sleep before he took a moment to remove his clothes. He then gathered her back into his arms and held her closely. Her pain wakened an old memory in him, a memory of sitting in his father's lap the evening after his mother's funeral. Neither of them had cried—men didn't cry—nor did they speak. But the strong arms had sheltered him, comforted him. Catherine had never had that. Charles was grateful that he could comfort her now.

His father had endured his pain in silence, his laughter dying with his wife—his laughter and his anger and his tears, all buried with her. But even in his grief he'd never abandoned his children. He'd lent them his strength until the day he died.

Charles asked for nothing more as a man than to be like him.

A few days later Catherine asked Charles a question that had been bothering her. "Must I advertise in the London papers to find a suitable staff for the orphanage?"

Charles pondered for a moment. "Well, if you want a tutor for it, you may be obliged to send to London. I am by no means sure that you need one. However, I should think that most of the staff can be supplied locally."

"But I don't know anyone locally."

"True, but that presents no difficulty. Just mention it to Mrs. Hawes. I assure you, you will have more applicants than you can interview. And, of course, Richard can help you. He will be happy to send any advertisement you wish to London. You will not need my help. I shall be busy with the renovations."

His advice proved to be sound. Every day a different woman presented herself at Wulfdale to apply for the position of matron at the new orphans' asylum, followed by a procession of farmers wishing to manage the farm. Catherine, delighted that she could both choose the best applicants and get to know the people of Wulfdale, plunged enthusiastically into the interviews. Between them and preparations for the reception, she had no time at all to be lonely or bored. She and Richard made endless lists, and he sent off several letters and a large number of invitations.

One day, as Charles and Catherine discussed the progress of the orphanage, Hawes appeared in the doorway to announce visitors. Helen and Adam Barbon walked into the drawing room.

"Hello. How nice to see you!" Catherine extended a hand to her sister-in-law and received a light kiss on the cheek in response. "When did you come home to Yorkshire?"

"We returned a few days ago. Adam escorted me."

Catherine shrewdly considered this information. It would seem that Charles's sister and his best friend were something more than casual acquaintances.

Charles held out a hand to Adam. His friend clapped him on the shoulder, but kept his right hand out of reach. "Forgive me for not shaking hands." Adam lifted his right hand to reveal a bandage. "I had a little mishap with a burning hearth rug."

"What, again?" Charles indicated a chair, and Adam sat. "Did you also set this carpet alight? Will you have some madeira?"

Adam laughed, accepting the wine. "You are not going to let me live that down, are you?" He turned to Catherine. "When we were lads in school, I once almost set fire to the dormitory. I was playing with fire as boys will, feeding the flames bits of paper. A scrap blew out of the fireplace and landed on the rug. But to answer your question—" he turned back to Charles "—this coal leaped out of the grate with no assistance from me. The rug was blazing quite merrily when I discovered it."

"You were fortunate. We had a fire at Wulfdale recently, and the occupant of the cottage was not so lucky."

Helen shook her head sadly. "We heard. Hetty Askrigg worked in the house when I was a girl. Very lively and pretty. Poor thing, to lose her husband and then her own life while her children are yet so young."

Adam nodded in agreement. "Yes. I remember her, too. A very pleasant woman. Of course…" He stopped and shrugged. "The whole thing is very sad. What will happen to her children?"

"They are going to live in my orphanage," Catherine stated with a little thrill of pride.

Adam turned a smile on her. "I heard that you have bought the old Buck property."

"Yes." Charles set his wineglass on a table. "Catherine is going to establish an orphanage in the old house and home farm. I am going to put sheep and wheat on the rest of it."

"I am looking for some property to buy, also," Helen announced.

"Really?" As usual, Charles's voice did not seem to vary at all. However, Catherine was becoming more attuned to him. She heard an undercurrent that she did not understand. He had fixed his whole attention on his sister.

"Yes. I…I would prefer not to live at the dower house at Lonsdale any longer." A glance passed between her and Adam, and she looked down at her lap. Adam frowned. Catherine pricked up her ears.

"Is Vincent being unpleasant?" Charles watched his sister closely.

"Of course. He is always unpleasant. It is just that now…well, he is drinking more and more…and I—"

"You are afraid of him." It was not a question. Charles kept his gaze firmly on Helen.

Adam gestured impatiently. "She does not need to fear him, nor to buy…" He shrugged, hiding his expression behind a sip of wine.

"Excuse me." Catherine spoke into the tense pause. "I don't know who Vincent is."

Helen smiled and turned from Adam to Catherine.

"Forgive us. Vincent is my stepson, the present Earl of Lonsdale. We…we do not get on very well together."

"Ha!" Adam's expression darkened. "No one can get along with that insolent pup!" He turned to Catherine. "Vincent's father spoiled him outrageously. He was always an obnoxious brat. At two-and-twenty he is a drunkard, a cad and a bully."

Helen shrugged. "That's probably true. I have spent too many years trying to understand and help him to see him clearly. I wanted to be a good mother to him, but I was so young. It would have taken much more wisdom than I had then."

Adam stood abruptly and paced around the room. "When will you stop blaming yourself? You *were* too young, and Vincent's father made any discipline impossible."

Helen smiled her gentle smile. "I don't blame myself, Adam. I'm just sorry that he is as he is. And I don't blame his father, although I can see that he was ill advised. He was so afraid that he might lose Vincent as he lost his other children."

Adam stopped before her, a sad smile on his own face. "*Your* children. You should save your pity for yourself."

"I have put that behind me." Helen touched his arm lightly, then looked at Catherine, clearly cutting off the subject. "I have an invitation to your reception. May I help in any way?"

Before Catherine could answer, Charles held up a hand and turned to Adam. "To avoid becoming enmeshed in the details of the entertainment, we had best escape immediately. Walk down to the stables with me and have a look at Catherine's hunter."

Adam readily agreed, and the two men left. Catherine watched their departure, shaking her head. She turned back to Helen, smiling. "Your brother never ceases to confound me. I can never tell when he is joking or if he is serious. I once thought him always serious, but I have learned my mistake."

Helen laughed. "He has been that way since I can remember. I was only three when our mother died. Charles was eight. They say that he never showed any emotion at the time or since. However, he does tease, as I can attest. Growing up with him, I learned to recognize it. He is really a very kind person—a big brother I can lean on."

"I am learning that. At first he seemed so cold, but...yes, he can be very kind." Catherine refilled their teacups, recalling the feeling of his protective arms.

Helen frowned slightly. "He is accustomed to being responsible for others, and he can be rather autocratic about it. That is something else I can vouch for. He practiced on me. I'm sure he and Adam want to discuss my problem with Vincent. Together they will decide that I should marry Adam and thus be saved from my stepson."

Catherine chuckled. "Charles *is* rather forceful about taking care of me. I suppose I should appreciate it—and I do. It is just that I am used to having a great deal of independence. My aunt and uncle, with whom I lived for many years, made little attempt to supervise me."

"And you are feeling resentful?" Helen set her cup down on the tray and looked perceptively at Catherine.

"No...not resentful, exactly. Well, perhaps a little. But he does so many considerate things..."

"That you feel guilty about being annoyed." Helen laughed. "I understand completely."

Catherine echoed her laughter. "Yes. That's it. Perhaps I am just finding it hard to accommodate another person all the time. I guess that is the nature of marriage.''

"Oh, yes. It is certainly the nature of marriage. I think that is why…'' Helen paused.

"You don't want to marry Adam?''

Another small silence ensued. At last Helen shook her head. "It isn't that. In a way I *do* want to. I guess I am like you—I am enjoying my independence. I wed so young I never before had any at all.''

"Were you unhappy in your marriage?'' *She probably had no more choice than I did. And that was a very impertinent question for me to ask.*

Catherine was on the point of apologizing when Helen shook her head again. "No, not unhappy. Lord Lonsdale treated me very kindly. I was not in love with him when we married, of course. Papa was not well, and he wanted to be sure I was safely bestowed. His lordship was twenty years my senior, but I came to love him. We lost two children to miscarriage, as did his first wife. Adam believes a weakness exists in the Lonsdale blood.''

"Oh, I am so sorry. That must have been very difficult for you.''

"Yes, but harder on Lord Lonsdale. That is why he spoiled Vincent so badly. Only he survived. But as I told Adam, I have left that behind.''

The conversation turned to mundane matters, and after another half hour Helen and Adam took their leave. Charles went to consult with his agent, and Catherine had time to think about the conversation. In the end Helen would probably accept Adam. It did not take much to see in Adam a man in love. And Helen looked at him with a tenderness that could not be missed. Another fact captured Catherine's awareness. She and Helen had something in common in their marriages.

And Helen had learned to love her husband.

Catherine considered her own feelings. They certainly had undergone a change since her marriage, but did she love Charles? The word had never been spoken between them. She did appreciate the kind things he had done, especially his comforting her, but she still felt anger toward him for manipulating her into the marriage without so much as an inquiry, let alone a courtship.

And protecting her as if she were a child. Odd. Catherine had felt unloved when her aunt failed to restrict her—knowing the woman didn't care enough to trouble herself. Now Catherine resented it in Caldbeck. Of course, she was no longer twelve years old, a fact he frequently appeared to forget. As Helen had pointed out, she felt both indignation and gratitude, neither of which was love.

But then there was the attraction she felt to him physically—his muscular body, the taste of his mouth, his strong hands. Her face grew warm at the thought. Poets often called that love. But was it?

And she felt lonely when his business occupied him elsewhere. Was *that* love? Or just loneliness?

Catherine had to admit that she didn't know.

The rising wind stirred his hair, but he did not feel the chill, nor the rain trickling across his scalp. His need for the night, the cold, the dark had not changed. But at last he had begun his work! And the taste was sweet. So sweet! She had welcomed him—until she saw her fate written in his eyes. Then she feared, struggled—puny, helpless. A beautiful fear.

He forced her toward her imperfection, her vileness, as he purified them both. She saw it as he freed her. He groaned as the fire again swept over him. But the rapture was fading. The evil reared once more, bitter, defiling, hungry. So much of it. So much.

Chapter Seven

Once started, the renovation of the old manor moved very rapidly. Several weeks later, Catherine brought her consideration of candidates for the staff to a close and announced her selections to Charles as they shared a light luncheon.

"I have decided on Mr. Kettlewell to manage the farm and on Mrs. Giggleswick for the matron. Richard suggests his older brother, Thomas, as the tutor. I understand that he is free at present, since his last charge has gone off to Eton."

Charles looked up from his baked eggs and nodded. "Kettlewell is a good choice. He has done very well with his own land. He is quite capable."

"Yes, I thought him so." Catherine smiled in satisfaction. "There is something rather grandfatherly about him, too. The children will love him."

"I believe Thomas Middleton will also do an excellent job, if you really want a tutor." Charles sipped his tea. "I know him. A very pleasant young man, and as I remember, a fine scholar. The only concern I have is with Mrs. Giggleswick. She was injured in an accident several years ago and now walks with a severe limp."

"It isn't that noticeable." Catherine bridled and rose to the defense of her chosen candidate. She had not asked the Earl of Caldbeck for his advice. He was *not* going to tell her whom to hire to care for her orphans! "It will not be a problem."

"But can she hold up to the work? Her leg never healed correctly. I would have rather thought Mrs. Clapham. She is certainly qualified."

So he had taken an interest in the applicants, after all! Confound him! He had promised to leave that to her. Did he think he could take over *everything?* Catherine's chin lifted stubbornly. "She is not as kind in her attitude toward children. Mrs. Giggleswick is so motherly. I really did not care for Mrs. Clapham."

Charles studied Catherine's mulish face for a few seconds. "I see," he said at length. "Perhaps you are correct. If you think the position will not be too much for Mrs. Giggleswick…"

"Oh, no!" Catherine insisted. "She tells me she took care of her own home and children for several years after the accident. Now that they are grown, and her husband has passed on, she needs something to do—someone to care for. I'm sure she will be just the thing."

"Very likely. Do as you think best." Charles finished his breakfast and stood. "Would you like to ride over to Buck Manor and inspect the repairs with me?"

Startled at his easy capitulation, Catherine stammered a little. "Oh, y-yes. Of course. I would love to."

"Good. I'll meet you as soon as you are ready."

As Catherine went upstairs for her riding clothes, she pondered the exchange with his lordship. She had been so sure he was going to give her one of those frosty looks that brooked no discussion. She hated it when he did that! She just froze in her tracks, and she hated that even more.

But instead he had deferred to her judgment. She had girded her loins for battle to no purpose! Catherine laughed aloud and ran up the stairs.

A scene of industrious activity greeted them at the old manor. Two men applied whitewash in the great hall, while several more created a racket with hammers and nails somewhere in the back of the same wing. Catherine saw two girls washing windows, giggling together as they worked. A plump woman on hands and knees scrubbed the old planks of the floor vigorously. As Catherine and Charles approached she got to her feet, pushed her fading blond hair out of her face with a damp wrist and curtsied.

Charles guided Catherine in that direction and made the introduction. ''Lady Caldbeck, this is Mrs. Ribble. She is overseeing the necessary cleaning of the building.''

Catherine nodded, and Mrs. Ribble again bobbed a curtsy. ''Welcome, me lady.'' With a pleasant smile the sturdy woman swept a hand around the spacious room. ''Does it suit you?''

''Oh, yes. It is going to be lovely.'' Catherine returned the smile.

''That it is. A champion place for the poor mites. We're to do the next room today, too, before the light goes.'' Mrs. Ribble indicated one of the doors with a glance, but Catherine was not sure which one. On the point of asking for clarification, she suddenly realized that her confusion was attributable to the fact that one of Mrs. Ribble's eyes did not move in concert with the other, making her gaze a bit misleading.

Not wishing to embarrass her, Catherine decided not to ask which room. ''It seems that you will soon be finished and ready for occupants. Will you continue to help Mrs. Giggleswick when the orphanage is in operation?''

"Aye, me lady, if you like. I'm fond of the wee ones, though the good Lord never saw fit to give none to me and Ribble.'' The woman sighed. "It is a grief, but when there's nothing to be done, we might as well be satisfied, choose how.''

Impulsively Catherine patted Mrs. Ribble's arm. "I know you will be an asset to the staff.''

The older woman favored her with a grateful smile— or at least, Catherine thought she did. The wandering eye made it hard to know whether she directed the expression at Catherine or someone unseen to her left.

Before she could be sure, a call from Charles, who had stepped out of sight, claimed Catherine's attention. She left Mrs. Ribble to her scrubbing and peered through each door until she found him.

"Is this to be the schoolroom?'' he asked as she came through the door.

"Yes. It is so warm and cheery.'' Catherine pointed to a newly restored bank of windows. "The light is good. It will be easy to learn here.'' She paused, considering. "My lord, I believe we should have all the Wulfdale children come in for lessons, not just the ones who live at the orphanage. Thomas could easily teach more students than we will have in residence for a while.''

Silent for a few moments, Charles then shook his head. "Their parents will not want that. They need every hand they can muster to put the crops in and to help with the harvest and the daily chores. Life is very hard for tenant farmers, Kate. The work is endless.''

Catherine frowned. "But surely their parents would like to see them learn skills that would help them in later life.''

"Perhaps, but they will not see the schoolroom as a source of those skills. And they are probably right. Think on, Kate. What opportunities exist for them, outside of working the land?"

Catherine's mouth drew into a stubborn line. "Surely there are opportunities, even for educated tenant farmers. They might become clerks, or…"

"Or what? Few positions for clerks exist. I and some of the other gentry might hire one or two, but we need people on our land. Most employment for the educated would be in the cities—cities of which these people have no knowledge. You know yourself the condition in which the poor exist in London. And what of the lasses? They cannot become clerks. No, Kate. I cannot agree."

"But…but, the girls might become housekeepers, like Mrs. Hawes. Or…"

"I guess it is possible, but I think it highly unlikely. Most of them will become wives and mothers, just as they have for generations." He put his hands on her shoulders and looked down into her face. "You are a kind and generous woman, Kate, but you cannot change some things."

Catherine tossed her head and shrugged away from his hands impatiently. "I don't see why not. Women need a way to support themselves as much as men do. Look at my own situation. I had no recourse but to marry you."

As soon as the words were out of her mouth, she wished them back in it. His lordship did not alter his expression, but she was suddenly conscious of a change in his eyes. A light had been darkened. She quickly touched his sleeve. "I—I didn't mean that the way… I mean, I was fortunate that you wished to have me. Another woman might not have been so lucky."

Charles continued to look into her upturned face for

several heartbeats, then he turned to the door, offering her his arm.

"No. They would not."

Charles led Catherine out into the dooryard, changing the topic of conversation. "I am told that Kettlewell is in the byre. I should speak to him while we are here."

They strolled across the farmyard, Charles completely self-possessed, Catherine vacillating between indignation at his attitude on education and cursing her careless tongue. It had never occurred to her that she could hurt him, but she feared that she had. She had not intended that at all. She sighed. Marriage was indeed a treacherous path to tread.

As they approached the byre, Catherine spied a mounted figure trotting into the yard. She turned to Charles. "Who is that?"

He followed the direction of her gaze. "Hmm. It seems that you are about to have the pleasure of making the acquaintance of the Earl of Lonsdale."

Catherine threw Charles a quick look to see if he were being sarcastic, saw no indication one way or the other, and made a face. "If you mean Helen's stepson, it is a pleasure I could do very well without."

"No doubt." Charles waited silently until the tall, dark-haired rider reached the byre and dismounted. The young man's hawklike countenance showed the unmistakable signs of dissipation.

He approached, leading his horse, and half bowed. "Servant, Caldbeck. I see the story that you're wasting your brass on a pack of orphans is true. Wouldn't have thought you such a gudgeon. But I see the tales of your lady's beauty were not exaggerated, either. Introduce me, will you, old man?"

Charles nodded coldly. "Catherine, may I present the Earl of Lonsdale—Vincent Ingleton."

Catherine reluctantly extended her hand. Vincent carried it to his lips, holding it too tightly and too long. She tugged discreetly, but he kept possession of it until her face flushed crimson. Grinning unpleasantly, he released her and turned to Charles.

"I can see why you've kept her shut up in that great barracks you call a house. Too pretty by half to let out of your sight—if you like red hair."

Catherine stiffened, but Charles did not rise to any of the deliberate provocation. "Have you been in Yorkshire long, Vincent? I thought you in London."

Vincent twisted his mouth in derision. "Forced to return to the home of my fathers. Pockets quite to let."

"Ah, the races, I take it. So you have decided to ruralize. Do you mean to make a long stay?"

Charles's face, as usual, betrayed no indication of his opinion of his nephew-in-law, nor any real interest in his plans.

"God, I hope not! A curst rum place to be stuck," Vincent said, rubbing a hand over his cheek. "No sport worth talking about."

Catherine, who had been stunned into uncharacteristic silence by the man's rudeness, studied his face. Several long, deep, half-healed scratches marred the debauched face. "Oh, my," she blurted. "What happened to your face?"

Vincent snarled. "Stupid chit!"

Catherine blinked in disbelief, but Charles answered his nephew coolly. "Since I believe that even you would not address Lady Caldbeck in that manner in my presence, I assume that you refer to someone else?"

"Damn lightskirt near our village. Didn't know when she was well off."

"Did the girl object to not being paid, or did she have the temerity to refuse your many charms?" Without actually changing, Charles's tone reflected utter contempt.

"Eh, she was playing hard to get." Vincent displayed no awareness whatsoever of Charles's scorn. "But I left her with something to think about. It will be awhile before she catches anyone else's eye."

Rage flooded Catherine. "You—you mean she refused you and you—you…!"

She broke off as Charles's arm slipped around her waist and squeezed slightly. "This is hardly a suitable conversation for my wife's ears, Lonsdale. We must return to Wulfdale, in any case, before darkness falls."

"We can't offend her delicate sensibilities, now can we?" Vincent sneered. "Just as well. I've a burning thirst. I'm off to the taproom." He favored Catherine with a sardonic bow. "My pleasure, Lady Caldbeck. Your most obedient servant, Charles." He vaulted into his saddle and, with a careless salute, departed at a canter.

Catherine rounded on Charles, fire in her eyes. "Did he really mean…did I understand correctly? He accosted some young woman and, when she wouldn't have him, he beat her or—or something?"

"Or something. His behavior toward women is only one of his many shortcomings."

"Can't you do something about him?"

"Not unless one of my people—or someone else— brings me a complaint. But he will go too far one day and pay the piper."

"But…but how can you tolerate him?"

Charles tucked her hand into the crook of his arm. "Very poorly."

Catherine allowed him to guide her toward their mounts. "Well, if Richard has sent him an invitation to my reception, I am going to tell him to send a retraction!"

"No, Kate. You won't do that."

"What do you mean, I won't do that?" Catherine dug in her heels and brought them to a stop.

Charles's voice was bland. "As little as I want him in my home, neither do I wish to quarrel with him. He is both a neighbor and a family member of sorts."

"So I am to tolerate him and his rudeness, also?" Catherine folded her arms under her breasts, her expression stormy. "I fail to see why I should."

Gently Charles nudged her back into motion, resuming as though she had not interrupted. "Nor do I wish you to attract his enmity toward yourself. He can be very vindictive, Kate."

"Surely he wouldn't…"

"As much as I would like to believe that my presence would deter him from doing you a disservice, I am not prepared to say what he may or may not do when he is drinking. As you heard, he is not trammeled by any degree of chivalry."

"Or even good manners! 'If you like red hair'," Catherine mimicked angrily. "Oh! What nerve! And he spoke as though that girl were nothing. As though he thought nothing of hurting her or—or whatever he did."

"No. He thinks of nothing but his own desires. But don't concern yourself overmuch. He probably will not come to the reception. He will find it too great a bore to appear in polite society. If you send a retraction, he will be certain to come, and I shall be forced to eject him—to everyone's embarrassment."

"And that is all you are going to do about him?" Catherine grimaced in disgust.

"At the moment." His tone was clearly unyielding.

The Earl of Caldbeck had declared the discussion closed.

The Countess of Caldbeck preserved a polite silence throughout dinner, relinquishing it only to answer direct questions. Catherine was *not* accustomed to allowing anyone else to have the last word in an argument. She could not decide which she hated more—Charles's arrogant manner or her inability to break through it. She did not usually consider herself so poor spirited! This situation could continue only for so long. The day of reckoning fast approached, and Charles Randolph had best prepare himself for it!

And how he could abide young Lonsdale was more than Catherine could see. *If you like red hair,* indeed! That comment alone should be grounds for a duel. But not to Charles Randolph, Earl of Caldbeck. Oh, no! My Lord Caldbeck simply rose above lesser mortals. Oo! He made her furious.

Catherine's disgruntlement did not improve the next day when she received in the post a handful of replies to the letters she had written soliciting support for her London projects—all of them politely evasive. The various gentlemen felt sure that this or that project was worthy in the extreme, but... But what?

Couldn't these people understand that children died on the streets of London every day? Even had she received her inheritance, she could not save all of them alone. Catherine considered going to Charles with the problem, but did not feel sufficiently in charity with him to approach him.

It was just as well, perhaps. The night of the reception loomed near, and she had countless things to do to get ready. Catherine exulted in the thought of her first big entertainment as mistress of her own home. That the home commanded respect due to long history, and that its master was the incumbent of a very old title, added to her enjoyment. Perhaps she should chide herself for vanity, but modesty had never been one of her strong points. She gloried in her beauty and in her position.

The night of the soiree was clear, but chilly, with a large moon lighting the way for the guests. Catherine sat before her mirror and, as Sally fastened it around her throat, admired the wonderful sapphire necklace Charles had given her. The stones picked up the light and reflected the brilliance of her eyes. She had ordered a dress from her favorite dressmaker to compliment the gems, and she delighted in the effect.

Pleats of blue silk crisscrossed her milky-white breasts, lifting them up and swooping from the tapered sleeves, which barely touched her shoulders, to just above her nipples. The sheer fabric flowed from beneath her bosom to cling gracefully to curved hips and thighs, while beading encircled the hem and formed a motif of vines across the skirt. Sally pulled Catherine's glowing hair to the top of her head in a drift of curls, letting the myriad ringlets determined to escape confinement form a halo around her face and neck.

As the two of them were admiring their handiwork, the door to Charles's chamber opened, and he stepped in, elegantly clad in his inevitable gray. The satin coat and knee britches shone silver in the candlelight, reflecting his smoothly brushed hair. He stood watching Catherine silently with his silver eyes until she dismissed Sally. Too excited to maintain her anger with him, Catherine stood and pirouetted halfway across the room.

"How do you like my dress? Doesn't it set off the sapphires to perfection?"

Charles followed her, nodding. "Yes, it certainly does that—and your eyes. I knew the sapphires were right for you."

He stood surveying her intently, saying no more. Catherine begin to feel uncomfortable under his unrelenting gaze. "Is something wrong, my lord?"

"That dress is cut very low."

Catherine flushed. "Well, yes... Yes, of course it is. That's the fashion. Don't you like it?"

"I like it very well...here. In the ballroom—" Charles lifted one shoulder slightly "—perhaps not. It reveals a great deal."

Indignation welled up in Catherine once more. This man was *not* going to tell her how to dress, on top of everything else. "Well, I can do nothing about it now. Our guests will start arriving at any moment." Her chin rose to a familiar, balky angle.

Charles looked at her silently for a few heartbeats, then bowed. "So they will."

He extended his arm, and Catherine rested her hand on it lightly, favoring him with a haughty glance. She had no idea why he had dropped the subject. If he were annoyed, she had no more notion of it than she ever did. Together they descended the stairs to the ballroom.

The Wulfdale gardeners had stripped the greenhouses to deck the rooms for the affair. The gardens had also yielded up a few late blooms, so that Catherine viewed the resulting adornment with pardonable pride. Mrs. Hawes and the chef had quite outdone themselves with the refreshments, and Charles's and Hawes's selection of

wines from the Wulfdale cellars would demonstrate the
taste and affluence of the Earl of Caldbeck to anyone's
satisfaction. *This will be a night to remember,* Catherine
thought a trifle smugly.

And so it proved to be.

The neighbors of Wulfdale would hardly ignore an invitation to the Earl and Countess of Caldbeck's magnificent home. Catherine, viewing the arrivals with satisfaction, could not but remember the anxiety she had
experienced when she'd attempted to entertain potential
donors for her charities. Would anybody come? Many
times very few guests, indeed, had appeared. She need
not have that sort of apprehension ever again. In spite of
the disappointing responses to her letters, she was confident that when she and Charles returned to London,
those same people would come to their London home at
her husband's invitation.

Catherine and Charles moved gracefully among the
visitors, he greeting old acquaintances, she making new
ones. Adam and Helen arrived together early in the evening, but Catherine stayed so busy learning the unfamiliar
names and faces that she had no opportunity to converse
with them. Many of the gentlemen and a few ladies
played cards at tables set up in the adjoining parlors, and
a small group of musicians provided a background of
music for laughter and conversation.

Long after the rest of the company arrived, Catherine
noticed Vincent saunter into the room, obviously already
in his cups. She sighed with irritation, but he seemed
content to lounge around the card rooms, watching the
play and saying little.

Spotting Lord Arncliff, Catherine slipped through the
crowd to greet the magistrate. She liked him. He stood
talking with a group that included Charles and two other

men whom Catherine did not know. When she joined them, Charles introduced to her their neighbors, Sir Kirby Stalling and Mr. Malham.

"Lovely occasion, Lady Caldbeck. Lovely," the tall, angular, dark-haired Malham exclaimed, bowing over her hand. "And what a captivating hostess you have, Caldbeck. You make us all envious."

Charles acknowledged the tribute with a silent nod, drawing Catherine's hand into the crook of his elbow.

Arncliff quickly stepped in with a greeting and a compliment, adding, "It is a shame that we first met under such tragic circumstances. Have you settled Mistress Askrigg's children in your new home for orphans?"

Catherine smiled happily. "No, but they will be moving in next week. The renovations are almost complete, and the matron is already established there. We are planning a trip to visit a textile mill in Skipton soon. Children who have fallen to the care of the parish are often put to work in the mills, you know. I have heard that some of them are dreadfully mistreated. I intend to see for myself and perhaps bring some of them here."

Sir Kirby cleared his throat, glancing covertly at Catherine's bosom. "But, of course, Lady Caldbeck, it is only right that the indigent should work for their keep. I cannot recommend the coddling you propose. Those youngsters will be worthless when they grow up."

Catherine considered her adversary. Stalling appeared to be in his midforties, and stocky, with pale blue eyes and streaked blond hair. He struck her as just a bit pompous. More than a bit. Bullnecked and bullheaded. She doubted anything she said would change his mind, but perhaps she could gain support from the others and forward her argument with Charles.

"Oh, but I intend to have them instructed in all manner

of skills—farming, sewing, and in the basics of reading, writing and ciphering. Perhaps geography, also. They will be ready for any number of careers.''

"Humph. Hardly." Sir Kirby frowned. "You will make them dissatisfied with their station in life—that's what you will do. No good will come of it, you may mark my words. You have obviously been reading the nonsense propagated by Robert Owen.''

Malham stroked his chin thoughtfully. "Owen's ideas have proved very successful in his own holdings, but I don't know…. Of course, farming and sewing will be useful to the children, and I can see where reading might be of use…but where would it end? If you provide education for these children, others will also want it. There cannot possibly be positions enough for all of them.''

Catherine, hearing the echo of Charles's words, made the mistake of glancing at his face. She decided that she saw a gleam of triumph in his expressionless countenance and bristled.

"And why not educate all of them? Knowledge can only improve one's abilities.''

"There is a certain value to the growing opinion that all lads should be taught basic knowledge," Lord Arncliff allowed. "I have read about it in several recent periodicals.''

Catherine knew she should leave well enough alone. She should accept that small gain and withdraw from the lists, but her blood was up. She forged on.

"Not only the boys, but girls, also. They may need a means of supporting themselves in later life.''

Arncliff appeared to be pondering that thought, and Malham shook his head doubtfully. Stalling, however, drew himself up in righteous indignation. "Lady Caldbeck, you go too far! God did not intend for the lower classes to read and write or rise above their station. Certainly he did not intend that women do so! Nor that they support themselves. Ridiculous! That is for their husbands to do.''

Smiling a bit too sweetly, Catherine asked, ''What if a woman has no husband?''

''Any woman who knows her proper place can have a husband. Even Hetty Askrigg with that ugly birthmark on her face had a husband.''

''But her husband died and left her and the children. And now see the situation the children are in.'' Catherine drew a deep breath, intending to fight on, but let it out abruptly when Charles squeezed her fingers. She pulled her hand away, but took another breath to steady herself and remind herself of her duties as hostess. She couldn't risk being rude to a guest. ''But you gentlemen must excuse me. I haven't visited with Helen and Adam yet. Lord Arncliff, Sir Kirby, Mr. Malham.'' Nodding at each gentleman, she moved away with what she hoped was dignified grace.

A chorus of ''Lady Caldbeck,'' ''My pleasure,'' ''My lady,'' followed her retreat. She left them with a smile, but was inwardly fuming. Men! Could none of them see anything but tradition? And why must selfish people always justify themselves by calling on God? Times were changing, and they had best learn to change with them!

She approached Helen with relief. Her sister-in-law smiled knowingly. ''Now who has put your back up, Catherine? Surely not one of our stalwart Yorkshire squires?''

Catherine inclined her head toward the group she had just abandoned. ''That odious man!''

''Which odious man?'' Adam arrived bearing two glasses of champagne that he cheerfully bestowed upon the two women, looking around for a footman to bring a glass for himself. "Or are all men odious?"

"Most of the time, yes." Catherine grinned ruefully and pulled in her horns. "I was referring to Sir Kirby at the moment, however."

"Ah, and what has Stalling been doing to incur your wrath?" Adam signaled a footman, and at last supplied himself with a glass of wine.

"He has been telling me that God does not want me to care for and educate my orphans. And that any woman 'who knows her place' can have a husband."

Adam and Helen both laughed aloud.

"Poor Catherine!" Helen gave Catherine's arm a sisterly pat. "No wonder he set you off. You are quite right. He is perfectly odious. I always felt sorry for his wife."

"Does he have a wife? I don't think I met her."

"No, she died in a riding accident last year. They had no children, so of course, he is an expert on them." Helen chuckled.

Adam grinned. "Did he tell you about his sainted mother?"

"No!" Catherine returned the grin. "Does he have one of those?"

"Fortunately, no. She has also gone to her reward. Actually, she was a termagant of the first consideration, but to hear him tell it, she was a veritable angel. She was quite excellent at quoting scripture."

Laughing, Catherine shook her head. "I should have withdrawn with honors when Lord Arncliff suggested that at least the boys should be educated."

"Oh, he is such a dear." Helen sipped her wine. "He wants the best for everyone. His wife really was a saint, but she died also, poor thing, of a lingering illness."

Adam smiled, but added, "I think you must accept that

you will find little support for your work, Catherine. But I should think you would be used to that.''

''Alas, I am. Theirs are the same tired arguments I always hear.''

Helen gave her a little hug and chuckled. ''You are a brave girl, Catherine. Excuse me now, if you please. I wish to speak to Mrs. Malham. She and her husband are really very nice people. She is pretty and lively and very kind. You will like them.''

As her supporters wandered away, Catherine looked about to make sure that all was well with her guests. She couldn't decide whether the room was too warm or if she herself was overheated from the argument, but decided it was the room. Not immediately seeing a servant, she decided to open one of the French doors onto the terrace herself.

The door opened outward easily, and Catherine stood with her hand on it for a moment, enjoying the frosty air. Suddenly, strong fingers closed around her wrist, and she was dragged unceremoniously into the night.

Catherine swallowed a shriek as she was spun around and found herself facing Vincent Ingleton. He grinned at her lewdly.

''Step into my parlor.'' He held up a champagne bottle, swaying slightly. ''Want a taste?''

Catherine almost sighed with relief at the familiar face, then thought better of it. What she knew of the Earl of Lonsdale did not quiet the resurgence of fear crawling up her throat. She pulled back, trying to extricate herself from his grasp. Vincent clamped his fingers tighter and inexorably drew her to him.

''Come now, Vincent! Give over, do!'' Catherine tugged at her wrist with more force. ''This is not funny. Let me go.''

"Don't be in such a hurry." Vincent managed to get his other arm around her waist, still holding the bottle.

"Don't spill that on my dress!" Catherine ordered, hoping to distract him. He laughed drunkenly.

"Of course not, me lady. So sorry, me lady. Begging pardon, me fine lady." He jerked his arm, and the bottle flew across the terrace and crashed against the parapet. Catherine used the moment to try to wrench loose, but Vincent anticipated her. He yanked her up against himself, twisting her arm behind her back.

"You are drunk. Stop this instant!"

"Drunk." He nuzzled her neck. "Drunk on old Charles's champagne. Devil of a head in the morning."

"Vincent, this has gone far enough. I must return to my guests."

"Don't be in such a hurry," Vincent purred. He tightened his hold, putting pressure on her twisted arm.

"Ow! You are hurting me. Let go!" Catherine no longer tried to keep her voice down. She could see that she would be unable to stop him without calling for help. An incident appeared inevitable. "I shall call out if you do not let me go."

"No, no. You don't want old Charles's bed. Too cold. Too old." He giggled at his own cleverness. "Too old, too cold. You need a man with hot blood to go with that hair." He grabbed her hair and forced her mouth under his. He probed aggressively, trying to push his tongue between her teeth.

Catherine squirmed and twisted, trying to free her mouth without opening it. Pushing hard at his chest with her free hand, she aimed a kick at his shins. Her satin slipper, however, proved no match for his booted leg. Panic welled up inside her. What was she to do?

At that moment an expressionless voice sounded behind her.

"That will be enough, Vincent."

Vincent lifted his head and smirked at Charles, not releasing Catherine's bent arm. "Fine woman, Charles."

"I told you to let her go."

"I don't know about that. I think she would rather have me, wouldn't you, my lady?" Holding Charles's eye, Vincent very deliberately placed a hand on Catherine's breast. She jerked back instinctively.

Before Catherine's mind could take in the fact, a blur passed before her eyes, and she heard a thud. Suddenly released, she stumbled backward, colliding with Charles. He steadied her, and she saw Vincent sprawled on the paving stones, rubbing his jaw and looking murderous.

"Go into the house, Kate." Charles grasped her shoulders and turned her toward the door. The ice in his voice cut like a knife.

Catherine hurried toward the door, pausing to look back over her shoulder. Vincent was struggling to his feet. Charles watched impassively, saw her hesitation and spoke again.

"I said *go*."

Catherine ran for the door.

Chapter Eight

She made it through the rest of the evening with some difficulty. As soon as she was back in the ballroom she signaled to Adam. He hurried across the room and disappeared through the terrace door. She was looking around for her strongest footmen when both Charles and Adam came back through the door, apparently none the worse for wear. Neither of them spoke to her about what had transpired, and she gave thanks that the episode had ended quietly. By the end of the reception, however, she found herself galvanized with the energy of her earlier excitement, of having been mauled, and of pent-up anger.

She ascended to her bedchamber with a determined tread. She was going to have a few things out with Charles Randolph before he was much older! He acted as though the occurrence with Vincent was *her* fault, ordering her into the house in that steely voice. That was the last and final straw!

Without undressing, she sent Sally to bed, and was stalking back and forth across her room when Charles came through his door, his cravat untied and his shirt unbuttoned. She rounded on him like a whirlwind. He watched her with mild interest.

"Well, there you are at last! I have been waiting for you, my lord. I wish to explain some things to you."

Charles inclined his head with polite attention.

"Oo! You are so sure of yourself, aren't you? Well, you are not so wise as to have the right to treat me like a child!"

His lordship nodded gravely.

Catherine's rage immediately escalated several degrees.

"Ordering *my* maid to prepare *my* bath!" She seized a pillow and bounced it off the wall.

"Threatening to take my hunter away!" A second pillow followed the first. "Telling me to take a nap." A strong kick sent one slipper to join the pile on the floor. "Who do you think you are? Oh, my husband. Oh, yes. After you *tricked* me into marrying you—oh yes, you did!" His lordship folded his arms across his chest. "You tricked me. And now you want to control my whole life." When the second slipper did not leave her foot as she swung it, she grabbed the shoe and flung it to join its fellow.

Charles leaned a bare inch to avoid being struck.

"And that is *my* orphanage. You said so! The Lady Caldbeck Home for Orphans. I *will* educate them, do you hear? And as many other children as I can." She stamped her foot and whirled away from him.

"And if your hidebound stubbornness were not enough, you have the audacity to blame *your* nephew's outrageous behavior on *me*. I didn't want him in my home in the first place, but no! I must allow him to come, and see what happened. What he did was *not* my fault. You have no reason to question my honor."

Charles held up one finger. "I never said it was your fault, nor have I questioned your honor."

"Well, you implied it. Ordering me into the house like a bad child. And look at you! Just look at you!"

Charles's manner revealed mild inquiry.

"Ooh! You are so infuriating! You just stand there like a statue with a face of wood and—and…" Words failed her. Casting around for something else to throw, Catherine's eye fell on a small china trinket box that rested on the end table near the sofa. She snatched it up and was in the act of drawing back her arm when her wrist was seized for the second time that night in an unbreakable grip.

Charles pried the ornament out of her fingers and replaced it on the table, saying, "That belonged to my mother."

As Catherine drew in a frustrated breath, Charles's gaze fell on the smirking china shepherdess. He lifted it off the mantel, put it in Catherine's hand and stepped back.

Catherine narrowed her eyes first at her husband and then at the figurine. "I warned you!"

She raised her arm and heaved the offending figure into the fire. It shattered with a satisfying smash.

A pregnant silence ensued. Catherine stood breathing heavily for a few seconds. Then she slanted a glance at Charles's immobile face. Shaking her head in amazement, she sank into a chair and began to laugh. "My lord, you are the outside of enough. You truly are."

She laughed until tears rolled down her cheeks, while Charles watched her solemnly. At length he stepped in front of her and knelt. Catherine caught her breath and looked at him uncertainly. He lifted her skirt above her knees and moved between her legs. Catherine choked on a breath as he put his hands behind her hips and slid her forward in the chair, pressing her against himself.

"Poor Kate. Such an impossible husband." He reached for the top of her bodice. "Telling her that her gown is cut too low. You forgot that." With one hand he easily liberated a rounded breast from the pleats. "Such a trial she must bear." He covered the firm pink nipple with his mouth, sucking gently. Sensation suddenly flooded Catherine's loins, and she gasped.

"Tricking her into marriage, only to abuse her." Charles released that nipple and slid one finger under the bodice on the other side. He brushed it across the second nipple for several heartbeats, then slipped the silk downward, lifting the breast. His mouth claimed that straining bud while his fingers pressed the other one. Catherine dropped her head back and gripped the arms of the chair. Suddenly she tingled from her neck to her toes. She pressed her hips forward.

Charles lifted his face, and with a hand on either breast, touched the tip of his tongue to the tears of laughter still sparkling on her cheeks. He lifted a drop away, and then tasted the other cheek. Moving to her mouth, he stroked her lips with his tongue, his fingers pulsing on her nipples.

All thought fled from Catherine. Passion flowed through her mind and her body, driving out all other emotion. Her mouth opened of its own accord, but Charles continued to tease only her lips. When she was twisting against him in the chair, he moved one hand and unfastened his britches.

"Poor Kate. She has lost control of her whole life," he murmured against her lips. "We must remedy that."

He altered his position to lie on his back on the floor, pulling Catherine with him. Snagging a sofa pillow from the pile on the floor, he placed it under his head. "We

can't have the Countess of Caldbeck rendered power-
less.''

The Countess of Caldbeck sprawled on top of him,
looking at the earl questioningly. Charles lifted her by
the waist and set her astride him, then carefully lowered
her over his hot, firm shaft.

He then lay perfectly still. Puzzled for a moment at
this new approach, Catherine also remained unmoving.

She looked down into the pool of sapphire blue silk
covering his chest and thighs. The fabric brushed softly
against her bare legs, sending whispers of awareness upward. Her bodice fell to her waist. As she hesitated,
Charles reached up to touch a tight nipple.

Catherine had to move! She couldn't bear staying still
another instant. She shifted experimentally and was rewarded by a pulse of Charles's hips. She rested her arms
on the floor and lifted her own hips, leaning forward as
she slid along the length of him until she was near to
losing him. Her breasts fell forward above his face. He
lifted his head from the pillow and took one of them into
his mouth. Catherine moaned, and her whole lower body
clenched. This occurrence elicited a groan and another
thrust from Charles.

Catherine began to understand. *She* controlled events.
She set a rhythm, moving upward until he could nibble
her breast, clenching, then slipping down again. She
knew Charles was carefully holding on to his own control, and she became determined to defeat it. She stroked
him relentlessly, offering her breasts, then moving them
away, enticing, forbidding, luring. His mouth reached for
her. His fingers tightened on her bottom. Even as he
struggled to hold himself back, he pushed upward with
more and more force. Catherine closed her eyes in satisfaction.

With each cycle her feelings rose, until they coursed the length of her body, tightening every muscle, tantalizing every nerve. She could no longer think or see or hear anything but her own low sounds and Charles's response. Desire engulfed her.

Suddenly Charles was moving, driving into her faster and faster. The world turned black. She could hear her own voice crying out, Charles's echoing hers. Stars sparkled in her vision as she stiffened, trembling and throbbing, and then collapsed across him.

He wrapped his arms around her and held her close, still pulsing slightly under her. As he quieted, Catherine lay against him gasping, listening to his ragged breathing and the pounding of his heart.

Eventually they both regained their breath and a modicum of composure. Catherine rolled to the side, and Charles rose and extended a hand. She let him pull her to her feet, and stood gazing at him uncertainly. He enclosed her in his arms again, resting his lips against her forehead.

"We must talk," he murmured against her skin. "But let us do it more comfortably." Catherine nodded, and they helped one another to undress without speaking again. When they had reached the refuge of the curtained bed, Charles, leaning against the headboard, lifted her hand to his lips.

"Poor Kate. Do you truly feel badly treated?"

Catherine sighed and shook her head. "No, I know I'm not badly treated. It's…it's hard to explain. I'm sorry I said all those things." She grimaced. "I seem to be forever apologizing for my temper of late. I do know you try very hard to please me and care for me."

"Yes, I do. But perhaps I have been rather overbearing about it. I'm afraid I have that tendency."

"Perhaps a little." Catherine smiled at the understatement. "The real problem is that I never know if you are angry with me or...or what? You look at me so, I don't know, uncompromisingly? Sometimes I feel a bit intimidated."

Charles stroked her hand. "I did not think you so easily daunted. I must be very fierce indeed."

Catherine chuckled. "I'm not, usually. I was a little afraid of you at first, but I'm not anymore. No, I think it is more that I no longer feel that I control my life. You are the master here, while I..." She struggled for words. "I am here at *your* decision. And I find it hard to trust anyone with my welfare. I learned early not to rely on my aunt and uncle. It is hard to allow someone else to order my life."

"I have no wish to order your life or to be your master, and I have no objection to compromise. We can achieve that if we understand the need." Charles looked down at her seriously. "I do feel very much responsible for your well-being, however. I did not intend to trick you, but as you say, my actions brought you here. It was I, after all, who made marriage to me seem your only choice. I knew what was happening to your uncle and your fortune. I might have given you some warning."

"Why didn't you?"

"Because I feared you would not accept me if you had time to seek an alternate solution to your problem. You might have chosen to marry someone else."

Catherine sensed an unaccustomed tautness in him. She looked up into his eyes. "There was no one else I wanted," she said firmly. "But I have never understood your determination."

Charles sat quietly for several moments, looking away into the distance. Finally he turned his gaze back to Catherine. "I have a need for you, I think, Kate, for your passion and emotion. You express what I cannot."

Catherine sat up and took both his hands in hers. "Is that lack very hard for you?"

"Sometimes. As you have seen, it can lead to misunderstanding."

"That first day—when you kicked the door in—were you angry then?"

Charles looked mildly surprised. "Why, no. I simply lacked the time to wait for you to come about. It was an intellectual decision."

"An intellectual decision?" Catherine shook her head in amazement. "Do you never let yourself feel things?"

"Yes, of course I do. I know I do not show it, but I definitely have emotions. Tonight, when Vincent touched you, I wanted to kill him and then take you right there on the terrace. A very primitive masculine instinct, I suspect."

Catherine smiled. "Yes, it sounds very primitive. At least you had the satisfaction of hitting him."

"Yes. I often express myself in action. I hit him several times, in fact." Charles rubbed his bruised knuckles absently. "Adam arrived in time to save him from worse. It wasn't very sporting of me, drunk as Vincent was."

"I should think that 'primitive' does not take 'sporting' into account at all."

"No, it certainly does not." Charles reached for her and gathered her into his arms. "I want you to be happy, Kate. I may have brought you here for my own, very selfish reasons, but I did not intend to sacrifice you. I was vain enough to believe that I could give you happiness. Do you believe you can at least be content with me?"

Catherine leaned back to look into his eyes. "I don't think it is in my nature to be 'content.' I shall always fight for what I want. I am just not sure what that is right now. But I am not unhappy. I enjoy being your wife and your countess, and I appreciate having that position, as well as your concern for me. And I want you to be happy, too.''

''Thank you. That means a great deal to me.'' Charles tightened his arms, pulling her head against his chest.

Catherine lay quietly, listening to the comforting rhythm of his heart. She was just drifting toward sleep when an earsplitting howl jarred her awake. She and Charles both sat bolt upright, staring at the foot of the bed, whence the clamor seemed to emanate.

''My God!'' Catherine clapped her hands over her ears as the dreadful lament sounded again, filling the room, echoing off the walls. ''Are there still wolves in Yorkshire?''

Charles relaxed against the bedstead. ''No, not for centuries. It's naught but that curst dog.'' A third wail assailed them. ''It must be directly under our window. Shall I throw a boot at it?''

Catherine giggled. ''You would spoil your good boot, silly. Perhaps it will go away.'' They listened cautiously, but the sound did not repeat.

''Thank goodness. The creature is gone.'' Catherine leaned back against the bed.

Charles looked at her with a new intensity. He lifted her hand and kissed the inside of her wrist, moving his lips along her arm until he reached the inside of her elbow. ''It appears to be a night for howling.''

Catherine sat up straight and glared at him indignantly. ''I did *not* howl!''

''Then perhaps I should try harder,'' quoth his lordship, reaching for her.

* * *

The sound echoed off the dark hills, reflecting the pain in his soul. Gone was the holy ecstasy. Gone the triumph, the release, the sweet fear. The taste of ashes scorched his tongue. The profane craving again stirred in the depths of his being, cruel, malevolent. Aching. Aching for Her.

She was yet beyond his reach. But soon. First, patience. Yes, patience.

Chapter Nine

Catherine indulged herself with an exhausted sleep late into the morning. For once, she decided to have a breakfast brought to her bedchamber. The late hour, the excitement of the party, her quarrel—if that was the word for it—with Charles, and the spectacular reconciliation had all left her drained.

He had been more open with her last night than ever before, letting her know how strong his hidden emotions were. She had not considered that, having brought her to Wulfdale as an unenthusiastic bride, he felt obligated to make her happy.

When she'd told him that she did not know what she wanted, she had not spoken the exact truth. She knew what she wanted. What she did not know was what she might hope for. Had she, at last, a chance for the loving husband and family she craved so much?

She saw Charles in a very different light this morning. She laughed aloud, thinking of how he had handed her the smirking shepherdess. Yes, his lordship understood her much better than she understood him. He certainly did not fear her temper. And she no longer feared him.

But she was at times acutely aware of the silent power he radiated.

And of a power he wielded every time he touched her. Her face grew warm as she remembered the sureness of his touch, her helplessness as she dissolved into passion, the strength of his hands and body. She found herself listening for his step every night as he came to her. For that matter, she listened for his step anytime he was absent. And her heart leaped in her chest each time he appeared. Suddenly Catherine stiffened as recognition struck her.

Heaven help her, she *was* falling in love with him!

The Earl of Caldbeck felt distinctly self-satisfied, possibly even a little smug. His countess was proving to be just the woman he had thought her since the day he'd first set eyes on her. As Charles shaved, his mind roved over the events of the previous night, relishing each one. He had known she was spoiling for a fight. And he enjoyed the explosion every bit as much as he had expected.

God, she was beautiful—flashing eyes, flushed cheeks, flaming hair and flaming passion. Whether throwing things or twisting in rapture against his body, his fervent lady stirred him to the depths of his temperate soul. He smiled to himself. Perhaps he had not made her howl, but the memory of her soft, moaning sighs started him throbbing with desire. If Charles knew how, he would be humming to himself.

As he pulled on his oldest broad-collared shirt and stained gray buckskin trousers, his valet maintained an aloof and disapproving silence. Charles knew that as much as the ever-proper Hardraw deplored the thought of a gentleman doing the work of a common laborer, he was absolutely mortified by having his master appear less than impeccably groomed.

Amused, Charles waved a hand at him. "Come now, Hardraw. Give over and find my work boots for me."

Hardraw sniffed. "That pair of boots has become quite disreputable, my lord."

Charles motioned impatiently for him to produce the objectionable footwear. "Now, Hardraw. I am confident that my reputation can withstand scuffed boots."

"No doubt, my lord." The valet lifted the old boots from the cubby in the dressing room with thumb and one finger. "But I can no longer even get them clean. I fail to see the necessity of ruining good clothing with manual labor." He set the footgear at Charles's feet and stepped back, crossing his arms.

Sensing mutiny in the offing, Charles refrained from insisting on Hardraw's help in donning the boots. He drew them on himself—easily, since they were comfortably stretched. He gave the valet an assessing look. "As I have told you many times, Hardraw, one gets soft if one does not use one's muscles." He then astonished the good Hardraw by punching him lightly on his ever-increasing midsection. "You should try it yourself."

Hardraw drew himself up, very much upon his dignity. "I have not the luxury of being eccentric, my lord. No *gentleman*—" he stated, emphasizing the word carefully "—would hire an eccentric valet."

Charles considered this point of view. "Perhaps not, but you already have employment with an *eccentric* gentleman. Perhaps assisting the kitchen boy to turn the spit—"

"My lord!" Hardraw permitted himself a very small smile. "I perceive that you are joking me, my lord."

"Very perceptive, Hardraw," Charles said dryly,

reaching for an old coat and waving his valet away when he moved to help him put it on. "I don't need this yet." He narrowed his eyes at the door leading to Catherine's bedchamber. "I believe I shall see if her ladyship is up and about."

"My lord!" Hardraw exclaimed, genuinely shocked. "You are not going to visit Lady Caldbeck looking like that!"

Charles weighed this advice. "Yes," he decided, "I believe I have sufficient credit with her to carry it off. It is not always clothes that make the man, Hardraw."

Hardraw could only shake his head mournfully. "You are teasing me again, my lord. You must find yourself in exceeding fine humor."

Yes, all in all, Charles was quite pleased with himself. He had won Kate's body and her fire. He would now set himself to win her loving heart.

Catherine's heart jumped into her throat when the door opened and Charles strolled into her room. The sight of the muscular pillar of his neck within the open collar and the smooth muscles of his thighs under the tight buckskins he wore almost stopped her breath. He exuded virility. How could she ever have failed to see it?

She rose from her chair—yes, the chair that his lordship had used to such good effect last night—and moved to meet him as he sauntered across the room. He paused halfway to her and tossed his coat onto the sofa, waiting.

"Good morning, Kate. I trust you slept well."

"Yes, thank you—" Catherine sent him a roguish glance from under her eyelashes "—after I was finally allowed to sleep." She came to him and, standing on tiptoe, put her arms around his neck and kissed him lightly on the lips.

"Hm." Charles rested his hands on her hips and pulled her closer. He dipped his head, increasing the pressure of the kiss.

"Hmm." Catherine sighed, clasping her arms tighter. Charles slipped his hands under her negligee, sliding them across her soft, round, satin-covered bottom.

"Hmmm." He drew his head back and looked down into her eyes. Catherine gazed up into his face, a happy little flutter starting somewhere in her middle.

"My lord, you look very—" Suddenly she broke off in astonishment.

"Charles!"

"What?"

"Charles!"

"What, Kate?"

"You smiled!"

Charles started slightly. "I did?"

"Yes! You did. You are still doing it."

"I guess I am." He tilted his head in thought. "How odd."

"I think it is lovely. You must be happy."

"I am." He pulled her hips harder against his swelling body. "You have never greeted me with a kiss before. I am quite taken by surprise."

"Oh. Surely I must have…" Catherine flushed and tried to step back.

"No, I am quite sure you have not. I have always been the initiator." Charles held her firmly, preventing her retreat. "Don't be embarrassed. I like it very much."

"I…I'm glad you do. I wouldn't want to become…well, unbecomingly bold." Catherine ducked her head, suddenly unsure. She might be falling in love with him, but she had only the slimmest evidence that he might return her feelings. Drat! Must she act on *every* emotion? Could she not show *some* restraint?

Charles lifted her face, his own serious once more. "You are certainly not that. Very responsive—magnificently responsive—but never overbold."

"Well, if it made you smile..." Her uncertainty began to dissipate.

"Yes," he replied, clasping her against the length of him, "you made me smile." He took her mouth once more, teasing with his tongue. At length he released her, smiling again. Catherine wonderingly touched his lips with one forefinger, and he took the tip of it between his teeth, nibbling gently. "Smiling is not so difficult, after all," he said after a moment. "But how am I to maintain my terrifying aspect if I take up smiling?"

Catherine chuckled. "I feel sure your lordship will manage."

"Probably. But you said I look very...something, before I interrupted you with my unprecedented smile."

"Yes, you look very...what did you say last night? Primitive. Yes, you look somehow very primitive."

"I must wear work clothes more often if this is the effect of them." He held her close for another moment, then, with hands on her shoulders, set her resolutely away from him. "But I shall get no work done at all if this continues."

Catherine giggled. "No, indeed you won't. What are you going to do today, to dress so?"

"I am going to help rebuild one of the stone walls on the Old Buck property. Most of them are in sad repair. We have little time before it snows. I want to make the most of it."

"Do you often do your own work?"

"Yes, I am in the habit of doing so regularly. It keeps

me fit, as I have just been explaining to Hardraw.'' He shook his head. ''He can hardly bear it—for me to go out in old clothes.''

''And you tease him, I've no doubt.'' Catherine chuckled.

''Of course,'' Charles responded with his usual gravity. He gave her a quick kiss on the forehead. ''I shall not be back until dinner.''

Catherine watched his dignified exit with renewed hope.

When Hawes sent to inquire as to Catherine's wishes for a midday repast, she learned from the maid that the chef was packing a nuncheon to be taken to Charles. On the spur of the moment she directed that her own meal be packed with his.

She wanted to see Charles at work.

She wanted to see him with his men, wanted to see his austere face as he concentrated on the task, wanted to see the play of his muscles beneath his clothes.

Pushing her previous lethargy aside, Catherine rang for Sally and set about donning her riding dress. She emerged to find James Benjamin walking her hunter in the front drive.

He helped her to mount, and climbed into his own saddle. ''Eh, m'lady, it's a fine day for a ride. John David is bringing the basket in the gig.''

Catherine expressed agreement, and they set off to enjoy the rare spectacle of an earl working with his hands.

As it happened, the spectacle of an earl working with his hands drew a large crowd. The day was bright and clear, a perfect fall day with a brilliant blue sky resting against the glowing green of the hills—the perfect day to be outside before the impending nip of winter made it unpleasant. Though the air was chill, a golden sun warmed Charles's back and shoulders. He enjoyed physical labor. As it stretched his muscles, it liberated his spirit. At times he felt almost unbearably constricted, his every thought and feeling imprisoned inside him.

Today, however, was not one of those days.

Today he had smiled.

Today Kate had greeted him with a kiss.

Yes, this morning all was well with his world.

And it seemed that half of Yorkshire had come out to enjoy it with him. Charles experienced a little thrill of pleasure as he spied Kate riding up the dale toward him. He continued his work as she directed the laying out, under the spreading branches of an oak tree, of the picnic retrieved from the back of the gig. When she settled her skirts on the blanket and leaned back against the bole of the tree, he signaled his men to cease their labors and take a rest.

As he stripped off his gloves and walked toward the oak, he became aware that his men were smiling behind their hands. His first impulse was to give them a chilly look, but he thought better of it. Let them enjoy seeing their master in the toils of Eros. It was a novel experience for all of them.

Charles sat down beside Kate on the blanket and reached for a boiled egg. A little distance away, where they could watch the horses, James Benjamin and John David availed themselves of the contents of a basket prepared for them by the chef, and the tenants on the other side of the wall delved into food brought with them.

Hardly had they begun to eat when their first visitor appeared, on horseback. Charles groaned inwardly as he became aware of Vincent trotting down the road toward them. He did not want his pleasant mood spoiled by that insolent brat. Kate paused in midbite and looked at Charles tensely. Charles shrugged.

The young earl rode to within a few yards of them and paused. Charles nodded at him coldly, and Vincent, after a moment's hesitation, touched his riding crop to his hat in formal salute and spurred his gelding into a gallop.

As they watched him disappear down the dusty path, Catherine let out an audible sigh of relief. Charles reached over and squeezed her hand. "Don't let him disturb you, Kate. I shall not allow him to annoy you again."

She gave him a slightly tremulous smile that sent a twinge of pain through his heart. Damn the man! He did not want Kate overset.

She straightened her shoulders, and the smile grew stronger. "I know you would not let him, but...I don't want you to have to hit him again. He might..." She stopped thoughtfully. "It is a wonder, as offensive as he is, that someone has not killed him in a duel."

Charles shook his head. "Boot's on the other leg, I fear."

"What do you mean? That *he* has killed his man in a duel?"

At her look of alarm Charles cursed himself for a fool. He should not have told her that. "Don't be concerned, Kate. He is not going to call me out."

"How can you be so sure? It seems to me that he would scruple at nothing."

"No, it is not a matter of scruples, even though it is not at all the thing to duel with one's uncle-by-marriage." He looked her squarely in the eye. "The reason he will not challenge me is that he does not wish to die."

Kate looked at him with big eyes. "He believes you could kill him?"

Charles returned the look levelly. "He knows I could."

"How can you be so sure? He must shoot well."

"Yes, he is a very good shot, but it is not hot blood that wins a duel, Kate. It is cold blood."

Catherine digested this information, as well as its implications. "Have you ever—"

She broke off as Charles sent her a long look, knowing that the ice in his heart must be reflected in his eyes. After a moment he drew in a breath and lifted Kate's hand to his lips. He kissed the back of it with polite reserve, longing to increase the intimacy, to taste her lips, but aware of their audience.

"The point is, Kate, that you need not fear for my safety where Vincent is concerned. He is afraid to meet me, and too proud to shoot from hiding. But look." Charles pointed down the road. "We are to have more company." Even at a distance he recognized Adam and Sir Kirby Stalling. "That is a strange combination."

"Yes, it is." Catherine smiled. "I had the distinct impression that Sir Kirby was *not* one of Adam's bosom friends."

"Hardly. Stalling is the greatest bore in nature." Charles got to his feet as the riders approached, drawing rein near the picnic. As the two men dismounted, James Benjamin hurried over to take charge of the horses, leading them away to where Charles's and Catherine's mounts stood.

"Good afternoon!" Sir Kirby smiled effusively, apparently on his good behavior.

"Stalling." Charles extended a hand to his neighbor, and then turned to his friend. "How are you, Adam?"

Adam shook hands. "Better, thanks. My burn is healed, as you see. Lady Caldbeck, I hope I find you well?"

Catherine smiled at the two in turn as each of them bowed. Stalling, with what Charles thought must be intended as a hearty laugh, pointed to Charles's garments. "Making us all look lazy again, I see." Charles nodded, but did not answer. Stalling turned to Catherine. "We all know his lordship's little ways, my lady. Never mindful of his dignity. No need to blush for him." Catherine opened her mouth to reply, and Charles waited with interest to hear what her rejoinder to that observation might be. But Sir Kirby pressed on, sparing her the necessity of an answer. "A nice day to be out, though, I must admit."

"Yes, it is," Catherine answered with a notable lack of enthusiasm.

Adam grinned at her. "I was just out for a ride myself when I encountered Sir Kirby. He was kind enough to give me the pleasure of his company."

Charles cast a look at his best friend. Stalling's intelligence was not generally considered to be of a high order, but Adam's sarcasm came very close to being obvious. Charles did not wish to arbitrate a quarrel between them. A glance at Adam's target reassured him, however. The barb had missed its mark. Stalling cleared his throat, a sure sign that he was preparing to pontificate on some subject. Adam turned a shoulder to Sir Kirby and rolled his eyes at Charles. Catherine covered a small cough.

They were never to learn, however, what wisdom Sir Kirby was about to bestow. For the third time within a half hour hoofbeats were heard, and the group turned as one to look up the road. Richard Middleton came toward them aboard one of Charles's grays. He pulled up near them and bowed from the saddle, apparently hesitant to join a group of his employer's friends.

"Hello, Richard." Charles strolled to the horse and patted it on the neck. "Got him out for some exercise?"

"Yes, my lord." The secretary smiled his shy smile. "I had errands in the village."

Suddenly Charles spun around.

A hubbub of noise and motion had erupted from the group of workers on the far side of the wall. From the corner of his eye Charles had seen the man named Ribble leap to his feet and bound over the stone fence. Running to where the horses stood idle, the laborer sprang into the saddle of the gray stallion Charles himself had ridden. Before the stunned James Benjamin could react, the man kicked the animal into a gallop, jumped the wall and rode away across the fields.

Startled, Charles's gaze followed the direction of his flight. A greasy column of very black smoke boiled up from behind the next hill.

"That's Ribble's place," someone shouted.

"Richard! Get down!" Even as Charles barked the order, his secretary was falling off the gray and Charles was vaulting into the saddle.

He sailed over the wall and raced in pursuit of his tenant and his horse.

Chapter Ten

Chaos erupted. Adam and Sir Kirby were running for their horses. John David struggled to pull the gig around onto the road, and Richard, left afoot, dashed toward him. The workmen set off at the best speed they each could make.

Catherine scrambled to her feet. ''James Benjamin, wait!''

The groom screeched to a halt in his bolt for his own mount. Catherine ran to her hunter, and he hastened to provide a leg up onto the sidesaddle for her. She followed Adam and Sir Kirby over the wall and across the hill. She could hear her groom's horse pounding behind her.

As she gained the crest of the hill, she saw that a cottage was, indeed, blazing, the thatched roof completely engulfed. The man named Ribble rode down the hill at breakneck speed, heedless of obstacles and footing. Charles followed at a slightly more cautious pace, but his gray easily outdistanced the rest of the pack. Catherine's hunter cleared fences and ditches gracefully, and she was gaining on Adam and Sir Kirby. The riders flew down the hill and over the low walls like a string of broken beads rolling and bouncing.

She saw Ribble reach the cottage and fling himself off the gray stallion as she neared the bottom. Before her horrified eyes, he darted through the door into the inferno. Charles pulled up not far behind him. Catherine's heart sank as she realized that he might follow Ribble into the fire. Before he could do so, however, Ribble staggered out, his clothing aflame, something clutched in his arms. He fell to his knees a few yards from the cottage. Charles leapt from his saddle, shrugging out of his coat as he hit the ground.

The rest of the riders thundered into the dooryard just as Charles threw his coat over Ribble, beating at the burning clothes. The men all ran to his aid, while Catherine slid down from her mount, struggling with the entangling train of her riding dress. A few of the faster workers had topped the hill and were charging down it at a run. As Catherine ran to the stricken man, Charles rose, grabbing her and pulling her away from the conflagration. Adam and James Benjamin were trying to lift Ribble to his feet to move him away from the flying sparks.

When the other tenants reached the scene, some of them found buckets and attempted to control the fire. The cottage was clearly lost, so they concentrated on the outbuildings, dashing water onto the thatch. Two of Ribble's fellows came to Adam's and James Benjamin's aid, coaxing and tugging the stricken man farther from the flames. He stumbled backward, still cradling something in his arms.

Realization hit Catherine like a blow to the stomach.

What Ribble held so tightly to his chest was a body—the body of a woman. The naked, burned body of a woman. Mrs. Ribble! The cheerful, helpful, child-loving Mrs. Ribble. Oh, God, no!

Catherine twisted out of Charles's grip and ran to where the woman's husband, again on his knees, sobbed against her lifeless face.

"Dorrie...Dorrie...Dorrie..." The man cried the name again and again.

A sob rose in Catherine's own throat. She knelt beside the grieving man and started to put a comforting hand on his back. But he was burned, too! She snatched her hand away before it touched him, gazing helplessly at him and his wife.

Charles came up behind her and placed his hands on her shoulders, standing silently. One by one the other men abandoned fighting the fire and came to stand in a circle around them. No one looked up as John David and Richard drove the gig into the yard, and no one spoke.

And then Catherine saw something else.

Dorrie Ribble's body was smeared with blood. It trickled down a limp arm, and Catherine could see more on her legs. She gestured, looking up at Charles. His hands stiffened on her shoulders. He stepped around Catherine and squatted in front of the Ribbles. Lifting the bloody arm, he regarded it for a few moments, then reached across the woman's body and gently pushed her husband back. The man resisted at first, tightening his hold, until at his friends' murmured encouragement, he leaned away a little from his wife's still form.

A shocked gasp rose from the onlookers. A gaping hole was torn in Dorrie's chest. Blood no longer pumped from it, but had spread over her stomach and her horribly gashed breasts, leaving little doubt as to the cause of her death. Kirby Stalling turned abruptly away from the sight and vomited on the ground. Several others paled, and they all drew back a step.

Charles got slowly to his feet, his countenance more

somber than ever. He turned to his secretary. "Richard, take your mount and ride for the magistrate." Richard nodded and made for the horse he had been riding earlier. Charles looked around until his eye fell on James Benjamin. He beckoned to the groom. "You go for Dr. Dalton. Take him to Wulfdale. Ribble will need immediate attention." He paused, reflecting. "And I think Lord Arncliff will have need of him here, afterward. But first, we must get Ribble into the gig."

Ribble sobbed anew, shaking his head and clinging to his wife. The men exchanged helpless glances. Catherine leaned nearer and spoke as softly as she could. "Please, Mr. Ribble. You have cared for her as long as you can. Let us have her now." A tear slid down her cheek, leaving a cool track in the soot that had settled on her face. Ribble turned his head toward her, but did not seem to see her. Catherine swallowed a sob and touched his face with a compassionate hand. "Please, Mr. Ribble, we will be very kind to her."

With a groan the bereaved man slumped backward. Several hands reached to steady him, and others lifted his wife's body out of his arms and laid her on the ground. As Charles spread his coat over her, Ribble looked at Catherine, aware of her at last.

"You'll see that she is treated gently?"

"I promise. I shall wait with her until the magistrate has finished." From the tail of her eye she saw Charles shaking his head, but she ignored him. "I promise."

Ribble nodded finally and allowed himself to be led to the gig, still weeping.

Charles signaled to John David. "Take it as easy as you can. Put him in a room and get Hardraw and Mrs. Hawes to tend him until the doctor comes."

Adam stepped forward. "I'll ride with him." He began

tying the rein of his horse to the back of the gig. "You stay with Catherine."

"I'll go with them." Sir Kirby, his face white, mounted his horse, but Adam forestalled him.

"I don't think you will be needed. You're looking a bit pulled yourself."

Sir Kirby nodded. "As you say. I shall be available to talk to Arncliff if you want me." He pulled his mount around and cantered off down the lane.

Adam grimaced. "The less help we have from him, the better. He will become insufferable as he recovers."

"Just so." Charles nodded, turning to Catherine. "Kate, are you sure you wish to stay?" His gaze strayed to the mutilated body.

Catherine looked resolutely into his eyes.

"I promised."

And stay she did. Never had Charles felt more proud of his bride. While he admired her poise and her charm, it was her heart—her warm, tender and courageous heart—that left him feeling awed and grateful.

He had sensed it in her from the moment he'd met her. Charles had considered using her charities to approach her, but while she might have appreciated his support, he held no illusions concerning his ability to charm women into matrimony. His greatest appeal to them lay in his formidable fortune. He had learned that the hard way. When he'd discovered her uncle's corruption and her own plight, Charles had struck without hesitation.

But Catherine—Catherine was different. True, it was the loss of her wealth that had constrained her to accept him, but she did not consider only herself. It was what he'd declared himself willing to do for her causes that had decided her. And she did not stint on her end of the bargain, but poured out her beautiful fire upon him without restraint. He now hoped for her love as well.

She stood guard beside the grisly remains of Dorrie Ribble the whole miserable afternoon. She did not look away when the magistrate and the doctor examined the wounds, but tears trickled down her already soiled face, adding to the grime. Charles positioned himself with an arm around her shoulders, wishing that he might hold her close and comfort her. He left her only for a brief, somber conversation with Dr. Dalton.

When at last the cart arrived to carry the body away to be prepared for burial, Catherine sagged against him with grief and fatigue. As he guided her toward her horse, the church bell began to toll. They paused with heads bowed. Boom, boom, boom… The bell sounded six times—the death of a woman. Silence. Then—boom, boom, boom… One peal for each year of Dorrie's violently curtailed life. They counted quietly.

When silence fell once more, Catherine lifted her head and looked into Charles's eyes. "Thirty-four. She was not even as old as you are."

Charles wrapped his arms around Catherine and pulled her to him. "A great tragedy," he agreed, stroking her back.

"Who could have done such a horrible thing? What sort of cruel, twisted mind could even conceive of it?" Catherine leaned back to look into his eyes.

Charles shook his head grimly. "I don't know, but I propose to find out. And very soon."

As soon as they returned to the house, Charles and Catherine looked in on the suffering Ribble where he lay in the care of Hardraw and Mrs. Hawes. It was impossible to know whether the farmer's grief or his burns caused him the most distress. He tossed on the bed and cried out, lost in semiconsciousness.

Charles recognized in himself a cold fury.

Never had his habitual restraint chafed as it did this night. He strode back and forth in his library like a wolf in a cage, wanting to snarl like one. Wulfdale had been attacked. One of his people—people for whom he held a responsibility—had been killed, and another was bereaved and injured.

The lawless past, when he would have been free to gather a small army and ruthlessly hunt the killer down and hang him, took on an appeal Charles had never before experienced. He longed to express himself in action, to ride out and wreak vengeance on the murderer. But he didn't even know where to start looking. Even the relief of shouting and throwing things, as Catherine might have done, was denied him.

He was, after all, still Charles Randolph.

Catherine retired to her chamber and ordered a bath, feeling filthy and sick at heart. They had decided against the formal serving of dinner, much to her relief. She was exhausted. Why did she feel that way so often lately? What had happened to the boundless supply of energy she usually enjoyed?

She picked at the food on her dinner tray. Nothing tasted good. Her stomach felt queasy. Visions of Dorrie Ribble's slashed body kept intruding into her consciousness.

Afterward, Catherine sat before the fire, alternately thinking and weeping. Poor Dorrie. And her poor, poor husband. How much he must have loved her. The thought brought on a renewed round of sniffles. Would she ever have that kind of love from Charles? Was the sober man she had married capable of such deep feeling?

The wind was picking up again. Catherine could hear it whistling and whining around her windows. Suddenly the eerie sound brought to her mind the awful howling of the previous night. She sat up straighter, her brow furrowed. They had heard the same baying the night before the widow's cottage had burned. Now another life had been lost. Could it be…?

Surely not. Catherine relaxed again against the sofa cushions. Coincidence. It must be coincidence. But somehow she could not get the notion out of her head. Where was Charles? All at once she wanted very much to talk to him, to feel his sensible solidness. Why had he not come to her room?

She glanced at the clock on the mantel. It was getting very late. Catherine got up and took a turn or two around the room, but waiting was not one of her better skills. She decided to take the matter into her own hands. Why should she sit and wait for him? This was her house, too, after all.

Tying the sash of her negligee more firmly, she opened the door that led to Charles's dressing room and thence to his bedchamber. The dressing room smelled of boot-blacking mingled with leather. Those scents mixed with the wool and starch of his clothes and the indefinable something that was Charles.

Catherine stopped a moment to inhale the fragrance, wondering why she had never come this way before. In part, of course, it was because Charles always came to her room after dinner. But there was more to it than that. The other reason was that she still felt rather like a guest, here at his lordship's invitation. Frowning, she pondered that for a moment, then drew herself up and approached his bedroom door.

She tapped lightly. Gaining no response, she repeated the knock more vigorously. Still no answer. She turned the knob and eased the door open, peeping into the spacious chamber.

Suddenly she erupted into laughter. Gray! Almost all of the furnishings were gray. Did the man never get tired of it? Only the heavy drapes at the windows and around the massive bed glowed a deep, dusky, muted purple. Rich, polished dark wood shone softly in the candlelight, negating the coldness of the gray. A very comfortable room.

And a very empty one. His lordship must be elsewhere. Giggling at the realization that Hardraw had neatly turned the covers back, in spite of the fact that his employer had not slept in that bed for many weeks, Catherine crossed the room to the outer door and peered into the sitting room they shared. *Hmm.* He must still be in the library.

She took the bedside candle from its table and, shivering a little in the draft from the dimly lit hall, made her way down the stairs. The servants had apparently extinguished the candles, banked the fires and retired to bed long before.

The house, so warm and gracious in the daylight, seemed hollow and cavernous in the dark. Unknown beings lurked in unlit doorways. Faint sighings emanated from the high ceilings, floating down through the gloom to brush against her. Small whisperings skittered around the looming walls and across her skin. She shuddered. Somehow she kept expecting to hear the terrible howl at any minute.

What ailed her, anyway? It was only a house—her house. A very large, very dark house. She increased her pace until she was almost running. Eventually, she arrived at Charles's study and once more knocked at the door.

"Yes?"

Catherine heaved a sigh of relief at the sound of his voice. Feeling more than a little foolish, she took a moment to catch her breath before she turned the handle and peeked around the door into the murky room. She could just make out a shadow by the window. "Ah. There you are. Are you alone?"

"Quite."

"Well, that is a very good thing. I'm not dressed. Why are you sitting in the dark?" Setting the candle on the stand beside the door, Catherine carefully maneuvered around the desk and several chairs until she came to stand in front of Charles, where he sat in a wing chair, staring out at the night. He reached up and pulled her down onto his lap, and she snuggled into his arms.

"You're cold." Charles held her closer.

"A little." Catherine drew her knees up so that one of his arms could cover them. "I missed you. Are you all right?"

"Well enough. Frustrated and angry."

"Angry? You don't seem so."

Charles shrugged. "I know, but I am. I have been thinking about Dorrie Ribble, trying to comprehend who might have done such a thing. And how I can bring him to justice."

"I've been thinking about it, too. And I just remembered something disturbing. The dog—the howling dog. We heard it again last night."

"And…?"

"We heard it the night Mrs. Askrigg died."

Charles sat silent for a moment, then tightened his

arms around her slightly. "Very strange. You're frightened?"

Catherine considered for a few moments. "No," she answered at last. "Well…not really frightened. It can't have been anything but chance, can it? It is just… unsettling."

"The whole matter is unsettling. It seems that we may have had more than one murder." Charles's imperturbable voice and manner had been having a calming effect on Catherine until he made that statement. She sat up straighter in his lap, the hair at the base of her neck lifting, and looked into his face.

"More than one… You mean…? Do you think that Jill's and Jesse's mother was also killed before…? Oh, heavens! That's horrifying! That means that someone is…" She let the sentence trail off, unwilling to put her thoughts into words.

"Horrifying indeed. It means that someone—probably someone in the neighborhood—is killing and mutilating women, from some dark impulse known only to himself, and then burning them. Or trying to. Dr. Dalton believes that Mrs. Ribble was also raped, although it was difficult to tell with all the other injuries. It appeared that she had been bound with rough cords."

"Oh, no! How she must have suffered. How could anyone treat another person so?" Catherine turned her face into Charles's shoulder, gripping his coat collar in a convulsive fist. "How could they?"

Charles stroked her hair. "That is what I have been sitting here trying to fathom. And why? The answer to that question may tell us who the killer is—if any of us can conceive of such motives. I have sent riders to invite the local landowners to a meeting tomorrow. Perhaps one of them will have some idea or information. But now—"

he allowed her to slip off his lap, and stood ''—let us go to bed before you freeze.'' As she moved away, he stopped and turned her to him. ''One more thing, Kate.''

''Yes?''

''Do not leave the house alone.''

Damn them! They knew. Now they would hunt him—hunt him like an animal. He kicked viciously at the dog slinking around his feet and snarled deep in his throat. But at last they understood. A destroyer, a dark angel, walked among them, redeeming, cleansing with fire and the sword, sowing fear.

Ah, the Fear. Her eyes wide with it, her body heaving with it, her smell rank with it. Now they *all* feared, and they would come to greater Fear—to feel it and smell it and taste it. He ran his tongue across his lips.

Soon She would taste the terror. She would be afraid of him. Him! Terrified of him, cowering at his feet, begging. He caressed himself hungrily. Soon. Soon.

Chapter Eleven

Charles spent the morning at the wreck of Ribble's cottage. The ground had been so trampled the previous afternoon that any sign of tracks had long since been obliterated. He did find, however, horse droppings in the cow byre. Knowing that his tenant did not keep a horse in the shed, Charles suspected that the murderer had arrived on horseback and had taken pains to conceal his mount while he was about his bloody work.

And there must have been a great deal of blood. Had the slayer ridden away covered in it? Surely someone in the district would have seen him. No one had come forward with that information, so what had the monster done?

Possibly he had removed his clothes to rape the woman. Had he wildly slashed at the woman while she lay tied and helpless? Then calmly washed himself and dressed again? Was anyone capable of that? The rage inside Charles was becoming a living thing, haunting him, clawing at him. God, how he longed to get his hands on the culprit!

Charles returned home silent, thoughtful and tense. He

shared a quick lunch with Catherine and prepared to meet his fellow landowners.

The men arrived singly or in pairs, depending upon who met whom along the road, and began to assemble in one of Wulfdale's larger dining rooms. Taking seats around the long table, they sipped tea or wine offered by Hawes and the footmen, and conversed with their neighbors.

Just as Charles prepared to call the meeting to order, the growing murmur of voices suddenly broke apart, and all heads turned to the door. Catherine stepped into the silence. She took a chair near the foot of the crowded table, arranged her skirts and demurely folded her hands in her lap. All heads turned back to Charles, eyes questioning.

He hesitated. His first impulse was to send her away, as the men seated around him clearly expected him to do. As always, he wanted to protect her—spare her this bleak conference and the ghastly description of Dorrie Ribble's terrible death that must inevitably be made.

Before he had decided how to respond, the vicar got up from his seat and approached Catherine. All eyes returned to her.

"Lady Caldbeck, it is very kind of you to be concerned about this terrible tragedy," the reverend said, "but I assure you, this will be no discussion for a lady's ears. Since his lordship is leading the meeting, please allow me to escort you to your drawing room. It will be much for the better."

Catherine smiled at the cleric, but shook her head. "Thank you, Reverend Middleton, but I prefer to stay."

Every head swiveled back to Charles. He raised one eyebrow a fraction of an inch. Catherine smiled at him. At last, he nodded. After the courage she'd displayed the day before, he could hardly convince himself that she would be undone by a mere reciting of the injuries. He drew a deep breath.

"Lady Caldbeck was present yesterday when the murder was discovered. Her observations will no doubt prove useful." Having said that, Charles nonetheless could not bear for her to be so far from his protecting presence in a roomful of disapproving men. He gestured at Richard, who sat beside him, preparing to take notes. The secretary quickly gathered up his writing materials and vacated the seat. Charles turned back to Catherine and extended his hand. "My lady."

Nodding graciously at the assembled gentlemen, Catherine made her elegant way to Richard's abandoned chair, while he took the one she'd left empty. Charles could not fail to be aware of the censuring looks directed at him. He glanced coldly around the table, and one by one, the critical gentlemen looked away.

"Very well, let us proceed." Charles nodded at the magistrate. "Lord Arncliff, if you will, please tell these gentlemen what occurred yesterday."

Charles took his chair and listened attentively while Arncliff related what he had seen, and announced that an inquest must be held shortly. Dr. Dalton described the body. The physician glanced in Catherine's direction only once, sparing no detail in relating his findings. Charles looked at her several times, but except for being a bit pale and keeping her gaze on her hands, she did not flinch. His pride in her grew by the moment.

"From the amount of blood, I'm afraid most of the wounds were inflicted while she yet lived," the doctor concluded. "We are dealing here with an unspeakably depraved mind."

The room erupted in a shocked buzz. After allowing

the group to express their consternation for a few moments, the magistrate again got to his feet. Charles tapped on the table for order, and quiet once more descended.

"I have already sent to Bow Street for a runner," the magistrate announced, "but it behooves us to set about finding this fiend before he can do further damage. We all need to question everyone on our property to see if any of them have seen or heard anything of use, or if they know anything concerning the victim that might help." He paused as if to weigh his next statement. "Perhaps I should say 'victims.' I believe we must also consider the possibility that the Widow Askrigg died at this animal's hands."

Another burst of noise ensued. Clearly some of the gathered men had already thought of that possibility, while others had not. Catherine touched Charles's sleeve. "My lord, a thought has just occurred to me."

Charles held up a hand for silence. "Yes?"

"We commented at the time that it seems strange," Catherine began, scanning the occupants of the room as she spoke, "that Mrs. Askrigg sent her very young children to stay with her father. He is so deaf and unwell that he can hardly have been adequate to the task of caring for them. Why would she have done that?"

Around the table brows furrowed, some in thought, some in annoyance at her interruption of their deliberations. Lord Arncliff regarded Catherine solemnly. "What does that fact suggest to you, Lady Caldbeck?"

Catherine turned to him. "Perhaps she was expecting someone—or was afraid."

The men's faces began to show more interest. The murmur of voices picked up again. The magistrate cut through the hum. "Was someone courting her?"

Charles shook his head. "I haven't heard of any such

thing, but I shall make inquiries. If there was, it may shed light on the matter. Has anyone else an idea or a suspicion?''

After some moments, Malham got to his feet. He waited until the crowd quieted and then looked uncomfortably at Charles. ''Lord Caldbeck, I hesitate to relate this story, concerning as it does a kinsman of yours, but it may have bearing on this discussion.''

Charles nodded frostily. ''Don't let that deter you, Malham. We need this matter resolved, and speedily.''

''Just so.'' Malham swallowed, his prominent Adam's apple bobbing. ''Well, I have this from one of my footmen. It seems that some weeks ago young Lonsdale was drinking with some of his cronies in a taproom favored by my man on his free evenings. Vincent was deep in his cups and started pawing…er, excuse me, Lady Caldbeck. Don't wish to offend…'' He looked uncertainly at Charles.

''Go on,'' the earl responded icily.

''Yes, well…Vincent forced his attention on the barmaid as she brought ale to the table. She tried to repulse him, but he wouldn't have it and grappled with her until she began to fight him in earnest. At that, he flew into a rage and knocked her to the hearth—they were sitting by the fireplace—and fell on her.'' A hostile mutter circulated around the room.

Malham waited for it to die down, then continued. ''It seems the girl was quite attractive—had a fall of hair down to her hips. Her hair was flung into the fire—I don't know whether intentionally or not. In any case, Lonsdale wouldn't let her up, and her hair caught fire. She might have been badly burned, save his friends dragged him off her, and the landlord had the presence of mind to empty a pitcher of ale over her. I understand that most of her hair was lost. I just thought that, since fire was involved…''

A resounding thump cut short the angry outburst of voices that exploded. The startled men turned as one to look at Catherine, whose fist was clenched on the table.

''Oh! Oh, the scoundrel! The beast!'' Her face shone, an outraged scarlet. ''Certainly we must consider him. He is capable of anything.''

''Nay, Lady Caldbeck.'' Kirby Stalling cleared his throat importantly. ''You cannot believe that a *gentleman* committed the crime we saw yesterday. Young Lonsdale is, of course, undisciplined to a fault, but he is an *earl,* after all.'' He looked around the room, obviously expecting agreement.

He encountered very little. A general shaking of heads seemed to indicate that, for once, the assembly agreed with Lady Caldbeck.

Adam Barbon's sardonic voice broke the thoughtful hush. ''Unfortunately, Vincent is a *gentleman* by birth only. His abuse of women is well known. However, without some evidence that connects him to yesterday's atrocity, we can hardly indict him, though I, for one, intend to keep a sharp eye on him for a while.''

An affirming drone surged through the group. Adam waited only a moment before continuing. ''I, also, dislike relaying the particular bit of information I have, but I feel I must. A day or two ago one of my tenants went to the Ribble cottage to discuss buying a ram. He said he saw Odd Harry running away into the dusk.''

This time it was the vicar who demurred. ''Oh, no, my lord, surely that poor, unfortunate creature cannot have done any such thing. He has always been gentle as a lamb. True, he is very strange, but—''

Adam waved an accepting hand. ''I know, Reverend

Middleton, we have all known him our whole lives, and there is no evidence that he has ever harmed a soul, but…''

"I can't think it," the vicar stated firmly. "Most probably she was giving him food."

"As do most of the women in the dale," Adam agreed. "Still, we have little to go on here. I certainly have no understanding of the workings of his mind."

Catherine tugged discreetly at Charles's sleeve again and looked inquiringly at him. He leaned down to her ear as the other conferees again consulted one another. "Odd Harry is a sadly deformed dwarf who lives in the district. At one time he assisted the blacksmith, but he began to withdraw from others more and more, until now one rarely sees him. The women leave food out on the stoop for him."

Catherine smiled. "As some do for the fairy folk."

"Just so." Charles nodded, his face solemn. "Only here it is more likely that a dwarf garners the bounty. I'm told that if a knife or some other implement is left out with the food, it will be sharpened or repaired in the morning. Occasionally, I have heard, even a horse will disappear, only to reappear in the morning miraculously reshod."

Catherine chuckled. "A very good fairy, in fact."

"Does anyone know where Harry is living nowadays?" Lord Arncliff searched the crowd in vain for an answer.

Adam shrugged. "I don't think anyone has known that for years."

Hearing no response from the rest of the men, Charles nodded. "We shall have to make a push to discover his whereabouts. I'm at one with Reverend Middleton in that I doubt he is our villain, but we should at least try to learn whether anyone knows where he was when the murders were committed. Perhaps someone knows where he hides in the daytime. It would be best if we could talk to him directly. Was anyone else in the vicinity, especially yesterday morning?''

Adams laughed curtly. ''You mean other than half of us here?'' He waved a hand around the table. ''I was there, you were, Stalling—not to mention a dozen of your men and your secretary. We might as well have been holding a bloody—er, beg pardon.'' He glanced at Catherine. ''A harvest fair,'' he amended.

''Vincent also rode by.'' Catherine's voice was firm.

''So he did. And anyone might have ridden off in another direction.'' Charles shook his head in frustration. ''I suggest that all of us instigate an investigation through our tenants, and then we will meet again.''

Agreement being vouchsafed in all quarters, the meeting broke up.

The next few days became extremely busy for Catherine and extremely frustrating for Charles. Despite the recent tragic deaths, she was more excited and thrilled than she remembered being ever before. A lifelong dream opened before her—the ability to make a real difference to the helpless, uncared for children of her world.

The Askrigg children were moved into the orphanage, along with two girls and a boy being cared for by relatives who could ill afford to house them. Catherine set about searching for a replacement for Dorrie Ribble, and a maid or two. She could see that, as word spread that the Lady Caldbeck Home was open for business, they would soon be deluged with candidates, and that a larger staff would be needed.

Also more space. Without bothering Charles, who was

concerned with the search for Odd Harry, she gave orders to the workmen to begin refurbishing a second wing of the huge old building as soon as they finished the first. She decided later, however, that she had best discuss it with him. She had no experience with the cost of such work, and only a rough idea of the expenses she would be facing as the institution grew.

For that matter, Catherine had no idea at all of the extent of her husband's monetary resources. They were apparently enormous, but common sense told her that no fortune was endless. Left to her own devices, she would happily buy furnishings, supplies and clothing far beyond the actual needs of the home. No need to strain both Charles's finances and his good nature.

She posed the question to him as they shared their evening wine side by side on the sofa in Catherine's bedchamber. He listened seriously, then commented in his dry way. ''You may continue. I appreciate your sense of responsibility, but I believe we may avoid the workhouse for yet a while.''

Catherine gave him a stern look. ''Really, my lord, this is no time to become inscrutable. I need to know what I may safely spend.''

Charles, who had leaned back and closed his eyes, opened one of them and gazed at her. ''Hmm. When you call me 'my lord,' I am on notice that you mean business. Very well. You may feel free to equip the Lady Caldbeck orphanage with anything short of a French chef. I doubt that his services would be appreciated in any case.''

''Charles! Do be serious.'' Catherine turned toward him, one hand on her hip, her lips compressed.

Charles closed the eye and sighed loudly. ''Alas, there is no justice. All my life I have been chastised for being too serious, now you abuse me for not being serious enough.''

Catherine grabbed a sofa cushion and raised it threateningly. "Charles...!''

A second later she shrieked as, before she even saw him move, she found herself dispossessed of the pillow and imprisoned in his lordship's arms. "Yes, Lady Caldbeck?''

She looked into his solemn face, inches above her own. "You...! You are quite infuriating, Charles Randolph!''

"I cultivate the quality. Will it satisfy you if I have my agent draw up a budget and present it to you?''

"Yes. I would appreciate that, thank you very much.'' Catherine heaved an exasperated sigh, then relaxed, her head on his shoulder.

Charles ran his fingers through his hair, as if brushing it out of his face—a quite unnecessary gesture, Catherine thought, as not a single hair of his head would dare escape his careful control. "I do not wish to think about business tonight,'' he finally offered. "I have spent three hellish days trying to find Harry, wracking my brain to discover where he may have gone to earth, and trying to keep other searchers from setting the hounds after him.''

"Oh, they mustn't! How horrible to be chased by dogs!'' Catherine shuddered. "Like an animal.''

"I agree. And not necessary. Nor effective. I do not believe he is responsible for these outrages, but he might have seen someone. He is a past master at slipping about with none the wiser. I do want to talk to him.''

"Has the runner arrived from Bow Street?''

"No. There has been some delay.''

"Oh, dear. I can see why you are frustrated. But don't be discouraged. Something will come to light.'' Catherine snuggled closer against his hard chest. "I have another question."

"And what might that be?"

"Must we postpone our trip to Skipton? The orphanage is ready and waiting for more residents."

"It will not wait long." Charles's arms tightened around her. "However, I see no reason why we cannot make a short trip. I know you have been eager to see the situation in the mills. We should be away three days at most, and if we do not go soon, it will be too cold. We might even have an early snow."

"I do want to go, but if you are too busy right now with the searching... Or if you fear the dogs might be loosed on Odd Harry in your absence..."

"No. I think the hunt is over for now. I have at last made my point that, aside from the humanitarian element, hounds are useless without something known to have his scent on it. It has been a senseless argument from the beginning. You may plan to leave day after tomorrow." He brushed her lips with his. "Now, let us consider something more pleasant."

Before Catherine could answer, his lips covered hers, effectively removing all need for conversation for some time thereafter.

Chapter Twelve

The manager of the woolen mill in Skipton greeted his noble visitors effusively. Mr. Earby apparently aspired to fashion. His brown locks were pomaded and curled, and he wore well-cut riding clothes and carried a stylish riding crop, which he used to indicate items of interest.

Charles had written to him to arrange the appointment, but had been deliberately vague as to their purpose. He found himself wondering cynically whether their welcome would be as friendly once the man discovered Catherine's real purpose. How pleased would he be to have his young workers carried away? Which Charles had no doubt they would be if Catherine deemed it necessary. This might prove to be an interesting day indeed.

The work area of the mill was surprisingly open and well lit. Charles had been expecting a gloomy atmosphere, and so was pleasantly surprised, even though the fumes from the gas lights created a pervasive miasma. The faces of the men and women toiling before the various machines looked tired and careworn, and an occasional cough could be heard above the rattle of the machinery. He saw several smaller figures that he took to be older girls and boys, but no really small children.

Obviously enjoying an audience and his own temporary importance, Earby led them from room to room and floor to floor, expounding on the mysteries of gilling and drawing, roving, spinning and the actual weaving itself. That, he explained, was done by hand on the huge looms at the top of the building.

Fascinated by the intricate process of roving, Charles paused to listen to the detailed explanation of how the wool fibers were elongated and twisted in preparation for spinning. Earby waxed eloquent on the superiority of his mill's product, while Charles peered closely at the complicated machine.

An unexpected sound from the other end of the room brought to his attention the fact that his countess was no longer by his side. He glanced toward the noise, only to see her advancing determinedly across the wide room, a little boy's hand grasped firmly in her own. Charles judged from her militant expression that the visit was, in fact, about to become much more interesting than the contraption he had just been studying.

Catherine's young charge, however, obviously did not share her enthusiasm for the encounter. He was trying hard to dig in his heels, but the smooth floor provided no purchase, and she towed him along relentlessly, her reticule clutched in her other hand and her dashing hat teetering on its moorings. Dust and lint coated the front of her skirt. The smile in Charles threatened to emerge, but a glimpse of Earby's face decided him in favor of restraint. His gaze moved from Catherine to her diminutive catch.

The boy's size startled Charles. He looked to be no more than four years old. Surely they did not have workers that young. Scrawny and bedraggled, his bony ankles protruding from grubby britches, the waif offered little to admire. Only a few strands of wispy blond hair adorned his head, and his scalp oozed from numerous sores. As Catherine pulled him nearer, Charles saw that his tiny hands were a mass of cuts and scratches.

Catherine drew rein before the manager and fixed him with a fiery glare. "Mr. Earby, will you please tell me what a child this young is doing crawling about under these dangerous machines? He cannot be more than four years old!"

Earby looked considerably less cordial, but hastened to respond. "No, no, Lady Caldbeck. He is past six years old, I assure you. He *is* quite small for his age, but he has been here for a year now. It is his function to go under the apparatus and clear the jammed fibers from the teeth and gears."

Catherine looked down as the boy struggled to free his hand, but maintained her grip. "Is that true? Are you six years old?" The lad ducked his head and wiped his nose on his sleeve, but made no other response. "What is your name?"

Still no answer. Suddenly the riding crop that Earby had been carrying so casually licked out and caught the child across the shoulders. "Answer the lady! You want another bang on the lug?"

The boy cringed and pulled hard against Catherine, but didn't answer. The overseer raised the crop again, and Catherine turned her own shoulder so as to intercept the blow, placing herself between him and his target. Earby quickly dropped the whip to his side, perhaps reading in Charles's face his intention of shoving it down his throat.

Earby stepped back, but Catherine's defensive movement caused her to momentarily loosen her grasp on the lad's little hand. Seeing a chance for escape, the panicked child dropped to the floor and dived under the nearest machine.

He was fast, but Catherine was faster. She plunged after him, dropping her reticule and falling to her knees. She grabbed a small foot just as it disappeared under the device. A brief tussle ensued. Catherine inexorably drew the small, squirming body back into the light of day. The small body kicked and grabbed at the machinery. Her hat slid farther over one ear, the plume curling under her chin, but like a terrier at a rathole, she refused to relinquish her prey.

Charles bent down to retrieve the reticule. Before he could straighten, he was arrested by the spectacle of his wife's enticing derriere emerging from under a roving machine. His eyes widened. Her rounded form swayed intriguingly from side to side under her skirts as she, still on hands and knees, tugged her burden away from the machine. Her petticoat frothed around her feet. Charles remained bent over, captured by the sight.

He was not alone. He was veritably surrounded by astonished and appreciative faces. Charles stood and cleared his throat loudly. The mill workers hastily resumed their work, even Earby averting his gaze, leaving Charles to enjoy the view alone.

Catherine finally gained her feet, bringing her prize with her. She set the child upright and regarded him sternly. "Now. We will have no more of that. What is your name?"

Earby shrugged. "He won't answer. The stubborn brat hasn't spoken a word in six months. His name is Willy."

Charles favored the man with one of his coldest stares. "What happened to his hair?"

The manager shrugged again. "We were attempting to cure those sores on his head. Hot pitch was applied to his scalp, and when it was removed his hair came with it.''

''*What?*'' Catherine fairly shrieked the question. ''You tore his hair out by the roots?''

''Lady Caldbeck...'' Earby's hostility began to show in his eyes. ''Hot pitch is an excellent remedy for sores.''

''Perhaps, but not under those circumstances.'' Catherine glared. ''And where did he get those sores in the first place? They look like cuts from that whip to me.''

The overseer folded his arms across his chest, his scowl deepening. ''My lady, surely you can understand the need for discipline. You have seen how stubborn he is.''

''Terrified, more likely. Where are his parents? How can they suffer him to be treated thus?''

Earby looked a bit smug. ''They are dead, my lady. He is fortunate to have food and a place to sleep.''

''A reminder that there are two kinds of fortune.'' Charles pointed at one of the boy's hands, indicating the injuries. ''And these?''

''Those are from the sharp edges of the metal. It is a hazard of the work.'' Speaking curtly, Earby grasped the child's upper arm and tried to pull him away from Catherine. ''Now, my lady, if you don't mind, it is time for him to return to work. He has been idle long enough.''

''Certainly not!'' Catherine tightened her hold. ''He is coming with us.''

''My lady, I have been very patient.'' Earby pulled harder on Willy's arm, all vestiges of courtesy gone. ''I need him back at his task. Too many of these indigent brats are trying to escape their duty. Only this week two rascals have run away from the Grassington lead mine. Now, if you will release him...''

"I will not!" Catherine hauled back on the luckless Willy. "I will not leave him here!" Earby jerked again. Catherine did likewise.

Charles watched this process with interest for several more tugs, wondering if his countess's hat was going to survive the encounter or wind up at his feet. Then he began to wonder if Willy was going to survive. He appeared to be in imminent danger of being torn in two. Charles decided the time had come to take a hand in the matter.

He lifted his walking stick and lightly touched Earby's fingers where they clutched the small arm. The overseer cast him an assessing glance. Charles said nothing, but let all the ice of his frigid eyes bear on the man. The silence quivered between them. At last Earby dropped his hand, the stick following it for a heartbeat.

"Very well, my lord. It will be as Lady Caldbeck desires. I'm sure I will find an employee who can talk to be less trouble, any road." Earby's murderous gaze met Charles's frosty one. "Take the whelp and good shuttance." So saying, he turned his back and marched away.

"Well. That settles that. Thank you. How do you do that? It is a trick I must learn." Catherine smiled up at Charles as she pushed ineffectually at her hat with her free hand, then made a futile attempt to brush the dirt from her skirt. They were just turning toward the door when she heard a soft voice behind her.

"Me lady."

She turned around, but could not discover the source of the whisper. Then she heard it again. It appeared to be coming from a woman working behind her. "Here." Catherine thrust Willy's hand at Charles. "Don't let go."

Charles took the hand and regarded Willy with his most intimidating expression. Confident that the boy would not dare to budge, Catherine left them and approached the woman. "Were you speaking to me?"

The worker nodded, her hands flying over her work. "Aye, me lady, but I mustn't let him see me."

"Oh. I understand." Catherine nodded and raised her voice. "That looks very interesting. Explain it to me, if you will." Then, sotto voce, she added, "We will pretend you are answering my question. What is it you wanted?"

"There's another child as needs your help. Laurie. She works in the room there." The worker nodded her head almost imperceptibly toward a door, her hands never slowing. "She come to the mill ten years past when her folk all died. Too young—her bones was all soft." The woman shook her head sadly. "Her poor legs are so bent from standing now that soon she'll not walk at all. He'll turn her off, that road."

"How awful," Catherine whispered. "I shall talk to her." She touched the woman on the shoulder. "Thank you. If you ever need me, come to me at Wulfdale, just north of Grassington."

The worker nodded gratefully. "Thank you, me lady."

Catherine made for the door behind which Laurie might be found.

Charles leaned back against the headboard in their bedroom at the inn in Skipton and regarded his bride with one eyebrow elevated. "And what," he wondered aloud, "do you think the much harassed Mr. Earby is going to say when he discovers that we have absconded not only with Willy, but with Laurie as well?"

"Humph. I don't care what he says. It quite breaks my heart to see her poor legs. They are so bowed that she is no taller than a young child, although she is nearly fifteen. Besides, she has almost reached the point where she can no longer work. He would put her out then, anyway.''

''A comforting consideration. Perhaps he will not set the minions of the law after us then.''

''If he does, it will be worth it.'' Catherine tossed her head and crossed the room to sit on the side of the bed. Charles reached out to stroke a satin-clad thigh.

''Nonetheless, it would behoove us to make an early start in the morning.'' He felt the amusement bubbling up within him as he studied his unrepentant wife. ''I am not sure I would think it worthwhile if I were clapped in gaol. I did not realize that I had married such an outlaw.''

Catherine smiled. ''Surely I am not that bad.''

''Perhaps not. The more I consider the episode at the mill, the more I think that there were some redeeming aspects.'' Images of the scene flickered through his mind, the humor growing.

''What redeeming aspects?''

Charles put on a thoughtful mien. ''Yes, the more thought I give it, the more I am sure that the memory of your tempting bottom emerging from under a roving machine would be entirely worth any price.''

''My bottom!'' Catherine's hands flew to her hips, and she burst into giggles. ''I didn't realize… I *have* sunk myself quite beneath reproach! Do tell me that my skirts did not… Alas, I fear my rashness has made a complete fool of me once again.''

''One of your more endearing qualities. You do it with such appeal and grace.'' Faster and faster the images flooded Charles's mind. A rusty sound emerged from his throat. ''Kate, had you but seen your elegant self…'' Another unfamiliar sound burst from him. ''Your bottom wriggling in the air, your hat over your ear, your petticoat tangled around your feet…and a death grip on that poor hapless lad's ankle.''

Suddenly he was laughing. The peals echoed around the room, satisfying, liberating. He had forgotten the feeling—his mother's playful hands tickling him, his baby sister making faces, his father playing horse on his knees for him. The pleasure of it came back to Charles in a rush as he looked into Kate's astonished face. He reached for her, pulling her across him and flipping her onto her back. Still laughing, he threw himself on her and pinned her wrists to the bed. Between chuckles he kissed her lips, her throat, her breasts. ''Ah, Kate. I count it well worth it, indeed.''

They prudently kept their resolve to be away from Skipton early in the morning, Willy and Laurie entrusted to the care of Sally and Hardraw. Sally was delighted to play nursemaid, but the worthy Hardraw looked a bit nonplused.

They were making their way across Grassington Moor when the carriage slowed and came to a halt. Charles opened the door and called up to the coachman. ''Why are we stopping, Jem?''

''I dunno, m'lord. The other carriage has pulled off the road.''

Charles directed his gaze behind them and saw Hardraw emerging from the coach, a less than pleased expression marring his dignified countenance. Charles walked to meet him.

''What's afoot?''

''It's the little lad, my lord. He is feeling…uh, unwell.''

As Charles looked, Sally could be seen helping Willy down the steps. She directed him to sit on a convenient boulder, and waved smelling salts under his nose. Predictably, after one whiff the boy turned his head away and protested noisily.

Charles nodded. "Travel sickness. Not unusual for children in a closed vehicle, I'm told. Did he cast up his accounts?"

Hardraw looked distinctly pained. "Not yet, but I fear the event is imminent."

"Oh, well. A bit of fresh air will set him right soon enough. We might as well all take the opportunity to stretch our legs." Charles narrowed his eyes at his henchman speculatively. "Some of that exercise we were discussing last week, Hardraw. Just the opportunity you have been seeking."

Hardraw permitted himself the veriest hint of a smile. "Just so, my lord."

Returning to Catherine, Charles helped her from the carriage and explained the situation.

"The poor thing." Catherine shook out her skirts and stretched. "Sally said he ate the most prodigious breakfast. I've no doubt that awful man has been starving him, but perhaps eating so much was not wise before traveling."

Charles took her arm. "Sally has the situation well in hand. I propose that we investigate that knoll." He pointed to an outcropping at the crest of a low hill.

"Of course!" Catherine retied her bonnet and lifted her skirts a few inches. "That is just the thing! My own stomach feels the need of some fresh air. Perhaps it was the fish from last night. I ate very little breakfast."

They set off up the gentle slope arm in arm. A few minutes later they reached their objective and looked around curiously. They found themselves in a circle of embanked earth perhaps thirty feet in diameter, studded at regular intervals with large stones.

"Look at this," Catherine exclaimed. "It is a stone circle!"

Charles looked. "Yes. It must be that. I have heard that there are some on Grassington Moor, but I have never known just where."

"I wish I knew what they were used for. There is a strange feeling about it." Catherine sat on one of the low stones, her chin resting in her hand.

Charles lowered himself to the grassy embankment beside her. "You are much more susceptible to atmosphere than I am, but, yes, I always sense something in such places that—" He broke off as a flicker of movement caught his eye. Just beyond the circle, behind the crest of the hill, something bobbed up and then quickly retreated. He squeezed Catherine's hand lightly. "Hmm. Do not look now, but I believe we are being observed."

Catherine shifted on the stone as if trying to find a more comfortable position, and followed the faint motion of his head. "Yes," she whispered. "I see it. Someone's head, I think."

"I believe so." Charles stood and casually dusted his coattail. Then, without another word, he sprang over the embankment and sprinted over the top of the hill. A small figure dashed away from him, scurried over a stone ledge and disappeared.

Reaching the ledge, Charles paused to consider where his quarry might have gone. As he stood catching his breath, he became aware of earnest whispers and muffled sobs. They seemed to be coming from directly under his feet. He slipped cautiously over the stone. A dark crevice appeared just beneath it. He strained his ears.

"Come on, Timmy. Hurry!"

More muffled sobs.

"Pluck up! It isn't far. He'll see you!"

A dissenting murmur.

Charles eased his face closer to the dark opening. The crying became louder. He could see just the corner of a tattered shirttail. His hand shot out, grasping the fabric, and he pulled. The shirttail emerged, accompanied by a struggling body. A scream of terror shattered the peace of the morning.

He hauled the child out of the cavity, being careful to maintain a firm grip. He was rewarded for his efforts with being pummeled by flying fists and kicking legs. Terrible shrieks split the air. Before he could gain control of the skirmish, another body, slightly larger, flew at him from the crevice, adding its strength and shouting at him.

"Let go! Let him go! You got no right—"

Charles had begun to question the outcome of the encounter when he heard Catherine's voice, and one of his small assailants turned his attention to her. She raised her voice above the din. "We aren't going to hurt you. Ouch! Stop that!"

Finally succeeding in subduing his tiny, but fierce, opponent, Charles looked around to see Hardraw advancing on the fray at a run. The valet reached Catherine and took a firm grip on the collar of the dirty ragamuffin she was trying to control. A tense silence ensued while all parties caught their breath.

"Well," Catherine exclaimed at last. "I think we have found the Grassington runaways."

Charles nodded in agreement. "I believe you are correct." He turned a frosty eye on the elder boy. "Very well, lad, what do you have to say for yourself?"

The boy looked to be possibly ten years of age, thin and pale, grubby beyond belief. He stuck his chin out defiantly. "We ain't done nothing. You better let us be." Then, in a softer voice, he murmured, "Ah, Timmy, don't take on so."

"I collect that this is Timmy?" Charles indicated the sobbing child he held firmly under one arm. "What is your name?"

"Ain't none of your…" The boy took a look at Charles's face and seemed to reconsider. "Thom," he answered sullenly.

"Have you two, indeed, left the lead mine?"

Thom shut his lips stubbornly, then evidently changed his mind and sighed. "You'll find out, any road. It's Timmy. He's feared of the dark. He cries the whole day. I had to get him away."

"I see. He is your brother?"

"Aye." Thom nodded.

"But he is so little!" Catherine protested. "What can he do in a mine?"

"He's a trapper."

Catherine frowned, perplexed, and Thom cast her a look of disdain at such ignorance.

"He opens the air doors so we can come through. He's only five. Myself, I'm a hurrier," he added proudly. "I'm strong."

"I can attest to that." Charles set Timmy on the ground, turning to Catherine. "A hurrier pushes the loaded carts. How old are you?"

Thom hesitated, considering. "I'm ten, I think."

Charles looked in inquiry at Catherine.

"Of course! Certainly we will take them with us."

"You won't take us back?" It was a wail of despair.

"No!" Catherine dropped to her knees beside the brothers. "We will take you to Wulfdale. We have a home there for children. Timmy will not have to stay in the dark, and you will both learn better ways of supporting yourselves. Have you parents living?''

Thom shook his head, still suspicious. Catherine racked her brain to find the most convincing argument. Her gaze fell on Thom's skinny frame.

"Mrs. Giggleswick is a very good cook."

"Aye?" Interest quickened in the child's face.

"Aye."

"All right, then. We'll stay there awhile."

Chapter Thirteen

Catherine found herself with much to contemplate, sensing a growing change in her relationship with Charles. She turned to his arms for comfort more and more readily, and he opened them to her with increasing ease. And she noticed other things as well. Little touches, shared amusement.

Yes, her hopes for love were blossoming in spite of her dwindling caution. But before she felt willing to pitch herself full-fling into loving Charles Randolph, she wanted an answer to one dismaying question.

Did he or did he not have a mistress?

She had little reason for suspicion. He certainly came to her bed with reassuring regularity, but he occasionally disappeared on "business," and when he did, he rarely described his day to her beyond more than a few words, indicating that she would have little interest in his doings.

Very likely, she wouldn't.

That would depend, of course, on just what his doings entailed. A visit to her sister-in-law was definitely in order.

The resulting conversation with Helen, a few days after their return from Skipton, proved to be a great deal more informative than Catherine ever imagined it would be. She was sipping tea and wondering how to broach the subject on which she desired enlightenment, when Helen casually asked, "How is Charles behaving?"

Catherine started guiltily and almost choked on her tea. After Helen patted her hastily on the back, she expounded on her question. "Is he still trying to manage your life for your own good?"

"Oh. That." Catherine blotted her lips on the tiny tea napkin. "I would say that I detect a certain improvement. We had a bit of a turn-up, and I told him how I felt. He assured me he did not wish to control me, and I believe he is trying to live up to that."

"You know, I believe you are good for him."

"I hope so." Catherine twisted the corner of her napkin and stared out the window for a few seconds. "There is something…something I wish to ask. I—I hardly know how to do so."

"Hmm. Why don't you just *ask?*"

"It…it is a rather delicate subject." Catherine took a deep breath and dived in. "I never heard any talk in London of Charles having, well, of his having a mistress."

"Ah." Helen nodded in understanding. "And you wonder if he has one in Yorkshire."

"Yes." Catherine looked into her sister-in-law's eyes. "Yes, I do."

Helen leaned over and patted her hand. "You are worrying for nothing. I doubt he has been celibate, but it has been years since he has had a particular friend."

"Years?"

Helen looked into the fire as if pondering her next words. Finally she turned back to Catherine. "Many years. He was very young—in his late twenties. I fear it was a bad experience for him. He thought himself very much in love at the time. Then he learned that she did not return his feelings. It was his money, you see, that she cared for.''

''Oh, dear. How sad.'' A lump rose in Catherine's throat.

Helen nodded. ''She told him as much when he found her with another man. They fought a duel, but—''

''A duel! Charles? Was Charles…did he—?''

Helen shook her head. ''The other man missed. He was frightened and shot in haste. Charles could have killed him easily, but he deloped. He realized that she wasn't worth killing a man over, but the whole thing hurt him deeply.''

''Of course it did. He *does* have feelings, though I confess, it is difficult to know what they are. Hmm. I begin to see… Why he used his money to court me, I mean, rather than his charm. To be honest, I don't know that I would have appreciated his charm until I got to know him. And I doubt I would have ever known him as I do now.'' In spite of herself, Catherine could feel herself turning red again.

Her sister-in-law mercifully pretended not to notice. She passed a plate of tea cakes to Catherine. Catherine shook her head. ''No, thank you. My tummy is not quite right today.''

''You look a little pale. Do you feel ill otherwise?''

''No. I've just been a bit tired of late. I don't know why. I'm usually very energetic. Perhaps it is the changing weather.''

''Perhaps.'' Helen shrugged, adding matter-of-factly, ''Or perhaps you are with child.''

''What?''

Catherine had been in the act of setting her tea on the

end table. The cup rattled alarmingly against the saucer, and Helen made a quick reach and took them out of her hand before the tea spilled on their skirts.

"I said perhaps...." Helen's brow creased. "Catherine, are you all right?"

"No. I mean, yes, of course. I mean I...I can't be increasing!"

Helen was clearly baffled by her distress. "What is it, Catherine?"

"Nothing. It's nothing. I'm sure that's not the case. I'll be fine tomorrow." Catherine racked her brain for a way to change the subject, but her mind refused to co-operate, coming up completely blank.

Helen stepped into the breach with a commonplace comment about one of her neighbors, and in a very short time thereafter Catherine had responded mechanically, thanked her for the tea and told her goodbye. Helen looked confused and concerned, but Catherine could not begin to explain her feelings to her.

She couldn't even explain them to herself.

Back in the carriage, her nausea grew worse than ever. She opened the window and let the cold air blow in her face. With child. It couldn't be. It couldn't be!

But, of course, it could be.

Considering the amount of time she and Charles spent entwined in passion, it most certainly could be. In fact, the only wonder would be if she *weren't* increasing. She had simply shut her mind to the possibility. Her monthly courses had been irregular and disrupted since her marriage, but she thought that attributable to all the changes that had been thrust upon her.

She *was* pregnant! Catherine covered her face with her hands. A baby. A child. A new little, helpless life grew within her. It was happening. That which she had avoided all her adult life was happening. She was creating a child.

She lifted her face and wiped tears from her cheeks. She thought she had accepted that possibility when she accepted Charles. She had thrown herself into their ardor with her whole heart, and she had loved every minute of it. Now that she faced the reality, terror clutched her.

What if she died delivering the child? What if Charles had no interest in an infant? What if her poor baby was left with no one to love it? A sob escaped her. She and Charles might both die. She couldn't bear the thought. She simply couldn't bear it. Several more sobs erupted. Surely God would not be so cruel. Surely not!

But He had let her parents die while she yet needed them. And those of countless other children. How could He? She sobbed harder, angrily. Could one be angry at God? Surely He would strike her dead where she sat. She dashed the tears from her face and glared defiantly out the coach window. She was furious at Him! So there!

Evidently, since no lightning bolt appeared, she would live to tell the tale. Catherine sighed and pulled off her bonnet, leaning back into the gray velvet cushions, toying with a fiery curl. What foolishness! As if God cared whether she was in a rage with Him. In any event, her anger would not solve the problem.

A baby. She was going to have a baby. A smile broke through her tears. A sweet, tiny life. How she would love it. If only… *Oh, please, God. Please don't let me die. Please don't leave my baby alone.* The tears again coursed down her face as she folded her hands protectively over her womb. *Give me the strength. Oh, please, please give me strength!*

He was tired and cold. Charles rode into the Wulfdale stable well after the dinner hour and set about unsaddling his gray stallion, grateful for the light and warmth of the stall. Samuel Josiah, his groom, appeared when he had only begun, and took the task away from him with an accusing frown. Charles noted the scowl with amusement. Far be it from Samuel to allow his lordship to groom his own horse at any hour.

Letting himself in a side door of the house, Charles encountered Hawes. "Good evening, my lord."

Charles shrugged out of his greatcoat and handed it over to the butler. "Good evening, Hawes. Has Lady Caldbeck retired for the evening?"

"I am not certain, my lord. She had a light meal sent up to her room. Her maid said she was not feeling quite the thing."

Charles stopped abruptly and turned back to his butler in alarm. "She's ill?"

"I wouldn't think it serious, my lord," Hawes quickly reassured him. "Sally indicated only a minor indisposition."

Charles was already moving rapidly up the stairs, concern speeding his way. What if Catherine were sicker than she had indicated? Come to think of it, she had not seemed quite her lively self for several days. And she had looked pale, and… He drew himself in. He was rapidly working himself into a full-blown worry. No need to borrow trouble. Nonetheless, he continued upward in haste.

Charles had pushed himself and his mount on the road home in spite of the numbing cold. He might have put up at the inn where he took dinner, but he craved his waiting wife. He had been frustrated all day.

He had warmed himself with a picture of her greeting him with a welcoming kiss, slipping her arms around his neck while he slid his hands over her soft bottom. He had, in fact, dwelt on the image until the nether portions of his anatomy had become distinctly uncomfortable. Perhaps that was not the wisest fantasy to engage in while riding a hard and unforgiving saddle through a frigid night. Had he been a different man, he might have laughed aloud at himself.

When he persuaded Catherine to marry him, he was intent on availing himself of her beauty and her exuberant nature. He had not realized how comforting domesticity would be. Yes, there was definitely something about having a woman in his house.

Charles did not even go into his own bedchamber, but tapped briefly at Catherine's door and then opened it a crack, peering around it. She sat in a large chair pulled up near the fire. Her elbow rested on the arm of the chair, and her chin rested, in turn, on the heel of her hand. She stared into the fire pensively. The glow of the flames caught in the strands of her vivid hair, turning it into a blazing penumbra around her delicate profile. Charles paused, drinking in the sight.

Beautiful. Truly beautiful.

She turned as he came through the door, but did not get up and come to him. Smothering a stab of disappointment, Charles crossed the room to her and knelt before her chair, gathering her hands in his. His anxiety increased when she did not speak, but regarded him silently with listless eyes. "Hawes told me you are not feeling well. Should we send for Dr. Dalton?"

"No...no, I'm not ill. I just..." Her voice faltered, and she returned to gazing into the fire.

Something in her voice caused Charles's fears to escalate. "Kate? What is it? Tell me."

She shook her head without speaking. A tear escaped to trickle down her cheek. The sight of it relieved Charles's mind slightly. She was unhappy, not ill. Her sensitive heart had been touched by something. He tightened his grip on her hands. "What has overset you, Kate? Come now. Tell me about it."

Again she did not answer, continuing to shake her head. Another tear joined the first in its journey toward her chin. Charles began to experience the bafflement and frustration known to husbands since Adam and Eve. "Kate, are you angry with me? Have I done something?"

Catherine nodded, then quickly shook her head again. She sniffled and choked on a little sob, never looking at Charles. He contemplated her helplessly. Was that a yes or a no? It must be a no. If she were angry with him, he would be in no doubt at all. He would be dodging pillows. Instead she began to cry harder. His lack of progress begin to wear on his patience.

"Kate. Kate, you must tell me what is bothering you. You are going to make yourself ill if you are not already." When his only answer was renewed sobbing, he put his hands on her shoulders and gave her a gentle shake. "Stop this, Kate. Tell me."

Catherine looked up at him with streaming eyes. She opened her mouth twice before any sound emerged. At last she managed a forlorn wail.

"I'm going to have a baby!"

Charles rocked back on his heels, stunned. "You're going to… But, Kate, why are you crying? That's wonder—" As Catherine covered her face with both hands and started sobbing again, a sudden conviction struck Charles like a sledgehammer blow to his heart.

She did not want *his* child.

She did not want his child.

His beautiful, loving wife did not want to carry his child.

Catherine had sat in her room alone all evening, her fears held at bay primarily through numbness. She held on, praying for Charles to come home and help her accept what must be, but when he at last arrived, she couldn't force the fateful words from her throat. As soon as she choked them out, her terrors all came crashing down on her again. As she sobbed miserably, she gradually became aware that Charles no longer knelt beside her. He had risen to his feet and stood gazing down at her. She drew a composing breath and lifted her eyes to his frozen face.

For the first time since she had known him, Catherine harbored no doubts at all about his feelings.

His face was a mask of pure, unadulterated pain.

"Charles…" Resolutely, Catherine pushed the sobs back into her chest. "Charles, are you…" With sudden insight she exclaimed, "I have wounded you. How? What have I done?"

For a moment she did not think he would answer. Thought and emotion warred in his expression. Finally, he spoke in a very careful voice. "You do not want my child."

Catherine was thunderstruck. "No…no! I mean, no, it is not that."

He seemed not to have heard her, but continued speaking. "I knew that you did not wish to marry me, but I thought…I have been thinking that perhaps—"

"Oh, no, Charles!" Horrified, Catherine reached for him, clutching his big hands in her slender ones. Somehow she must wipe that anguish from him. "It is not that at all. Please don't think that."

When he still did not respond, she jumped to her feet, throwing her arms around his waist. He stood immobile, his arms hanging limp at his sides. The anguish now scoring his impassive face wrenched another panicky sob from Catherine. "Please. You mustn't think that. You mustn't! Oh, Charles! Say something!"

Gradually the haze of pain befogging Charles's brain began to clear enough for him to hear Catherine's importuning words. He realized that her arms clasped him fiercely, that her tear-filled voice implored him to answer. Drawing a shuddering breath, he rested his hands on her shoulders and looked into the clear sapphire of her eyes.

"Yes, Kate?" To his own ears his voice sounded rough, choked. He cleared his throat, trying to speak around some sort of obstruction. "What did you say?"

"I said that you don't understand. I'm glad that it's your child. Glad! It isn't that at all." She pounded her fist against his chest. "You must believe me."

Charles gave his head a puzzled shake, as if trying to wake up. Glad. She was saying she was glad the child was his. Wanted him to believe that. Then why was she still crying? He stared into her tear-swollen face, trying to comprehend.

"I don't understand, Kate."

"I'm afraid!"

Charles began to see a crack of light. The terrible aching in his chest began to fade, the relief almost as painful as the sorrow. "Afraid. I see." He spent a few moments just breathing hard, like a man who has just escaped destruction by a hairbreadth. "Perhaps we should begin this conversation anew."

He turned them about, sitting in the chair and drawing her onto his lap. She laid her head on his shoulder and sighed.

"Now, Kate. Please explain this awful distress to me. Are you afraid of childbirth? Of the pain?"

Straightening, Catherine shook her head. "No... No, not the pain—or at least, not very much."

"What then?"

Another sob broke loose, and Catherine hid her face against his neck. "I'm afraid I shall die and you will not want to care for an infant and you will die too and nobody will want it and no one will love it or take care of it and it will be miserably unhappy and..."

The words came out in a torrent, and she covered her mouth with her hand as if to dam them and hold back hysteria.

Ah! The glimmer of light expanded to a reasonably large window. Charles held her closer, stroking her hair. "As *you* were. Now I comprehend."

Catherine nodded against his throat. "Yes. As I was. I don't want my baby to be unhappy." She sniffed and brought her voice back under control. "That's why I didn't marry before. I wanted a child so much, but I was frightened for it, and then, when you offered for me, I told myself it would be all right and I didn't have any other choice and you kissed me and I wanted..." The words again seemed to take on a life of their own, and Catherine gulped and stemmed the flow. "I love having your baby. I've always wanted one."

"And now you shall have one." Charles, correctly interpreting this tangled skein, felt his heart swell with gratification. She loved having his child. Clinging to the words, he lifted her face so that she could see him. "You will have *my* child, and we will both love it very much. We will take very good care of it, and I shall take very good care of you. And of myself."

Catherine attempted a smile, but it didn't quite materialize. "But what if something *does* happen to us?"

Charles straightened her on his lap, speaking very earnestly. "Kate, none of us can foretell the future. If I could promise you that nothing evil will happen to us, I would, but you know better. We will simply do everything we can and then trust in God."

Catherine stared at her hands for a few heartbeats, lips compressed. "I am not sure God cares."

Covering both her hands with one of his, Charles considered for a moment before speaking. "I do not believe God is always directly involved in what happens to us. He has given the world order, and events occur according to that order. And most things can be made to work to our good."

He paused, wondering if he were wise to continue. He decided to risk it. "I'm sure your losing your fortune seemed an utter disaster at the time, but it resulted in our marriage, and I am grateful that it did. Without it you might never have had the child you wanted, and…and I never would have had you."

He looked uncertainly into Catherine's face. She hesitated for a moment, then put her arms around his neck and pressed her cheek against his.

"And I would not have had you."

Charles's arms closed around her convulsively, crushing her to him. Her arms returned the pressure, and they sat thus for several minutes, simply drinking in the closeness. There was nothing more to be said. It was enough for now.

At last, when a spark popped from the fire, Charles raised his head to be certain it had not landed on the rug. Seeing all was well, he began to stroke Catherine's back, thinking how he might reassure her. "There are some measures we can take, Kate, to insure our child's welfare. Your jointure is secure. If something happens to me, neither you nor our children will be destitute. In fact, if the child is a boy, he will inherit the earldom and Wulfdale and its income.''

''What if it is a girl?'' Catherine sounded thoughtful, but no longer distraught.

''I have already set aside a portion for our daughters, just as your father did for you—except that I have made certain it is administered by responsible individuals. Our daughters will not find themselves in your boots.''

Catherine sat silent for a short while, then said, ''That is very well thought of. But who will care for them—love them?''

''You and I will.'' Charles spoke firmly. ''If something should happen to me, you will care for them. And if something happens to you, I shall love and treasure them for my whole life.'' He laid his fingers over Catherine's lips. ''No, no more what-ifs. We must decide who we most trust to love them if we both are lost, and provide for that.''

After a long silent moment gazing into the fire, Catherine murmured thoughtfully, ''Whom do I most trust? I must think about that. Liza is the kindest person I know. Perhaps she and George...''

''That is one possibility. Helen is another.''

''Oh, yes. Helen is very kind, and she is family, too. Who else?''

''We will think about it, as you said.'' Charles got to his feet with Catherine in his arms. ''Now you are going to bed. You have exhausted yourself. I intend to begin taking the most particular care of you as of now. You will soon be wishing me at Jericho.''

Catherine chuckled. "And just when I have gotten your promise not to order my life."

Charles dipped his head for a quick kiss. When he lifted it, he was smiling. "I must be more cautious about my promises."

Catherine traced the curve of his lips with a fingertip. "You're smiling again."

"Am I? Perhaps it will become a habit." He laid her on the bed and set about removing her nightclothes. "I have much to smile for recently."

"And to laugh about?"

"Yes, it seems that I do." Charles stripped off his own clothing and slid into the bed beside her. He pulled the covers over them both and, leaning on one elbow, drew the ribbon from her hair and spread the glowing locks across the pillow. Winding a curl around his finger, he delighted in the play of the light across it.

"I hope our daughters have hair like yours." He lifted a handful and buried his face in it. "Like living flame. And skin like yours. You smell so good—your hair, your skin, all of you." He moved his lips to her throat and inhaled. The scent enveloped him, bringing a flood of desire.

He kissed a trail across her breasts, and Catherine lifted her hips. Charles raised his head, shaking it. "No. I don't want to tire you further. I just want to…to feast on you. To cherish our child."

Catherine relaxed. Pushing the quilt aside, he let his caresses drift down to her soft abdomen. His child. His child lay cushioned within her protecting womb. He kissed her navel, then outlined the curved flesh with kisses, taking in the increasing fragrance of her body. If he were to hold to his good intentions, he must stop. He lifted his head, but her arms tugged at him, pulling him to her.

"Charles, I am *not* that tired."

He looked into her languid eyes, and then, surrendering to her and to himself, he covered her with his body and entered her slowly and carefully. He loved her with every stroke, gently, guardedly, overcome with protectiveness. As his own feelings heightened, her sweet sighs became soft whimpers, finally bursting into a long, drawn-out moan of pleasure. His followed within seconds, and they lay together, bodies and minds woven together, until sleep claimed them.

From the blustery hilltop he watched the lights in the windows of the hulking mansion blink out one by one as the occupants within extinguished their candles and retired for the night. The moon hid beyond the edge of the world and the usurping stars looked down at the frosty earth—observing, glittering, pitiless. The gale roared across the hills and through the trees and in his ears.

The blast tore at him with sharp teeth, but he paid it no mind. What was a little cold to him? The cold and the dark protected him. In the gloom no one laughed. No one called down reproach upon him. No one recognized the evil.

But he knew it. It had eaten at him inch by inch. Day by day. Year by year. But he had found his power at last. Now he would strike. Strike in secret, destroying the imperfection. Strike and strike and strike!

He growled low in his throat, clutching at himself, snarling.

She lay beyond the darkened windows. Lying warm. Safe. But he was ready to begin, ready to plant the seed of fear and then…then… He groaned. But the fear must have time to grow. He could wait. Until then, he had much work to do. Yes, much work.

Chapter Fourteen

To Catherine the world looked completely new. The sunlight streaming through the windows held a new brightness. When she gazed out at the countryside, the trees and hills glowed with fresh hues. Her hot chocolate had more flavor than she could ever remember before. It soothed her throat and stomach, quelling the nausea that had been plaguing her.

Love grew within Wulfdale.

Neither she nor Charles had spoken the word, of course, but it hadn't been needed. The seeds were sown. Love would grow, just as the seed of new life within her did. Charles's lovemaking had taken on a new quality the night before, a softness, a sweet tenderness. Catherine hugged the memory to herself joyfully.

And her panic about the baby had abated. Charles's calm planning had reassured her. She was no longer alone. Her child would not be alone. They would make a list of all the kindest people they knew, and they would write a will to cover every contingency. This would be the most thoroughly bequeathed child in history. The thought did not remove all of Catherine's anxiety, but it diminished it from a knife in her heart to a small prick.

All would be well. Now she wanted to experience, un-marred by fear, her enjoyment of the knowledge that she would soon be a mother.

However, the grim reality of the murders could not be pushed aside. At breakfast, perceiving Charles to be in a brown study, she questioned him as to the source of it.

He stared at his eggs and beef for a moment before answering. "It is these curst killings. The inquest re-vealed nothing new. The runner has arrived from Bow Street, but we are no closer to finding the culprit than we ever were. We cannot even find Harry."

"Has anyone questioned Vincent?"

"You are determined that he is the guilty party, aren't you?" Across the table, Charles's mouth pulled slightly at one corner. Did that represent a smile or a frown?

"Well, we know him to be a cad, and he had scratches on his face, as from a struggle with a woman."

"True, but that was before Mrs. Ribble was killed."

"It wasn't before Mrs. Askrigg died."

Charles actually looked startled. "Hmm! I hadn't thought of that. He said he had them from that woman in the taproom, but—"

"But Mr. Malham didn't mention that. And Vincent did not actually say that, either. He just said it was a girl near their village."

"No." Charles became pensive for a moment. "He did not." He wiped his mouth on his napkin and stood up. "I believe I shall seek out the runner and suggest he investigate that question."

"Good! I do not like Vincent." Catherine nodded in satisfaction and jumped to her feet. "I'll go with you."

Charles came around the table and intercepted her, placing restraining hands on her shoulders. "Not today. I have plans to meet Adam. Besides, it is too cold for you to be out.'' Catherine made a face, and he tweaked her nose. ''If Dr. Dalton says you may ride more, I shall not object. I have asked him to visit this afternoon, so I shall return before then. I want him to recommend the best midwife in the district to care for you—perhaps one who can stay here for a few months. And possibly a nurse for the baby.''

''Yes, that would be a good thing—but not a wet nurse. I do not want to turn my baby over to a stranger to feed.''

''No, I was sure you would not want to do that. But I want a responsible person to care for the child as it grows. You will not wish to be tied down forever.''

''No, I suppose not. But, oh, Charles…my own baby! I am beginning to believe it.'' She threw her arms around his neck and squeezed. Charles returned the pressure and dropped a kiss into her hair.

When she looked up, he was smiling.

Damnation, but it was cold! The wind still howled, biting and fierce. Charles pulled his gray wool muffler higher on his neck and hailed Adam as he cantered up the lane toward their meeting spot. ''Good morning.''

Adam pulled in his chestnut mount and returned the salute. ''Good morning to you. Has it occurred to you that we are both daft to be out-of-doors in this weather? We should immediately hie ourselves to the nearest inn and enjoy a pint of ale in front of a crackling fire—or better yet, mulled wine.''

Charles nodded in agreement. ''Actually, I had some such plan in mind.''

Adam rubbed his gloved hands together, trying to restore circulation. ''Champion! Let us be off without further loss of time. My hands are numb.''

"Not quite so fast." Charles held up one finger. "I wish to invite the Bow Street runner to accompany us."

"That doesn't sound too bad. He is putting up at the inn in your village, isn't he? That taproom is as good as any." Adam pulled his horse's head around and nudged him into motion.

Charles followed suit, spurring his mount abreast of Adam's. "The taproom I wish to visit is the one where Malham's man witnessed the incident with Vincent and the barmaid."

"Ah. I see." Adam wiped at his nose. "You think that story does relate to the killings then?"

"Possibly."

"Well, personally—" Adam smiled sardonically "—I am inclined to hope so. It would be most convenient for the law of the land to hang him. I'm none too keen on acquiring Vincent as a stepson-by-marriage—or whatever bloody thing he would become to me when I finally persuade Helen to marry me. Never let it be said that I stood in the way of justice out of fear of a mere deadly inflammation of the lungs. Lead on."

Charles led on, unconcerned. He had known Adam since boyhood and had never known him to hold back when circumstances required any form of action, nor to coddle himself. He would, however, probably continue the joking and complaining every step of the way. Charles had learned long ago to ignore him.

They had no trouble in locating the runner, and only a little in coaxing him out of the warmth of the inn. Zebidiah Maidstone, a tall, ungainly man perhaps forty years old, hauled himself bravely—if awkwardly—into the saddle, and the three of them set off. Charles pretended not to see Adam's amused glance, although he had his own doubts about the outcome of the runner's equestrian endeavors.

Alone, Charles and Adam might have made the ride in half an hour, but every time they dared a gallop, they soon came to fear that their new confederate would be quickly left behind on the frozen surface of the road. They finally sighted the inn for which they were bound, and all three heaved a grateful sigh, the runner's the most profound of all.

They made short work of handing their mounts over to the stableman and dashing into the welcome heat and bustle of the inn. The landlord hastened to take their coats and other wraps, while the men sought the fire, alternately warming hands and backs before the cheery blaze.

When they had all been provided with a flagon of mulled wine, Charles explained their errand to the landlord. "Mr. Maidstone is here to investigate the two murders we have had near Wulfdale. He is interested in your description of an incident that occurred here between Lord Lonsdale and your barmaid. Surely you must remember it."

"Oh aye, m'lord, I do that." The landlord rubbed his own pudgy hands together before the fire, shaking his head. "Terrible thing. The lass might have been burnt alive." He drew himself up indignantly. "Much his lordship might care!" He cast an apologetic look in Charles's direction. "No offense, m'lord. I hear he's some of your kin."

Charles nodded. "By marriage only. No offense taken. Please continue."

"Eh, he's a nasty piece of work, is what he is. Came around the next day, not a particle of remorse. Came to gloat. He'd have been happy if he'd killed her. Still comes in now and now, though I'm not so well suited to have him here. Not so easy for the likes of me to tell a lord not to come.''

The man looked uncomfortable, and Charles exchanged glances with Adam. He had a depressing suspicion that if anyone was ever to restrain Vincent, the task would fall to the two of them. Charles was more than tempted himself to lay the bloodshed at the door of Lord Lonsdale, just to rid themselves of him.

Maidstone tsk-tsked and looked grave. ''Shocking. Very. She able to defend herself at all? Scratch his face maybe?''

The landlord looked puzzled. ''Now how's a lass to do that with the great lout on top of her?''

''Is the lass here?''

The innkeeper turned to answer Charles. ''Nay, m'lord. When he came in the next day, she came all-a-bits. Went off to her old grandfather's place in Skipton and won't come back. I need her back here, and so does her mother need the brass I pay the girl, what with little ones still at home, but she won't come so long as his lordship's about. Little blame to her.''

''No. None at all.'' Charles looked at the runner. ''Perhaps we can ask his friends.''

''Aye, perhaps. Anyone know these coves' names?'' Blank looks met this inquiry. Maidstone sighed. ''Well, maybe we can find them. Much obliged to you, landlord.''

''My pleasure, my pleasure, sir, m'lords…'' The innkeeper signaled for their coats to be brought. ''I want to see the slam-trash that's done them bloody murders caught,'' he asserted, adding after a moment, ''no matter who. We've had no such scuggery in the Dales since I can remember.''

Just as the landlord lifted Charles's greatcoat to help

him don it, a fresh blast of frigid air swirled into the room, bearing Lord Lonsdale himself with it. There was a startled silence from all parties until Vincent shrugged out of his greatcoat and tossed it in the direction of the landlord. His hands already full, the innkeeper showed a moment of panic that the garment should fall to the floor before he could perform his duty. Charles stepped forward, smoothly intercepting the coat, and handed it back to Vincent. After glaring for a moment, Lonsdale took the garment from Charles, but sneered at him.

"Well, well, *Uncle* Charles." Somehow he gave the title an obscene ring. "What brings you out on such a bloody unpleasant day? Surely some great attendance to duty?" He pointed to the empty flagons on the nearest table and snapped his fingers at the innkeeper, who again looked perplexed.

Adam took Charles's greatcoat from the man and laid it over the back of a chair. The landlord made a hasty exit in the direction of the kitchen. Vincent snickered and sat, propping his muddy boots on a scrubbed table. "Nobly done, Litton. Or should I practice calling you *Papa?*"

"Thank God *I* didn't sire you. I'd hate to have that on my conscience." Adam favored Vincent with a twisted smile. "What brings you out? Haven't you made enough mischief here?"

"Not at all." Vincent took a cup of wine from the returning landlord, who stepped back and watched him with hostile eyes. "I can continue to get my revenge simply by being here. As long as I'm here, the chit can't come back to work. Maybe she'll starve." He took a long draught of the wine.

Maidstone rubbed his chin thoughtfully. "I collect that *this*—" with an impassive face that rivaled Charles's own, the runner breathed disdain into the word "—is Lord Lonsdale?"

Vincent scowled. "And who might *this* be? Is that the way you speak to your betters, oaf?"

"Haven't recognized any."

The words hung in the room like icicles. Adam grinned, and Charles found himself beginning to like the detective.

Vincent's feet slammed to the floor. "Of all the insolence!" He made as if to lunge at Maidstone, but something in the runner's quiet face stopped him. Balked, Vincent stood bristling. "Who the hell do you think you are?"

"I think I'm Zebidiah Maidstone of Bow Street."

Enlightenment spread across Vincent's face. "Bow Street! No wonder you're so devilish proud of yourself. You're supposed to be looking into the killings. What are you doing in here?"

"Looking into the killings…and into *you* a mite."

"Me?" Astonishment followed enlightenment. "You're investigating me? About those murdered women? You're fair and far off! I had nothing to do with that—" He broke off and looked at Charles and Adam, eyes narrowed. "Ah. I begin to understand. It's you two behind this. I should have known. You'd love to have me out of the way, wouldn't you?"

"Now that you mention it…" Adam's words were barely audible.

Vincent paid him no mind, but ranted on. "You—" he pointed at Charles "—you'd love to see me hauled out of Yorkshire. You know that red-haired wench you married wants me. Flaunting herself in front of me. If you hadn't interfered, you'd have been cuckolded in your own house very shortly!'' Vincent stopped for breath and gave Charles a measuring look.

Charles took a step forward, fists tight at his side. His nephew smirked at him. God! He couldn't kill him before an officer of the law. But Vincent would love for him to try. He always knew just when to seize an advantage. Taking a deep breath, Charles forced himself to relax.

''That's enough, Vincent. You try my patience.''

''Ha!'' Clearly Lord Lonsdale was enjoying the scene he was creating. ''No, not enough. Not nearly enough. I have only begun. We have yet to discuss your sister— oh, yes, my esteemed stepmother. You can't even get your best friend to take her off your hands. Why should he marry her? He beds her anytime he wants.''

Adam exploded past Charles. Before anyone else could react, he had Vincent by his coat, slamming him against the stone of the fireplace. ''You filthy cur! You may try your ability to break Charles's patience if you wish, but by God, I have none for you.'' He smashed him against the wall again. ''You will ask my pardon, and Charles's, and that of these good men if I have to beat it out of you one word at a time.''

''I'll be damned!'' Vincent recovered his feet and pushed Adam away, aiming a kick at his groin. Adam backstepped and swung a fist. Charles allowed him one blow before he grabbed his arm.

Vincent reeled back against the fireplace once more. As he moved to lunge at Adam, Maidstone grasped his wrist and twisted the arm behind his back.

''Give over, Adam. We have trouble enough.'' Charles stepped between the two combatants, forcing himself to interfere. Why did he always have to be the reasonable one?

Adam backed away, panting in anger. After a brief

attempt to free himself from Maidstone, Vincent evidently decided that he did not want his arm broken. He glared at Adam, wiping blood from his mouth with his free hand.

"You'll meet me for this, Goddamn you! Name your seconds."

"Ha!" Adam's bark of laughter sounded derisively in the suddenly quiet room. "Meet you? On a field of honor? You don't know the first thing about honor. I wouldn't lower myself."

"Afraid?" Even at a serious disadvantage, Vincent lost none of his sneer.

"Hardly." Adam, recovering his temper, met sneer with scorn. "I certainly cannot duel with the son of the lady I *am* going to marry, even if he had the honor of a man, rather than the bravado of a bully. One day, Vincent, you will go too far, and someone will shut that vicious mouth of yours for good."

"They may try!"

"Aye. They'll try, right enough. Sooner or later." Maidstone released the pressure on Vincent's arm slightly, propelling him toward the door. "Matter of time." He gestured for Vincent's coat and handed it to him. "Meantime, it'd be my recommendation that you stay away from here, guv'nor. Else I might decide you play a prominent part in this here investigation."

"What about them?" Vincent pointed to Charles and Adam. "Have you considered these fine lords? Caldbeck is cold as the North Sea. He's capable of anything. And ask Litton how many buildings he has admitted setting afire. And ask how many he has never admitted." He jammed his hat on his head and stormed out the door.

"Aye," commented Maidstone, "I'll ask him."

* * *

"And ask he did," Charles related to Catherine at breakfast the next morning. "I thought Adam would explode from attempting to control his temper, but he managed to answer with some grace. I think he convinced Maidstone that he had been responsible for only small conflagrations."

Catherine laughed. "Such as hearth rugs. But keeping his temper was quite an accomplishment! It is not every day one is accused of murder."

"Maidstone did not actually accuse him, just inquired politely and pointed out that Adam had been in the vicinity of Ribble's cottage the morning of the fire."

"But there was a whole crowd of people there that morning."

"True. And very likely none of them are guilty. I'm sure Adam is not."

Catherine paused thoughtfully with her fork halfway to her mouth, brows drawn together. "I cannot think it, either, but I suppose we must explore all possibilities." She pointed the fork at him. "But think, Charles. If we are to go back to Mrs. Askrigg's death, Adam did come here with a burn shortly afterward."

"So he did." Charles considered that for a moment, silently irritated. How could Kate even consider suspecting Adam of such a thing? The whole idea was ridiculous. His first impulse was to dismiss the notion out of hand. Then a very uncomfortable feeling began to steal over him. Was it possible to know someone for so many years—hunt with him, drink with him, sit by the fire with him, entrust his sister to him—and not recognize an evil of that magnitude? That was an extremely distressing thought.

An even more distressing one followed on its heels. Was Adam wondering the same thing about *him?* Damn!

What a coil! Not only was the vermin committing the vilest of crimes, he was sowing suspicion all over the dale.

Charles shook his head, casting off the mood. "No. It cannot be Adam. Surely I would suspect. I have known him all my life, and I just do not believe it. Of course, I have known all of those present that day all our lives. And…" He paused, staring into the middle distance for a few heartbeats. "It is a strange thing, Kate. I have just been wondering whether they are pondering *my* guilt. Are all of us looking at one another so uneasily?"

"Oh, no," Catherine declared. "No one could suspect you."

Charles looked appreciatively at his wife. "Thank you, Kate. I appreciate your loyalty, but consider…"

"Consider what? You could not have done it. You were with me on both occasions."

Charles raised an eyebrow. "Alas. It is my having an alibi. And here I was believing your certainty of my innocence to be wifely devotion."

"Oh, Charles! Do be serious! I know you are incapable of so foul an act. But I am glad that Mr. Maidstone is deprived of a reason to question you."

"Indeed. I am, in fact, quite overcome with gratitude for that fact." Charles poured himself another cup of coffee, offering with a gesture to refill Catherine's cup. She nodded. "But it is very difficult, Kate. I am mistrusting men with whom I have been associated for years—Richard, Vincent, Harry. Even Stalling, more's the pity."

Catherine chuckled. "I don't like Sir Kirby very much, but he hardly seems a murderer."

"No, being a pompous bore is annoying, but hardly criminal. Besides, he and Adam were together." Charles swallowed his coffee, contemplating.

"True, although only for a short while, apparently. Ribble left the house early to meet you at the wall, so there were several hours in which the killer could strike." Catherine sipped cautiously at the hot liquid. "What did Mr. Maidstone say of Vincent?"

"Very little. He does not like him. That is obvious, but I did not get the impression that he placed him very high on his list of suspects."

"Why ever not?" Indignation tinged Catherine's voice. "He is completely lacking in character."

"And he had the temerity to suggest that red hair was not to his liking." Charles carefully kept his face straight and awaited the explosion with anticipation. It should only be a moment....

"Well! Of all the things to say." Catherine primmed her mouth and sat up very straight. "If you believe, Lord Caldbeck, that I would make such a judgment just because someone indicated that they did not like my hair..."

Charles raised one eyebrow.

Catherine huffed and folded her arms beneath her breasts. He loved watching his wife when she was in a snit. She plunged on. "That is completely unjust, my lord, and you know it. With all the other things we know about him, all he has done..."

When she sputtered to a halt, looking as though she might bolt from her chair and leave the room, Charles regretfully decided it was time to cut line. He casually lifted his cup and watched her over the rim. "True. Do forgive me, Lady Caldbeck. How could I possibly have made such a mistake?"

Lady Caldbeck narrowed her eyes and put one fist on her hip. "Charles Randolph! Are you teasing me? You wretch!"

Charles maintained a suggestive silence.

"Oh, don't you try to look innocent. I know your ways. And I rose right to your bait." Catherine relaxed against her chair, smiling ruefully. "And, to tell the truth, that remark *did* put him in my black books for all time—even if he had done nothing else."

"As it should have," Charles agreed. He loved Catherine's honesty. "It was inexcusably rude. But in spite of Vincent's many shortcomings I rather doubt that he is the guilty party. There is nothing clandestine about his misbehavior. On the contrary. It is as though the whole purpose is to make others dislike him, therefore he must be as public about it as possible."

"How strange. Why would anyone do that?"

"I have no idea."

"Has he any friends?"

"Hangers-on, more like. He is a wealthy man—or he will be when his fortune comes into his hands. At the rate he is going, it will not last very long."

Catherine pursed her lips in thought. "He must believe that he must buy his friends. Perhaps he is convinced that no one will like him, anyway, so he is as obnoxious as possible to give them an excuse."

Charles considered for a moment. What would that be like—to believe that no one was willing to be your friend? To never have had the closeness that he had enjoyed with Adam for most of his life? He shrugged. "I suppose it is possible. It does not seem to be a motive for bloody murder. The mind behind these killings is undoubtedly insane."

"Yes. That is certain. But most likely it was *none* of the people we saw, Charles." Catherine leaned her elbows on the table and rested her chin in her hand. "It surely can't be Richard. I simply cannot picture him with a knife in his hand. By the way, does he always ride your grays?''

''Yes, often. The exercise is good for them. He is an extremely good horseman, and he can't afford blood horses, so I encourage him to ride mine. But now that you mention it, I have no idea why he was out that day. I left him with a great deal of work the day before.''

''He said he had errands.''

''No doubt he did, and so do I.'' Charles blotted his lips and got to his feet, laying the napkin beside his plate. ''I hope it is not as cold as it was yesterday. I told Maidstone that I would escort him about the dale today so that he may question the tenants. Someone is bound to have seen Harry in the last two weeks. At least we now know where he has been recently.''

''Really? Where?'' Catherine straightened in curiosity.

''In the Lady Caldbeck Home for Orphans.'' Charles made the announcement and waited with anticipation for the expected reaction. He was immediately rewarded.

''What? That can't be possible!'' His wife's eyes widened with alarm.

''Not only possible, but, apparently, a fact. I meant to tell you earlier. When the workmen opened the second wing, they found a room with signs that it had been recently occupied—ashes on the hearth, food that was stale, but not rotted. It looks as though he had been staying there for some time.''

''Well! No wonder I thought someone was watching me whenever I was in that courtyard. Odd Harry must have been peeking from a window.''

''Quite possibly. But he is not there any longer. I suspect the fact that we can't find him now indicates that he has, indeed, seen something.''

Catherine frowned, leaning back in her chair. "Why do you believe that?"

"I think he would be afraid. It is so much his habit to withdraw that it would be very difficult for him to come forward with information. It has been years since he has even spoken to anyone. But someone should have at least glimpsed him by now. He must be deliberately hiding rather than just avoiding people."

"No wonder he is called Odd Harry." Catherine toyed with her cup, staring into the swirling dregs of the coffee. "It gives me the shivers to think of being watched by him. Of his hiding behind some dark window and our not knowing he was there. I worry about the children. Are you really sure he is not our murderer? Living as he does might unbalance anyone."

"I did not think so at first." Charles paused, a hand on her shoulder. "But now I am doubting my judgment on the whole matter and suspecting everyone. Perhaps it is well that we have Maidstone. He should have no preconceived notions about us. In any case, we will make another attempt to locate Harry." He leaned down to kiss her cheek. "In the meantime, keep yourself and our child safe at home."

Chapter Fifteen

Delivery of a large parcel from a carrier later that morning provided distraction for Catherine. She had ordered several bolts of fabric and a large pattern book from her London dressmaker. Now it seemed that the materials would be used for maternity clothes.

She and Sally were happily spreading the goods around the sitting room in the master suite when Charles walked in, blowing on his hands to warm them. Sally quickly disappeared into Catherine's bedchamber.

"Hmm. What is all this?" Charles backed up to the fire, indicating with the toe of his boot a bolt lying near his feet. He leaned over and rubbed the emerald-green velvet between his fingers. "I like this one."

"Oh, I do, too." Catherine came and sat on the floor near him, pulling a length of the fabric across her. "It is one of my favorite colors. How does it look?" She held it up to her face.

Charles contemplated the effect seriously. "Very attractive. It sets your hair off nicely."

"What should I have made of it, do you think? A carriage dress or—"

"No, a ball gown, or an evening gown, perhaps."

"Do you think so?" Catherine tilted her head in thought.

"I definitely think so." Charles reached down to lift Catherine to her feet, pulling her toward him.

She came willingly, smiling up into his face, relishing the expression she saw there. True, it was no more than an increased intensity in his eyes, but she now knew it for the hunger it was. She opened her lips to him, rocking her hips against him as his hands cupped her bottom, moving her against his rapidly responding body.

Sally opened the door though which she had disappeared, started to step through and then hastily shut it again, retreating into the bedchamber with a giggle. Catherine jumped guiltily and would have pulled away, but his lordship prevented her, staring imperturbably into her face as his hands did provocative things to her derriere.

"Charles!" She tried unsuccessfully to step back. "Sally is bound to come back."

Her husband made no response other than to slide his hands farther down, wrapping them to the insides of her thighs so that his fingers stroked her through the fabric of her gown. Catherine gasped and collapsed against him, suddenly weak with desire. She managed barely a whisper. "Charles."

"Yes, Lady Caldbeck?" His breath caressed her ear, followed by his tongue.

"We—we really…shouldn't…."

"Should not what, my lady?"

Suddenly she realized that his hands had gradually stilled and that he was looking down at her with an unmistakable expression that could only be called self-satisfied.

"My lord, you look very pleased with yourself." Catherine attempted a stern look.

The corners of Charles's mouth lifted a bit more. "Yes. I am." He gave her a pat on the bottom and released her. "And with you, my lady."

"Oh, Charles. What am I to do with you?"

"If I might make a suggestion…"

"Charles! Not now."

"No," he agreed. "Not now."

After dinner that evening, as Sally brushed Catherine's hair for bed, Charles strolled through the connecting door wearing only a dressing jacket over his britches. He paused and leaned against the wall, enjoying a proprietary moment of watching the way his wife's glowing hair lay against her milky shoulders. The springy curls bounced with each stroke of the brush, bringing the deep shadows to life.

At last the maid pulled the shining mass to the top of her head with the ribbon his wife used for bedtime, and took her leave. Before Catherine could rise from the dressing stool, Charles stepped behind her and bent to kiss the little curls gathering at the nape of her neck. She ducked her head and giggled. He slipped a hand over her shoulder and cupped her breast. With a sigh she leaned back against him.

Watching her in the mirror, he took the second breast in his other hand, sliding his fingers over the satin-covered flesh until the nipples stood out clearly through the silk. Catherine closed her eyes and sat very still. Charles felt himself hardening. He enjoyed the arousal for a few more seconds, and then backed away. He had another purpose in mind for this evening. Catherine's eyes opened and regarded him with a question.

He lifted her to her feet and guided her toward the fire.

"Not yet. Not for a while. Where is the green velvet we were looking at this morning?"

Catherine frowned in puzzlement. "It is in my dressing room. Why?"

Making no further explanation, Charles strode to the door of the smaller room. He had no trouble locating the bolt, stacked in a corner with the others. He brought it out and laid it by the fire. Turning to where Catherine stood, hands on hips, watching this procedure, he set about pushing her wrapper and gown off her shoulders to the floor.

"Charles, what are you doing?" A little laugh spoiled the severe look she was trying to maintain.

He did not answer, but lifted the bolt of cloth and unwound several yards. When he judged that he had enough, he began to wrap her in the shining emerald stuff with one hand, while turning her with the other. He started at her feet and finished by draping the fabric around her breasts and tucking in the end of the cloth. Long before this process was finished, Catherine was laughing aloud, stumbling a little to keep her balance in the constricting folds. When she at last resembled a verdant mummy, he stepped back to admire his handiwork, nodding in satisfaction.

Catherine threw out an arm for balance, grasping his sleeve. "Charles Randolph, will you please tell me what you are about?"

Rather than speaking, for answer he reached into the pocket of his dressing jacket and pulled out a carved wooden box. Standing behind her, he removed what it contained and placed it around her neck.

"What is that?" She tried to see over her shoulder at him.

"Go look in the mirror."

"Don't be silly. I can't take a step."

"Very well." Charles walked to the dressing table and returned with the hand mirror. Holding it up for her, he watched the surprise bloom on her exquisite face, and was rewarded with a gasp of delight as she spied the magnificent emerald necklace she wore.

"Oh, Charles! It's beautiful. But where…?" She worked her other hand free and took the mirror. "It looks very old. Is it?" Her velvet cocoon began to slip. Charles tugged it back into place.

"Yes. It is a Randolph heirloom. I have been waiting for an occasion to give it to you." He poured two glasses of wine and handed her one.

"Charles! I can't drink like this." Catherine giggled and held the glass out for him to take.

"Very well, then, if you insist." Enjoying his own playfulness, Charles set both glasses on the table and began to unwind his wife. Having liberated her, he gathered the velvet into an awkward bundle and dumped it on the couch. When she reached for her nightwear, he stopped her and tossed it after the fabric. Then he shrugged out of his dressing jacket and added it to the pile.

Sitting in the big chair near the fire, he pulled Catherine into his lap, her feet dangling over one arm of the chair. The firelight glowed on her skin and set the gold and gems to blazing.

Picking up the mirror, which Charles had laid aside, she fingered the necklace as she studied it. "These stones are just wonderful! That's why you said the green velvet should be an evening gown. But, Charles—" she set the mirror down and looked into his face, smiling gently "—you can't keep giving me extravagant jewelry— pearls, sapphires and now emeralds. It is too much!"

Charles adjusted her position so that her soft breast

brushed against his hard, bare chest. After a moment of appreciating that sensation he gave thought to her statement, answering seriously, "I like giving you jewels. You are uniquely suited to wear them."

"Do you think so? Why do you say that?" Catherine turned toward him even more.

Her nipple pressed into his flesh. For several heartbeats the sweet pressure drove away all thought, but by using the greatest discipline he brought his mind back to what he wanted to say to her—the purpose of all the nonsense with the fabric and the gift of the emeralds. It was important, and he did not want to be sidetracked into passion.

"Yes, I think so. Your coloring enhances them to perfection. But that is not the only reason I give them to you."

"Oh?"

"The real reason lies in the fact that, as you know, it is very hard for me to adequately express my emotions." He searched her face, willing her to understand.

Catherine regarded him attentively for a few seconds before she answered. "I see. You told me before that you express yourself in action. What do you express through these gifts of jewelry?"

Charles spoke very cautiously, striving for just the right words. "How much I value you. What you mean to me. How you delight me."

"I delight you?" She looked pleased at the thought.

"Yes. Yes, you do. You are my dear delight, the mother of my child, and..." he paused and drew a deep breath "...my love." The words were almost a whisper. Charles closed his eyes and held his breath—waiting, fearing, wanting.

"Oh, Charles!" Catherine dropped the mirror and

flung her free arm around his neck. "I love you. I do!"
Tears coursed down her cheeks.

Charles clasped her to him as though he would never
loose his hold. She clung to him, hiccuping little sobs
between her words. "I have wanted so much for you to
love me. I want us to be...to be a real family.... I was
afraid you didn't."

"I know. But I do." The words made little sense, but
he didn't care. "I have wanted you since the first time I
touched you. Dancing. In a room full of people. I was
afraid to tell you, afraid you would not..."

He gave up on the words and claimed her lips, kissing
her with feeling from the bottom of his soul.

Their mutual declaration of love opened up a whole
new world. Despite the recent tragedies, Catherine had
never felt so happy. The feelings flowed between them
deeper and sweeter than ever before. Catherine found
that, her heart overflowing, she could just sit and look at
Charles for hours, loving the shape of his shoulders, his
serious face.

She wanted always to be touching him, and feared that
perhaps she was clinging too much. But Charles didn't
seem to mind. He never came into the room without em-
bracing her, no matter who else was present, and she
often looked up to find his intense gaze on her. Catherine
had never dared to wish for so much.

Two days after that momentous evening, they were
enjoying a quiet repast together in their private sitting
room. Charles broke off a comment as Hawes came into
the room with a tray of fresh bread rolls and a small
parcel under his arm.

He set the package on an end table and offered the
rolls to Catherine. "A curious thing, my lady. One of the

kitchen maids found this bundle outside the kitchen door a short time ago. It is addressed to you.''

"Really? How strange. Who left it there?"

"I have no idea, my lady. I sent John David out to look around, but he found no one." The butler sniffed disapprovingly. "I fear he did not go very far in the dark."

"And as cold as it is, who could blame him?" Catherine smiled. She recognized that John David was perhaps not the bravest member of their staff, but she was too happy to be critical. "But what can it be? Has someone sent me a gift? Please bring it to me, Hawes. I'll open it at once."

Hawes obediently fetched the parcel and gave it to her. She turned away from the table to rest it on her lap, eagerly tilting it this way and that, searching for clues to its source. It was wrapped in plain paper and tied with coarse string, her name lettered awkwardly. She slid the string over the ends of the package and began to unfold the paper.

As it opened, her brow wrinkled in puzzlement. "Oh. This looks like my purple scarf. I must have lost it, and someone…" Catherine lifted a fold of the silk and froze. She swayed, her face prickling as the blood drained from it. Charles jumped to his feet, knocking his chair over backward.

"What is it, Kate?"

Without answering, she dashed the parcel from her lap and covered her mouth with both hands. The room slanted crazily, and she leaned her elbows on the table for support. Charles's strong hands closed around her shoulders, steadying her. She could only point wordlessly at the object on the floor.

"My God!" Hawes backed away, his eyes wide.

Settling her against the back of her chair, Charles followed her pointing finger with his gaze. "Damnation!"

In a pile of ashes wrapped in the scarf lay a butcher knife, filed to a vicious point. A faint stench rose from it. Cinders adhered to the sticky blood that darkened the blade and handle.

The three of them stared at it as though a viper had invaded the luxurious room.

"Who…who?" Catherine swallowed and forced the words past the constriction in her throat. "Why?"

"To frighten you, obviously." Charles knelt and swept the knife and scarf up in the discarded paper. He handed it to Hawes. "Put this in my study, and send someone up here to remove our food and clean up this mess. Bring the mulled wine to Lady Caldbeck's chamber immediately." He lifted Catherine to her feet and placed a firm arm around her waist. "Come. We will finish our meal later."

Catherine allowed herself to be led into the next room, her thoughts spinning. Who would want to frighten her so? How had she made so awful an enemy? She was trembling all over as Charles pulled a chair nearer the fire and pressed her into it, his own hands not completely steady.

Catherine looked up into his solemn face. "Who hates me that much?"

He knelt beside her and took her hands in his. "I don't know, Kate. It makes no sense, unless…"

The sentence trailed away, and Catherine looked deeply into her husband's face. "Unless what?"

Charles shook his head, not replying.

Catherine sat up straighter and looked him in the eye, a terrible conviction growing in her. "The murderer sent it, didn't he?"

Charles drew a long breath. "I believe we must assume so."

"But why me?"

His grip tightened on her hands. "I am not sure, but we must treat it as a threat, Kate."

"A threat?"

"He is warning you—threatening you. And trying to terrify you."

"He is certainly succeeding in that!" A modicum of anger began to replace her shock. "The wretch!"

Charles's eyes warmed a tiny bit. "I believe he will find his work cut out for him when he attempts to terrify *you*. The Countess of Caldbeck is made of sterner stuff."

Catherine smiled, but shook her head. "I assure you I am quite petrified with fear. But I am angry, too."

"As am I." Charles rose and lifted her to her feet. He guided her to the sofa and sat down with her, an arm wrapped protectively around her shoulders. "It is bad enough that he has attacked my people, but to menace my own wife is too much by half. I will see him at the end of a rope if I must move heaven and earth to find him! I will see him in hell!"

Catherine was so startled at this unaccustomed vehemence from the staid earl that she pulled back to look into his face. His jaw was set, and his mouth formed a grim line. His free hand, clenched into a fist, pounded softly, but steadily, against the arm of sofa, emphasizing each word. The ice in his eyes glittered in the firelight. For a moment Catherine again felt the fear she had known when she first met him. She was looking at a very dangerous man. Then, even as she watched, he drew a calming breath and pulled her close to him. "I will not let him hurt you, Kate."

Just as he bent his head to kiss her forehead, a dreadful, but now familiar, howl split the air. Catherine screamed, and Charles jumped to his feet.

"Damn!" And then quite calmly he stated, "I am going to find that animal and break its neck. I have had enough of its infernal racket." Charles strode in the direction of his dressing room.

Suddenly a horrible dismay filled Catherine. "No! No, Charles! Don't!" She sprang from the sofa and made a grab for his arm. "Please. Don't go out there." He turned back to her as the baying sounded again. She pressed her hands over her ears, repeating, "*Please,* don't go."

"Why not? Surely you are as weary of it as I am?"

When Catherine did not hear the cry repeated, she cautiously lifted a hand from her ear and clutched Charles's shirt. She knew she sounded foolish, but she was trembling with dread. "If you go out there, you might see it, and then…" She could not go on. She gazed imploringly at him. "I know how stupid it sounds, but…"

Charles looked at her for a long moment. "Very well. If you are frightened, I won't go. You are distressed enough already. But surely, Kate, you do not believe that Padfoot story? You certainly are not stupid, so why are you so afraid of a howling dog?"

"I don't know." Seeing her husband temporarily safe from arcane powers, Catherine breathed a sigh of relief. "It is just that when we heard it twice before, a woman died each time. Who is to say that they did not see…?" She shook herself to throw off the eerie feeling. "Oh, I know they could not! What is the matter with me?"

Charles sat back down and pulled her down beside him. He touched her cheek gently with one finger. "You are understandably overset. Who would not be when confronted with so grisly a trophy?"

"A trophy?" Catherine wrinkled her brow. "I had not thought... Is that what that knife is?"

Charles nodded. "I would think so."

"What a warped mind!" Catherine shivered, wrapping her arms around herself, chilled at the thought of such malevolence directed at her. "What have I done to make him hate me so much? I do not believe I have injured anyone here."

Charles pulled her closer. "It is nothing you have done, Kate. The man is mad. Who knows what his thinking may be. By threatening you, he also challenges me, so perhaps it is someone with a grudge against me. I don't know who that would be, but both Mrs. Ribble and Mrs. Askrigg were my tenants. I am—was—responsible for their welfare. I am fighting a sensation of guilt because I did not somehow prevent their deaths."

"But that doesn't make sense!" Catherine turned quickly to face him.

"Yes, in truth, I think it senseless, also. No one could anticipate such insanity. But I am now warned." He lifted Catherine across his lap and drew her tightly against him, his muscular arms shielding her. "He will have to come through me to touch you."

Chapter Sixteen

Even in Charles's arms Catherine slept fitfully, half wakened by nightmares. Dim and elusive images of knives, wicked and glittering; of smoke, and ashes stained with blood. Several times she bolted upright in the bed, the echo of the horrible howling resounding in her ears. Each time, Charles reached for her, solid and comforting, but neither of them fell asleep again for a long, tense while.

Morning dawned bleak and cold. Catherine arose into the cloudy dawn shortly after Charles went to his own room to dress, the terror of the night yet clinging to her. There was no use in trying to go back to sleep, even though her eyes burned and her nausea had returned. She did not want to be alone—alone in the high-ceilinged room, in the dim, curtained bed. Alone with the growing foreboding. She dressed and made her subdued way to the breakfast parlor.

Charles rose to greet her, taking her in his arms for a minute before pulling out her chair. "How do you feel, Kate?"

She shrugged. "Not well. I'm tired and my stomach

is upset again.'' She took a tiny sip of tea and nibbled at a scone. ''Eating a little seems to help, though.''

Charles eyed her shrewdly. ''I was not thinking of your stomach. Are you anxious?''

''Oh. Well…yes, a little.'' She grimaced at her own dissembling and tried for a bit more candor. ''More than a little, actually. The light of day seems to be helping that, but I do wish the sun would come out. The sky is so somber.''

''It is harder to be afraid in the sunshine,'' Charles agreed. ''Perhaps we can spend this gloomy day together here in the house, safe and warm. Would that make you feel better?''

Catherine smiled wanly. ''Probably.'' She crumbled a piece of the scone into her plate. ''I feel sure that I'm being foolish past permission. No one can reach me inside Wulfdale. I know that. It—it's just that…''

''It is just that a veritable monster has threatened you. You would be more foolish not to be frightened. I assure you, I intend to take that warning very seriously.'' At that moment Hawes came into the room. Charles turned to him. ''Yes, Hawes?''

The butler bowed apologetically. ''I'm sorry to interrupt your breakfast, my lord. It seems that we have another crisis.''

''Oh, no!'' Catherine wailed. ''What now?''

''Oh, nothing as serious as the last one, my lady,'' Hawes hastened to assure her. He returned his attention to Charles. ''It is the Mukers' daughter. She has wandered away again, and they are concerned. They are not sure when she left the house, and it was very cold last night. They are asking for some men to help them search.''

''The Mukers?'' Catherine looked in question at Charles.

"Tenants," he replied. "They have a daughter who is simple. She is perhaps sixteen now—very pretty except for a rather vacant look in her face—but her mind is that of a very small child. She is prone to straying away from their home, sometimes at night when they are not watching her." He turned back to the butler. "Of course. Send several of the grooms on horseback. They will be more effective that way, and we are not planning to need them today."

Hawes bowed. "Very good, my lord." He turned away, but found his path blocked at the doorway.

Richard Middleton stood there, or rather leaned there, his shoulder against the door, and his face the color of cold tallow. Charles got to his feet and took a step toward his secretary.

"Richard? What...?"

The young man drew in a shaky breath and blurted, "There—there's another one, my lord."

"Another what, Richard?"

Catherine felt the floor falling away under her feet. She did not need to hear the answer to Charles's question. She struggled to rise, clutching desperately at the edge of the table, willing her knees to remain stiff.

"D-d-dead, my lord." Richard wiped his perspiring forehead and moved a few inches into the room. "All cut and burned and...oh, God!" He choked to a stop.

Wind roared in Catherine's ears, and darkness whirled around her. Her gorge rose in her throat. Very faintly, as if from far away, she heard Hawes exclaim, "My lady!" as she followed the floor down, down, down into oblivion.

Charles had never seen so grim a sight, not even the body of Dorrie Ribble. Still bound and gagged, tied hand

and foot to the trees that capped the hilltop, this corpse lay naked and exposed to the freezing wind that wept and sighed in the branches. Sharp stones bit savagely into the soft flesh, and a pile of charred branches and clothing covered the bleeding torso.

The fire had not lasted long, by no means long enough to hide the hideous deed, but long enough to fill the air with the unmistakable stench of burned flesh. The jeering crows that had rested in the branches as he rode up had flown, but still circled in the sky. Charles stood rigid, jaw clenched, knuckles white where he gripped his riding crop, his feelings frozen as he grappled with the enormity of the act. Who could possibly commit such an outrage?

Several men stood by silently, while from farther down the hillside the girl's mother could be heard sobbing, as some of the village women tried to comfort her and prevent her from climbing the slope to see her daughter. Muker, his face pale, watched stoically as Maidstone poked at the burned wood with the toe of his boot. Charles wanted to console the man, but felt stymied by his stolid endurance. Comfort might destroy the grieving father's tenuous control.

Besides, there was nothing to be said.

Suddenly Maidstone turned away from the body and kicked viciously at a stone. The rock flew into the trees with a hollow clatter. ''Damn the bloody bastard! Damn his eyes!'' Another rock sailed away from the runner's foot. ''This poor innocent! What harm has she ever done to nobody?'' He drew a steadying breath, laying a hand on Muker's shoulder. ''I'm sorry, me friend, very. I'd hopes of nabbing him ere he struck again.''

Muker nodded dully. ''Aye. Ain't no more you could do.''

"You know anyone who wishes you ill? Anyone she might have followed off?"

Muker shook his head. "She'd have gone with anyone, anyone at all." He sighed and wiped a tear from the corner of his eye with one finger. "Maybe it's better thus. She ain't never had no chance at a normal life, any road." He shuddered slightly. "But she had a nature sweet as one of God's angels. She did that."

He turned away, and one of the tenants standing by took his arm and led him down the hill toward his wife. Charles approached the fuming Maidstone, feeling the resonance of the runner's anger growing in himself. "Does this bring us any closer to finding this beast?"

"Nay, me lord, I doubt it." Maidstone continued kicking at the pebbles, his jaw tight. "Not unless someone saw the bounder. We can but try the dogs." He shook his head in frustration. "But with this crowd standing around, they ain't going to know which scent to follow." He paused speculatively. "It's worth a try, but it's a slim chance. Who was it found her?"

"My secretary."

"He here?"

Charles shook his head. "He was shaken to the soles of his boots. He told me where to look, and I left him at my home."

"Hmm." Maidstone rubbed his chin thoughtfully. "What was he doing up here so early on a cold morning? It's fair fit to freeze a man's— Well, it's devilish cold up here. What would have brought him up here, any case?"

Charles compressed his lips. "I don't know. But we shall ask him."

Having shown Maidstone into the library and provided him with a glass of brandy to combat the cold, Charles hurried upstairs to look in on Catherine. After reviving her from her faint with a dose of hartshorn, they had bundled her into bed, Sally sitting close beside her. Then, warning her sternly to set foot to floor for no reason whatsoever until he returned, Charles had sent riders to inform the necessary officials, and had ridden to the hill behind the village where Richard had told him the unfortunate young woman rested.

Charles was worried. His only experience with breeding women lay in watching his sister lose child after child to miscarriage. Not a comforting thought. He had left word for Dr. Dalton to visit Catherine the moment he finished with the Muker girl, but the doctor had not yet arrived. Charles tapped lightly on Catherine's door, then opened it a crack and peered in.

"Charles, is that you?"

He sighed with relief to hear her voice sounding strong and impatient. "It is I." Charles stepped through the door and crossed to the bed. Sally vacated her chair, and he sat in it, reaching for Catherine's hand. "Are you feeling more the thing?"

"Much better." Catherine leaned forward restlessly. "And I am quite tired of this bed. I see no reason I should not get up, but Sally kept insisting that you would be angry at her if I did."

"Sally was entirely correct. Had I returned to find you up and about, it would have gone hard for both of you." Charles let the chill in his voice express his seriousness. "I told you I would take the most meticulous care of you, and I am not going to risk your miscarrying because of this fiend." He expected a rebellious retort from his wife, but it was not forthcoming.

She leaned back against the pillows, looking at him sadly. "Tell me what you found."

Charles shook his head, his lips tight. "I will not describe what I found. Suffice it to say that the Mukers's daughter is dead."

"Oh, dear. Was it as before?"

"Worse."

The monosyllable hung in the air between them. Then Catherine closed her eyes and let her head fall back. "How could it possibly be worse?"

Charles got to his feet. The anger he had felt over the previous two killings was nothing to what he felt growing over this one. It welled up in him like bile, threatening to spill out in every direction. He could not trust himself to continue the conversation with a wife whose condition might be fragile. He could not bear for a lack of control on his part to be the cause of her losing the child.

He started for the door, his voice curt. "Dr. Dalton will be here shortly. If he says you may get up, then of course, you may. I must meet with the runner and Arncliff. Maidstone wants to question Richard."

Catherine's eyes flew open. "Richard? He can't believe that Richard had anything to do with it?"

"I don't know." Another wave of anguish rose in Charles's chest. "Why was he up on that hill this morning, Kate? Why?"

"Now, young 'un, all I need from you is a simple answer." The runner paced the floor in front of the fireplace in Charles's library. "What business had you out there so early?"

Richard sat in a chair before him, forearms on knees, his head hanging, his gaze on the floor. "I told you. I...I couldn't sleep. I went out for a ride, and saw smoke up on the hill…and heard the crows. I rode up to see what was afire, and I found—I found…'' He shivered as if cold. ''You know.''

''And that's all you can tell us, Richard?'' Lord Arncliff's voice was gentle, but doubtful. ''You just went out for a ride? In this weather?''

Richard gave the magistrate a quick glance. ''Yes, my lord. That's all.''

Maidstone cast a questioning look at Charles, who sat behind the barrier of his desk, leaning back in his chair with fingertips propped together before his face. Charles's mind refused to clear itself and provide his usual logical thinking. He hated not being able to trust his own judgment.

Could this quiet, studious young man—a youth he had known from childhood, to whom he had opened his home, his confidence—could he, by any stretch of the imagination, be capable of such barbarity, such ferocity? A sharp pang pierced Charles's chest at the thought. He did not want to believe it, and not wanting to… He shrugged.

Maidstone, receiving that ambiguous answer, turned back toward Richard, speaking sternly. ''All right, young 'un. You can go…for now. But don't go far. I'm gonna want you again.''

Richard nodded. ''Yes, sir. I understand.''

The runner jerked his head toward the door. Richard got hastily to his feet, bowed to his employer and the magistrate and quickly took his leave.

Maidstone sighed in exasperation, shaking his head. ''Fool young 'uns.'' Charles reached for the brandy decanter and offered another glass all around. The three of them sat and sipped in thoughtful silence for several minutes. Finally Maidstone turned to Charles. "You know him best, me lord. What do you think?"

Charles rolled the brandy on his tongue, welcoming the sharp bite, wishing it would clear his senses. Finally he forced himself to speak. "I don't know," he admitted. "Because I know him so well, I fear my judgment may be clouded. What is your opinion?"

The runner swallowed a mouthful of brandy, his eyes narrowed in thought. "I think he ain't the one. He didn't come in with no blood on him, did he?"

Charles shook his head. "Not even muddy boots."

"That's what I thought. No, he ain't the one, but he ain't telling everything, neither."

"That's my impression." Arncliff spoke from the depths of the armchair he occupied. "Damn, but this is a bad business! What in the world could he possibly have to hide?"

"Maybe nothing. Folk keep secrets for all sorts of reasons, most of them bad. He's that scared, though, that he'll spill it soon." The runner tossed his brandy back and wiped his mouth on his sleeve. "Guess I better go ask about. Maybe somebody seen something. I can only hope. Me lords." He bowed to the two gentlemen and made for the door.

Arncliff got to his feet. "Well, I have work to do myself. There'll be another inquest—for whatever good it will do us."

Charles rose and extended a hand. "Thank you for coming."

Arncliff shook his hand, but grimaced. "I'd like to say it's been my pleasure, but that doesn't seem to be quite the word for it. Well, good day to you."

After walking the magistrate to the door, Charles returned to his study and poured himself another brandy.

Which was very likely a mistake. Spirits were not known to improve the process of clear thinking. Nevertheless, he sat again at his desk, taking a modicum of comfort from the fiery liquid. Perhaps it would damp the rage coursing through him.

Women. Always women. Good women! Gentle, helpless against the strength of a man. Vulnerable, meant to be cared for and cherished. What cowardly brute was doing this to Charles's people, violating the women his position obligated him to protect? What abomination dared to so desecrate the vessels to which God had entrusted the nourishing of new life? Charles leaned back in his chair and closed his eyes.

And who…who on God's earth would commit an act so bestial against an unfortunate innocent like the Muker girl? She had gone her own way—simple-minded, childlike, guileless—living in her own world, hurting no one. A nature as sweet as an angel, her father had said, a perpetual infant, a source of pleasure to her parents which outweighed the burden she created. And then…then… some *animal* had ripped apart that world! Ripped apart her world and her body, defiling her, stealing both her innocence and her life.

And that same animal dared threaten Catherine, his wife, the love of his life, and their unborn child. The child he had promised to protect.

Charles's hand tightened around the glass, threatening to break the delicate crystal. If he could but close his hand around the throat of the one who—

He shuddered and carefully set the glass on the table. He must have a care or he would become just such a beast himself. He wiped a hand across his brow, startled to find himself sweating. Damnation! He jumped to his feet, kicking over his chair, his brain threatening to explode. He could not contain himself any longer. He must act. Act or go mad!

At that moment Catherine opened the door and came into the room. He glared at her, unable to keep the anger from his face. She gazed at him with her clear sapphire eyes, and he knew she saw into his soul. She mustn't...mustn't see... He grated out a dismissal. "Go, Kate. I am not myself. Go before I do something..." He did not know the words for it. "Just go."

She watched him steadily, not moving, taking in his trembling body, the fists clenched at his sides. "Before you do what? Show your anger?"

Charles could not trust himself to speak. Catherine glanced around the orderly room, her eyes stopping on the riding crop leaning against his desk. Returning her gaze to his, she picked it up and handed it to him, stepped back and turned the key in the door.

Charles stood for the space of ten heartbeats, breathing heavily, opening and closing his hands around the whip, struggling for control as a red haze spread across his vision. Then, with a strangled exclamation, he whirled and slashed the crop into a small candle stand sitting by the fireplace.

The stand toppled noisily to the hearth, the candles rolling in all directions. Seeing his target out of reach of his weapon, Charles brought his boot down on the fragile wood. He stamped again, and then again, splintering and pounding the shards into the floor. Past thought, he gave up all attempt at restraint, letting his muscles express freely the fury in his heart.

When the candle stand had been reduced to tinder, he swung around, seeking. His gaze fell on the desk, and he brought the whip down on it, blow after blow crashing against the polished surface. The pent-up anger of his whole life flowed into his arm. He threw all his strength into striking, punctuating each impact with a muffled curse, each utterance more vile than the one before. Suddenly, with a loud crack, the crop snapped and broke. Charles stared at it for a second, then, with one last oath, flung it across the room.

As he stood spent and panting, Catherine approached him, stopping only inches away, and looked soberly into his face.

"Well done, Charles."

Charles stood grasping for breath for the moment it took for her words to penetrate the fading haze. Then he wrapped his arms around her and crushed her to his chest.

Later, at bedtime, Charles tried to apologize to Catherine, terrified that he might have frightened her with his violence or disgusted her with his foul language. In truth, he had frightened himself. He had not known how dangerous he had become. Somewhere in the unexamined recesses of his mind, he had believed that, if he ever relinquished his iron self-command for even a moment, his fund of accumulated anger would impel him to kill someone. What a relief to discover that it had not. What a relief to suspend the burden of constant discipline.

But that Catherine had seen him so out of control! Would she continue to trust him? Could she continue to love him?

Catherine would have none of it. She was quite firm. "You have a right to be angry about these horrible atrocities, and you have as much right as I do to express it. You are not disgusted with me when I lose my temper, and ordinarily I have far less cause." And then, very gently, her soft fingertip against his lips, she added, "You cannot keep it all inside forever, Charles. You are only human. Very beautifully, very wonderfully human.''

He made love to her then, desperate to feel her accepting warmth, to feel the sincerity of her words in every touch, every sigh, to feel the shelter of her body. She came to him as she always did, joyfully and wholeheartedly, leaving him weak with gratitude. Without her encouragement, he could not imagine what he might have done. Without her love, he might never have had the courage to rid himself of the cancer that threatened to overwhelm him. He fell asleep giving thanks for his wife's courageous, generous spirit.

He closed his eyes and searched for the glory, the power, the righteous release. As always, they were fading. Fading too soon. Too soon. He groped for them, wrestling them from the darkness. It had been an exultant purging, a superb fear. The vessel's empty head had been filled with it.

Over too soon. When Her time came, it must not be over so soon. Slowly, slowly. Ah! The beauty of it! He shuddered as the heat spread through him. Yes. Soon!

Chapter Seventeen

In the morning Charles discovered that he could again think clearly. What a relief! Now that he was no longer fighting the fury, he once more had confidence in his vision of himself and his fellow man. He would almost enjoy accompanying Maidstone on a fact-finding mission, acting as guide around the dale for the runner.

But first he must see to Catherine's safety. He almost feared to leave her alone for a single second. He told himself that it was so unlikely as to be almost impossible for anyone to reach her inside Wulfdale. Even so, Charles set James Benjamin to follow Catherine, even in the house, and threatened her with a sound trimming if she tried to avoid his surveillance or so much as set foot outside the door.

She smiled, unperturbed. "Indeed, my lord, I am trembling in my slippers at the prospect. However, this is one time you need have no fear of rebellion. I am not going anywhere alone, I assure you." She rose on tiptoe to kiss him. "Now, do not keep Mr. Maidstone waiting."

The runner sighed as he climbed cautiously into his saddle. "It's back to askin' questions, me lord. At least it ain't so bloody cold."

"Why do you wish to speak with Lord Litton?" A niggling sense of unease had pestered Charles since the runner had asked earlier that morning to be guided to Adam's home. "We did not even see him yesterday."

"That's why. I got too many possibles. Got to clear out somebody. I'm starting with the lot as was nearby Ribble's cottage that morning. He was one of them."

"But Adam arrived at our picnic in company with Stalling."

Maidstone, who was lagging behind, nudged his horse into a bumpy trot to catch up. "I'm gonna talk to him, too. They was chance-met on the road—don't mean anything. Had plenty of time." Charles acknowledged that, and the runner went on. "You and Litton friends, eh?"

"Yes." Charles nodded. "The best."

"So what do you think?" Maidstone waited for a reply, eyes narrowed shrewdly.

Charles pondered his answer for a few hoofbeats. What might it be wise to say? Should he hold anything back? He decided on candor. "Not possible, Maidstone. I had a brief period when I was so confused by my feelings that I was ready to believe it of anyone, but my judgment has returned. I have known Adam Barbon since boyhood. He simply does not harbor that sort of anger."

Maidstone nodded but did not respond. They trotted along, each occupied with his own thoughts, enjoying the warming sun on their faces.

When they finally reached Adam's drive, Charles gave his attention to directing Maidstone to the old mansion, fine and well-kept, though considerably smaller than Wulfdale. Charles lifted the knocker and gave the door a peremptory thump. A minute later Adam's tall, white-haired butler appeared, smiling benignly when he saw Charles.

"Good day, Lord Caldbeck. It is always a pleasure to see you. Do come in." The butler stepped back, bowing. "How may I serve you today?"

Charles and Maidstone followed him into a large, but dimly lit hall.

"Good morning, Feetham. Is Lord Litton in?"

Feetham shook his head regretfully. "No, my lord. I am sorry to say that he is not. And I—I cannot say when he is expected."

Maidstone stepped nearer. "How about yesterday? His lordship home all day?"

The butler raised one eyebrow and favored the runner with a haughty silence. He then looked questioningly at Charles.

Charles cleared his throat. "Feetham, this is Mr. Maidstone of Bow Street."

Feetham looked startled. "Ah! Bow Street?"

Charles inclined his head.

"How do you do. Now how about it, guv'nor? His lordship here yesterday?"

The butler looked at Charles for further guidance, loyalty and necessity warring across his face. Charles nodded.

After a brief struggle with his conscience, Feetham uttered a grudging syllable. "No."

"Know where he was?"

The butler looked over Maidstone's shoulder at some point far behind him. "I'm sure I couldn't say, sir."

Charles touched the runner's sleeve. "I believe you would be better advised to put your questions to Lord Litton himself."

"Happy to—if I can find him." Maidstone narrowed his eyes at Feetham, who refused to look at him.

Charles could see that he would have to take a hand

in matters to achieve any progress at all. "Feetham, have you any idea where I might find his lordship?"

"No, my lord." Obviously Charles had fallen from grace along with the inquisitive runner.

"Very well. Perhaps Lady Lonsdale may have some idea." Charles watched closely as a flash of something flitted over Feetham's face. *Ah.* "Come, Maidstone. I believe we should call on my sister." He bid the indignant butler farewell and accompanied the runner down the stairs.

Maidstone groaned as he regained his saddle. "This Lady Lonsdale's yer sister?"

"She is the Dowager Countess of Lonsdale, and yes, she is my sister."

"She gonna know where to find Litton?"

"I think it likely."

The runner looked at him closely. "Any chance she'll know where he was yesterday—or the night before?"

Charles sighed. "I imagine so."

The clouds moved in, and as the sun diminished, the air grew much colder. Another uncomfortable hour brought them to the dower house at Lonsdale. Not far inside the walls of the estate, the small, but attractive home nestled in a well-kept garden. Both Maidstone and Charles were happy to be shown into Helen's cozy drawing room and to back up to a cheerful fire for a moment.

As Charles was certain he would be, Adam was there, looking far more comfortable than a man who was simply visiting was likely to look. He passed the brandy around with all the confidence of a host, a fact lost upon neither Maidstone nor Charles. Charles accepted his glass without comment.

Maidstone got right to the point. "You heard there's been another killing?"

Adam nodded. "Yes. One of the footmen brought the tale in from the taproom. The butler passed it on to us this morning." He sipped his brandy and shook his head sadly. "A shame…a damn shame! Why hurt a poor, unfortunate child like that girl? The man is a monster."

"Aye, me lord, he's that, no doubt." The runner studied his glass as if considering his next question. "What I'm needing to know, me lord, is where everyone that was at the Ribbles the day of her death was night before last."

Adam smiled sardonically. "Meaning, did I have the opportunity to kill this one also?" He tossed back a swallow and looked levelly at Maidstone, his jaw set. "The answer is no, I didn't."

"With all due respect, Lord Litton, that don't quite answer me question."

Adam glared at him without answering. Maidstone's eyes narrowed.

"Oh, for heaven's sake, Adam!" Helen stepped into the breach. "Just tell him where you were."

Adam winked at her. "That would not be very gentlemanly of me, my dear."

Helen flushed, the deep red tinting her delicate skin to the roots of her dark hair, but stuck to her guns. "He was here, Mr. Maidstone, with me. He has been here since the three of you interviewed—if that is the word for it—my stepson."

"Let me get this straight." Maidstone looked around the group. "The young Lord Lonsdale would be your stepson?"

"That is correct." Helen shrugged ruefully. "And I, uh, inherited him when his father died."

"Now *that* was a real joy, I've no doubt." The runner grinned, then sobered guiltily. "Er, no offense, me lady."

Helen chuckled. "No offense, Mr. Maidstone. He can be quite…difficult, as you have seen."

Adam grinned. "Now you have landed me in the suds, my dear. After that confession, your severe elder brother will have no choice but to call me out to protect your honor." The grin broke into a laugh. "Eh, Charles?"

Charles sipped his liquor, his face solemn. "I am giving it serious consideration."

Alarm blossomed on the runner's face. "Now see here, me lords. I didn't mean to stir up no duel. You can't—"

"Ha!" Adam's bark of laughter echoed around the room. "Maybe his lordship will be appeased if I make an honest woman of her. How about it, Charles?"

"That would, of course, be up to Lady Lonsdale." Charles turned to his sister, his face serious.

"Me lords…?" Maidstone looked anxiously from one to the other.

"Stop it, you two!" A gurgle of laughter erupted from Helen. "Mr. Maidstone, do not let these two buffoons disturb you."

It was obvious from the look on the runner's face that he had never for a moment considered the Earl of Caldbeck a buffoon. He turned his gaze to Charles, who looked at his sister.

"Well, it is up to you, Helen. Should I put a bullet through him? Or would you rather accept him?"

"Humph." Lady Lonsdale looked severely at her brother. "Do not believe, either of you, that I will be manipulated into marriage by these antics! I will make my decision when I am good and ready."

"Damnation!" Adam hung his head and looked mournful. "I thought I had her this time."

Maidstone sighed with relief. "Well, I'm glad to have that settled. That's one less possibility to think about, and I'm glad it ain't you, me lord." He finished his brandy in a gulp. "Never really thought it. Had to ask. Now…" He looked around the room. "Am I gonna be lucky enough fer Lord Lonsdale to live hereabouts?"

"You are in luck, friend," Adam assured him, "Vincent's home is just up the drive."

"But before you go, you shall both join us for lunch," Helen said. "You need some hot soup and tea."

Warmed by the soup and tea, Charles and Maidstone set off up the drive in search of Vincent, accompanied by Adam, who said their mission might require a show of force. Happily for Maidstone, they had not far to go. They were admitted to the elegant dwelling, albeit unwillingly, by the Lonsdale butler. He proved to be even less cooperative than Adam's Feetham. Charles had just decided that they would, indeed, have to force themselves in when the man, apparently realizing that he was dealing with a law officer, reluctantly gave way.

The moment they were in the door, their noses informed them of the cause of the servant's hesitancy. The house reeked of spirits and other things that Charles rather not consider. As they followed the butler up the stairs, rustlings and groanings and the occasional snore could be heard emerging from the large room at the far end of the upper hall. The butler showed them to the door, announcing as he did so to no one in particular, "The Earl of Caldbeck."

The Earl of Caldbeck peered into the room and quickly withdrew. Maidstone and Adam followed suit. Then all three looked at one another, shaking their heads in amused disgust.

The Earl of Lonsdale was entertaining. Young bodies of both genders littered the chamber, sprawled hither and yon, many unconscious, a few beginning to rouse from their night's debauch. Those who managed to move at all did it very slowly and carefully, holding their heads at a rigid angle. Several hastened to the door with hands clasped over their stomachs or mouths. The investigative party prudently moved aside, giving them a wide berth.

The runner chuckled. "At least we got plenty of witnesses—if they were here night before last."

Charles regarded Maidstone with a sigh. "And if any of them were conscious. Do you see his lordship?"

The three of them ventured another glance inside. "Nay. Not I. Do you?"

Charles shook his head. "No, not unless…wait. Is that he behind the palm?" Charles set out across the room, stepping over prone forms and skirting anyone attempting to rise. Maidstone followed, Adam bringing up the rear. Reaching a couple lying half propped against a wall behind a potted plant, Charles bent down and grasped a shoulder. "Vincent. Vincent!"

He was rewarded with a snarl and an arm swung in his direction, but no other motion. Charles grasped the arm and jerked. His victim groaned and tugged back. "Go 'way!"

"Get up, Vincent. We need to talk to you." Charles pulled again, and this time the Earl of Lonsdale rose to a sitting position and scowled at his tormentor.

"Go to hell!" Vincent dropped his head into his hands. "Can't you see I have guests?"

"Ah. So that is what you call this?" Adam cast a disdainful glance around the room. "I thought I had stumbled into a brothel by mistake.'' Vincent glared at him, but did not respond.

''How long yer guests been here, me lord?''

''What business is it of yours?'' Vincent got to his feet, grimacing in pain.

''There's been another murder, Vincent.'' Charles nodded in the direction of the runner. ''Maidstone needs to know where you were the night before last.''

Vincent released a bark of laughter and immediately clutched at his head, groaning. He gestured at the slowly reviving company. ''He's beside the bridge if he is looking at me. I was here with my friends. I am having a house party, and I have twenty witnesses to prove it.''

''Maybe.'' Maidstone scratched his head, looking to Charles and Adam. ''You think we can get these culls sobered up?''

''I'll see to it.'' Adam went into the hall and shouted down the back stairs. In a moment two footmen appeared. ''Bring up some coffee,'' Adam instructed, ''and some porter wouldn't be amiss if you have some. I think we are going to need some hair o' the dog here.''

''Yes, my lord. Right away. His lordship always keeps porter on hand.''

''I should think so.'' Adam returned to the room muttering.

At this juncture the young woman sprawled at their feet made an attempt to rise. She got as far as her knees and grasped Vincent's coat to steady herself. He cursed and turned on her, knocking her hands away and shoving her back to the floor. ''Keep your filthy hands off me, whore!''

For Charles, that was the last straw. His nasty nephew had finally stepped over some indefinable line. He seized Vincent's arm and yanked him forward. ''That is enough,

Vincent. A great deal more than enough. You had no objections to her hands last night. Mr. Maidstone, if you will excuse us for a moment?''

''What…?'' Vincent stumbled along as Charles all but dragged him through the door and across the hall toward a small parlor. The young earl tried to free himself, twisting and cursing, but Charles was not having it. He pulled him into the parlor and slammed him into a chair. Vincent moaned and winced, shutting one eye. A somewhat startled Adam followed them, locking the door and leaning against it expectantly, arms folded across his chest.

''Now.'' Charles straightened his coat and spoke softly. ''I have had my fill of you, you insolent whelp.''

Vincent looked up in astonishment at the hitherto moderate relative looming over him. Then, collapsing against the back of the chair, he squinched his eyes shut and covered them with one hand. ''Really, Charles, old man, what is this to-do? I've got the very devil of a head. Can't this wait?''

''It has waited far too long already. I don't give a damn about your head. You are going to mend your ways, or I am going to make you wish you had.''

''Oh?'' Vincent roused himself and pushed to his feet, blowing his foul breath into Charles's face. ''And how are you going to do that, old man?''

''With pleasure.'' Charles grabbed a handful of Vincent's shirt and jerked him forward, slashing his riding crop across the seat of his nephew's britches. Vincent yelped and tried to spin away, but Charles would not let him. He landed two more blows on his target's backside before the young earl managed to free himself, staggering backward, his face purple with rage.

''You—you bloody…! I'll have satisfaction for this. By God, I will. Anytime…anyplace. Pistols…sabers…''

''No, you won't.'' Charles advanced on him again, his expression implacable. Vincent backed away. ''Meet you on a field of honor?'' Charles took another step. Vincent retreated farther. ''What do you know about honor? What honor is there in mistreating a harlot you brought into your home? Or a barmaid? Or bullying an innkeeper?''

Charles continued to close on his quarry. Vincent continued to withdraw. ''What honor is there in being rude to decent men and accosting decent women? What in harassing your stepmother? You think honor is a matter of avenging insults against yourself? It is not. It is a matter of having courtesy toward others, of treating inferiors kindly, of keeping your word, of paying your debts. Of treating women of all stations well.''

Vincent fetched up against the far wall, and Charles took hold of his shirt again, giving him a sharp shake.

''Ow! Ow, my head! Leave off, Charles.''

''*Uncle* Charles to you.'' Charles shook him again. ''You may as well begin a habit of courtesy with me.'' Vincent pushed at Charles's hands. His face began to pale.

Charles continued in a chilling voice. ''Your father should have done this long ago, but you no longer have him. All you have is an uncle-by-marriage. Me. And I intend to put a stop to your present behavior.'' Vincent opened his mouth, but apparently thought better of replying.

Charles leaned closer. ''You think I cannot? What strength do you build, drinking and whoring? Anytime you want to find out, we will try it. You and me, man to man, hand to hand. Do you comprehend? No pistols, no sabers—just one man against another.''

Charles paused for breath, but there was no response from Vincent, who looked at him with cautious eyes.

Charles took another breath and continued. "Now listen carefully, Vincent. You will begin by apologizing to the young woman you just struck. Then you will take the money that, by your pettiness, you have deprived that barmaid and give it to her family—no, double the amount—and you will apologize to them. If I learn that you have not done so, we will meet again—as we will if I ever hear of any such episode again. And you will apologize to my wife. And to your stepmother."

He paused briefly to give Vincent another shake. "And do not forget that I am friends with your trustees. Though I have never done so, I can control your purse strings. If I hear that you are not paying your debts, you will find yourself in the sponging house. And do not believe that I do not know what you do in London."

Charles sighed, his grip relaxing. "I know of no way in which I can prevent you from drinking yourself to death. Drunkards cannot be stopped. You will have to deal with that, or not, yourself. Do you understand me?" Vincent did not answer, and Charles shook him again.

"All right! All right. I understand you." Vincent glared sullenly as Charles slowly released his grasp.

"Very well. Let us return to the others."

Chapter Eighteen

"That is absolutely amazing! He did actually apologize to that girl?" Tonight Catherine poured brandy for Charles while he sprawled on the sofa, divested of coat, cravat and boots. She handed him his glass and settled back in the corner of the sofa where she could see him.

Charles swallowed a mouthful of the liquor. "Ah. That's welcome. It is getting colder again." He shifted to face Catherine, leaning back against his end of the seat, one leg drawn up. "Yes. I admit to a bit of surprise, myself. I wasn't sure what he would do when he was again amongst his cronies. I rather thought that bravado would reassert itself, and that I would have to make good my threats there and then. Happily, I did not. Perhaps his head hurt too much."

Catherine smiled. "What a cruel uncle to so abuse his nephew's poor head."

"Poor head?" Charles sent his wife a stern look. "I did not force all that wine down his throat. Serves him as he deserves. They had been drinking steadily for most of two days."

"But I take it that they did exonerate Vincent?"

"Eventually, though had it not been for the poet, they might not have."

"The poet? What *are* you talking about?" Catherine chuckled. "Surely Vincent does not consort with poets."

"Well, perhaps not intentionally." Charles allowed himself a trace of a smile. "It seems that this particular young buck is accosted by his muse in the small hours of the morning when he has been drinking. Once he started writing, he left off drinking, and so was sober enough to attest that Vincent had not left the house, but had fallen asleep in the middle of a card game. He slept the rest of the night with his head on the table."

Catherine shook her head in mock wonder. "What a great deal we poor females never experience. Did you carouse in your youth?"

Charles held his glass up to the light and turned it slowly about, as if seeking an answer in the amber liquid. His face became carefully impassive. "Let us just say that I do not care for headaches."

Catherine reached out and pinched his toe. "And you hope that I shall be satisfied with that answer. Or that I shall imagine deep depravity. I know your sly ways. Never mind. I shall ask Adam."

Suddenly Catherine felt that she was too far away from her husband. She slid to the floor and moved so she could rest her head against his knee. He cupped her cheek in his big hand and pressed her face against his thigh. After a moment she returned to the subject of the young earl. "It is a shame about Vincent. He is nice looking and intelligent. He could have many real friends, yet he drives everyone away."

"Yes. A great waste. I have been thinking about what you said earlier—that he seems to believe that no one will care for him, so he gives them an excuse." Charles's fingers toyed with her curls. "His father did him no favor in allowing him his bad habits. The boy simply proved to himself—and to everyone else—that he was unlovable. Which he certainly is now."

"Perhaps he will think about what you said to him." Catherine rubbed her cheek against the rough fabric of his britches.

"Perhaps. I have little hope, but I have every intention of enforcing my instructions to him. It is strange, Kate. For years I regarded him with so much antagonism that I hardly dared to correct him. I was afraid I would go too far. Now that my anger is vented, I feel only a determination to apply the discipline that he has lacked—that every lad deserves. It is not actually my place to do so, but who else is there?"

"Maybe he will not stop to think of that. Did you and Mr. Maidstone call on Sir Kirby?"

"No." Charles slid down until his head rested on the arm of the couch, and stretched both legs out along it. He stroked her hair gently. "By the time we had sorted out Vincent's associates, I needed to get Maidstone back to the inn. We will call on Stalling tomorrow. But enough of Maidstone and enough of bloody murder." He set aside his glass and, leaning down, caught Catherine under the arms, dragging her up along his body.

She wriggled her way fully onto the sofa, lying atop Charles with her head on his chest. She breathed in the warm male fragrance of him and tangled her fingers in the curling black hair that escaped his shirt. A husky sound reverberated deep in his throat. His hands found her bottom and began their seductive dance, stroking and sliding over the silk of her gown. She loved the sensual awareness it created in her. She snuggled closer.

At that he used his grip to press her forward until their

mouths met. She savored the taste of brandy on his tongue as he played it along her lips. When her heart began to race, he moved his hands to her waist and lifted her so that her breasts pressed against his face. Catherine rested her elbows on the arm of the sofa beside his head while he made short work of opening the ribbons of her gown.

He then returned his hands to her derriere. She gave herself up to the mesmerizing sensation of his lips on her skin, the smoothness of his tongue in the valley of her breasts, and at last, the warmth of his mouth on her nipples. Somehow her gown was now rucked up to her waist, and his hands caressed the inside of her thighs, his fingers tantalizing the gate of her passion.

Catherine moaned, and Charles uttered a soft oath. Rolling to the side, he eased her to the floor. She watched with hungry eyes as he jerked his shirt over his head, flinging it away. His britches and stockings he dispensed with in one motion. He dropped to the carpet beside her, pulling her across him.

He entered her as she lay atop him, driving upward with increasing speed and power as he feasted on her breasts. Desire built in Catherine, and when he tightened his hands around the back of her thighs and forced her hard against him, it peaked in a thundering crescendo of scintillating lights.

A soft scream escaped her. Charles forged into her unrelentingly, demanding every morsel of surrender. Every muscle in her body responded, clenching and quivering, again and again, until she collapsed helplessly onto him. He finished with one more powerful surge, locking her to him with arms of steel. They lay thus until, much later, a cold draft forced them to the bed. There they sank together into deep slumber.

* * *

The bloodcurdling shriek filled the air and resounded throughout the room, echoing off ceiling and walls. Catherine bolted from the bed, dimly aware that Charles had already risen. Grabbing her wrapper from the floor and clutching it in front of her, she stared around groggily for the source of the scream. She did not have far to look.

Sally was backing away from the dressing table, both hands pressed over her mouth. She continued backing until she collided with Hardraw, who had burst in from the adjoining dressing room, where he had likely been selecting raiment for Charles. When her back encountered his body, Sally uttered another screech, spinning around to face him.

He reached out and steadied her with a hand on either shoulder. "What in the world? What is it, lass?"

Sally babbled incoherently as Charles shot through the door, shirtless and with britches half fastened, shaving soap coating his chin. "Kate! Kate. Are you all right?"

A pounding on the door from the sitting room announced the arrival of James Benjamin. "M'lady! M'lord! Unlock the door!"

Catherine blinked at the commotion, willing herself to come awake. Pulling her wrapper over her gown, she stumbled toward the door to admit James Benjamin, but Charles intercepted her, catching her arm and turning her to face him. "What is it, Kate?"

"I don't know." She shook her head and rubbed a hand over her eyes. "It's Sally."

Charles stepped to the door and let James Benjamin in. He then moved across the room to where Sally clung, sobbing, to Hardraw. The valet patted her back soothingly. Charles laid a firm hand on her shoulder. "Sally, tell me at once what the matter is."

For answer the shivering girl pointed silently at the dressing table. Everyone converged on it, searching for the source of Sally's distress. At first they saw nothing, then every eye fell on a piece of red-tinged white tissue, every nostril detected a faint, unwholesome odor.

In the center of the paper lay a small, but unmistakably human, ear.

'"Oh, my God." Catherine's knees failed her, and she crumpled to the dressing stool.

"Damnation." Even Charles was temporarily stunned. James Benjamin backed up a step. "Nay then!"

Sally, although she had been pulled forward by Hardraw, refused to look, hiding her face against his chest.

"The bloody bastard!" Charles jerked the paper up, wrapping it around its ghastly burden. He shoved it in the direction of James Benjamin. "Take that down to my study, and send someone for Maidstone."

"Aye, m'lord." James Benjamin crammed the bundle into a pocket. "But I think I'll have a look about first."

"Yes. Yes, of course. Do so." Charles nodded. "Ring for John David and let him run the errand. I want you to check the premises carefully. I shall assist you as soon as I see to Lady Caldbeck." The groom hastened away.

He turned back to Catherine. She sat unmoving on the stool, hands clasped across her chest. Horror roiled in her belly and in her mind. She couldn't think, couldn't reply when Charles spoke to her.

"Kate." He gave her shoulders a little shake. "Kate, answer me. Are you going to faint?"

She shook her head and looked up at him. "You have soap on your chin." Her mind refused to deal with anything else. "Use my towel."

Charles made an impatient gesture, and Hardraw reached for the towel on the washstand, towing Sally along with him. She clutched his sleeve and refused to let go. Charles took the towel and wiped his chin. He cast an assessing glance at Sally. "Perhaps you'd better take her up to her room. She is obviously—"

"No!" Sally's wail interrupted him. "I don't want to be up there by myself. He might be up there!"

Charles heaved an exasperated sigh. "Now, Sally, you are clearly not—"

"Let her stay." Catherine looked up from studying the floor. "I do not want to be alone, either." Her heart fairly failed at the thought.

"Oh, never fear," Charles assured her, his voice grim. "You are not going to be alone for so much as a second. Not until this whole mystery is unraveled. But now I want you back in that bed. These shocks cannot be good for you."

That was a masterpiece of understatement. Catherine's stomach rolled, and she still felt too weak to stand. How? How had that monster come here? And left…left that hideous… He had been in her room. Actually in her sanctuary. She was safe nowhere—not even with Charles asleep in their bed beside her.

"Oh, Charles." She sobbed and reached out for him. He came to her, kneeling beside her, and wrapped her in his powerful embrace.

"It will be all right, Kate. I promise you."

"How do you know?" It was a cry of anguish. "He was here—right here, in my room. You were here, and he came right in and…and left that horrible… Oh, Charles. It must have belonged to the Muker girl. Unless… Oh, no! Surely he has not…" She gulped, fighting hysteria.

Charles smoothed her hair. "No. It is not…fresh. I don't know how he got in, Kate. I intend to find out today—soon. Surely he left some trail." He tipped her face up and looked seriously into it. "But I do know this—we are going to be much more vigilant. I never believed he could enter the house—certainly not that he could come in here with me in the bed. But I was unusually tired yesterday, and then we...well, I slept very soundly. But this is a big place, and there are very likely means of ingress that I have not considered. We will make a thorough search today."

He stood and lifted her in his arms. "Now, it is bed for you." He spoke over his shoulder. "Hardraw, do you feel equal to standing watch in this suite?"

"Yes, my lord. I have...uh, well, I have taken your advice about exercise. I believe I am considerably more fit than I was a few weeks ago."

"Good. I have limited troops at my disposal. I cannot risk bringing anyone in from outside. You may work in here—with all the doors to the suite locked. Open them only to someone you know well." He set Catherine on the bed and gestured toward the sofa. "Put Sally there. And call Mrs. Hawes to bring up some breakfast for her ladyship and some tea for Sally. I believe Sally has had her breakfast?" He glanced at the maid.

Sally nodded and allowed herself to be ensconced on the sofa. Charles stacked Catherine's pillows and gathered the bedclothes around her shoulders. "And you, my lady, stay exactly where I have put you. Understood?"

Catherine nodded and followed her husband's departure with anxious eyes.

Charles and Maidstone stared in frustration at the two objects lying on Charles's desk. Dr. Dalton sat nearby in a wing chair, smoking a pipe. He nodded. "I don't know about the knife. Possibly. But yes. The ear is almost certainly from the Muker child. He took both of them."

"Both?" Charles thumped the desk with his fist. "Then are we to expect the other one to appear when we least expect it?"

"Nay, I'd reckon not." Maidstone touched the paper with one finger. "He'll keep the one for hisself." He glanced at Charles. "Did it scare her ladyship bad?"

"Yes. Quite badly." Charles looked questioningly at the doctor.

Dalton gestured with his pipe, speaking in reassuring tones. "She is frightened, of course, not without reason. But I believe you need not fear for her child. I see no sign of miscarriage. Contrary to common thought, nature protects the unborn against most shocks. Lady Caldbeck is a strong woman and a brave one. She needs but time to recover from the alarm."

"Aye," Maidstone agreed. "Pluck to the backbone, that one. But there's to be a little one, eh? That makes matters worse yet."

Charles looked up in irritation that the man should know what they had as yet told no one but Dr. Dalton, but a moment later thought better of a chill retort. It would be all over the dale very shortly in any case. No need in taking his foul humor out on the runner. "Yes, it does make matters worse. But this latest incident... I confess that I am frightened myself. How could he come into the room without my hearing him? How did he get into my house?"

"Maybe he was already in the house. Somebody had that scarf, me lord." Maidstone narrowed his eyes and awaited a response.

"Damnation." Charles leaned back in his chair and blew out an angry breath. "Of course, that must be considered. We shall have to question everyone." He slammed his hand down on the desktop. "God! Can I trust no one?"

Hardraw shuffled his feet and looked uncomfortably at the carpet.

"Come now, Hardraw." Charles's patience was running thin. "I only asked you if anyone was with you for any part of last night."

His valet still refused to meet his eye. "Unless it is very important, my lord, I prefer not to say."

Oh, no. Not another one. Charles sighed. As much as he approved of chivalry in men, he was growing weary of it in men he needed to be able to trust—first Adam, now his valet. "Hardraw, how could anything be more important than this situation? I need to know that I may trust you completely. If you can give me any reason to know that you *could not,* without a doubt, have been abroad last night, then for God's sake, give it to me."

They were in Charles's and Catherine's private sitting room. Catherine sat gracefully in a chair opposite him, and Maidstone slouched in another a few feet away. The runner watched Hardraw with slitted eyes, waiting for his response.

The valet nodded and looked up at Charles, his ears red. "I was with Mistress Sally."

"Sally!" The astonished exclamation erupted from Catherine.

"Sally?" Charles tried to picture the staid Hardraw with lively Sally. In fact, he found it difficult to picture his very proper valet in any such much-less-than-proper situation. Apparently this explained the new interest in physical condition.

"I see." The words seemed understated even to Charles. "All night?"

Hardraw nodded guiltily.

Charles leaned back in his chair, steepling his long fingers against his lips. Now what was he to do? Theoretically it was his place to maintain decorum in his household. Certainly it was his responsibility to protect his female employees from unwelcome attention. A few days ago he might have taken Hardraw to task for this breach of propriety, but considering that his own sister… But Helen was a widow, and mostly definitely her own person. She clearly had made her own choice.

"Hardraw, I must ask what your intentions are with respect to Sally."

"Oh, the most honorable, my lord!" the valet exclaimed seriously, ears glowing. "I find that my feelings are engaged to an extreme degree."

Charles glanced at Catherine, who held up one finger and, rising, disappeared into her bedchamber. A moment later, remorseful sobs could be heard through the closed door. The men sat in silence until Catherine returned to her chair. She said nothing, but nodded.

"Very well." Relief swept over Charles. "I suppose the two of you will have to work that out between you. At least I know you were safely occupied—not that I have ever pictured you as a murderer. I am glad to have all doubt removed. Of course, neither had I pictured you as…never mind. I can rely on you to help me keep Lady Caldbeck safe."

"Oh, indeed you can, my lord."

Charles nodded in thanks and dismissed Hardraw, looking inquiringly at Catherine. She covered her eyes with one hand, smiling ruefully. "I never would have thought this of Sally. She has always been such a good girl. But I suppose…"

"Human nature is human nature, me lady. And there's

danger in the air. It do have that effect.'' Maidstone leaned forward in his seat, forearms on his knees. ''But I say this ain't no bad thing. We got to consider that this cur has satisfied hisself with others before. Mistress Sally or one of the other maids could be next. The morts all sleep together somewheres?''

''Yes.'' Charles got up and began to pace. Yet another concern. More women to protect. Was there no end to it? His resources were dwindling. ''They have rooms in their own wing on the fourth floor.''

''Perhaps it would be a good idea for some of the men to move into that wing for a while,'' Catherine suggested.

Maidstone nodded. ''Might be, at that.''

Charles stopped his pacing and stared at the two of them coolly. This was becoming ridiculous. ''And what situation will I be dealing with nine months from now? I foresee myself doing a great deal of enforcing of paternal responsibility.''

Maidstone grinned, and Catherine giggled. ''Oh, Charles. It surely will not be as bad as all that. We shall just have to let nature take its course.''

''That is precisely what I fear it will do.''

A guffaw exploded from Maidstone. ''Nature'll take her course anyhow, me lord. There's naught you can do about it.''

''Well, we have talked to everyone in the house.'' Charles looked at the runner. ''Except Richard, whom I sent to his parents' home. What do you think?''

''I don't think it's none of these. Though, of course, not all of them was with someone else. Somebody got in here, me lord, most likely not for the first time. And not for the last, either.''

A cold hand clutched at Charles's heart. ''He is letting us know that he can enter at will.''

"Aye. And to do that he must be somebody very sly."

"Harry."

"Aye, me lord. This here Odd Harry is beginning to interest me very much. From what I'm told, he slips around like the wind."

"Yes, he does that. And I've no doubt that he is hiding from us in earnest now. Otherwise, someone would have seen some sign of him. He is not even picking up food anymore."

Catherine shuddered. "Might he have gotten in here?"

"He is certainly a good candidate for it. I am beginning to fear that his mind has become deranged."

"Sounds like he's always been a bit touched in his upper works."

Charles sat back down. "We must find him."

"Aye, he'll try again, and soon. And we best have another go at your Richard."

"It seems that our Richard is in love—yet another gallant swain protecting his lady."

They were settling into the sofa in Catherine's bedchamber to share their bedtime wine. Catherine clapped her hands together. "How delightful!"

"Perhaps. I am not convinced that his father will find it so. She lives in the village."

"Oh, dear. Her birth is not genteel?"

"No. Why must young men inevitably fall in love with unsuitable girls?" Charles shook his head in disgust. "But I know the answer to that question. They do it because the girls make their favors available. I did so once myself, much to my father's dismay. Now I wonder what I ever saw in the chit. But that is neither here nor there."

He propped his feet on the ottoman, leaning back with

a sigh. "Richard told Maidstone and me that he rode out to meet her just after dawn that day. Daft thing to do, as cold as it was. If she came out, he never saw her. Apparently she had better sense. I shall send to the village tomorrow to confirm his story, but I have little doubt that it is true."

"It must be. Richard could not have done these things. Will you interfere with the romance?"

"Not beyond warning him of the dangers. I shall leave the role of villain to his father. I seem to have played it enough recently." Charles put an arm around Catherine's shoulders and drew her nearer. "It is not as though I do not understand the attractions of romance."

She snuggled into his warmth. "Who else has Mr. Maidstone questioned?"

"Stalling. Or at least he went there. I sent Samuel with him to show him the way. Stalling's butler said Sir Kirby had taken to his bed with a nauseous complaint. I collect that Maidstone came away very quickly."

"Hmm." Catherine wrinkled her nose. "I would think so. No one wants to contract that sort of ailment."

"Apparently Sir Kirby has been sick for several days, so it is unlikely that he has been out."

"So that leaves Odd Harry. Is a dwarf strong enough to do the things he has done? Dorrie Ribble was a stout woman. I would think she might give a pretty good account of herself in a struggle."

"Perhaps, but no woman is the equal of a man in strength. Besides, Harry is extremely strong. He used to lift enormous burdens when he helped the smith."

"Oh, dear. Can he possibly know a way into Wulfdale? Has he ever been inside?"

Charles considered. "He might have been, years ago, before he became the recluse he is today. It is possible that he can get into the house, but I believe he will find it very difficult indeed to get into our rooms—not with the doors locked and James Benjamin and Maidstone sleeping across them.''

''I do hope they will not be too uncomfortable.'' It had been arranged that the detective and the groom would sleep in the private sitting room, where the only doors that led to Charles's and Catherine's bedchambers were located. The chambers connected with one another through the dressing rooms.

''On the contrary.'' Charles sipped his wine. ''I hope that they are sufficiently uncomfortable to be kept awake. I plan to spend tonight here on the sofa myself. I do not wish to be lost in slumber if he again appears.'' He kissed Catherine on the forehead. ''Unfortunately, that also means I cannot be lost in passion as I was last night.''

Catherine sighed. ''I shall be unable to sleep myself if I must do so alone.''

''This is not open to argument, Kate. But do not despair. I assure you that when this problem is resolved, we will make up for lost time.''

Chapter Nineteen

The hours of the night wore on slowly for Catherine. The lonely bed served as a constant reminder of the reason for Charles's absence. He lay on the sofa, keeping watch. Catherine punched her pillow and turned to the other side. It would be of little use. She could not get comfortable. Strange. When she and Charles first began sharing a bed, she had found it hard to fall asleep with him there. Now she could not sleep without him.

Not that she wanted to. Panic gripped her at the thought of being helplessly asleep, prey to grasping hands and slashing knives. Whenever she began to doze, a sudden shock flashed through her, jerking her upright, setting every nerve alight, chasing slumber to the far reaches of her mind.

She flipped onto her back and stared upward at the canopy. Little slivers of light from the night candle danced through the spaces in the curtains. Perhaps she should get up and sit with Charles. But it would be so cold with the fire banked. Maybe she would just stay where she was.

Before she could decide, Charles, apparently hearing her stirring, tossed his blanket aside and came to the bed.

He sat on the edge of the mattress and stroked a hand over her hair. "Not sleeping, Kate?"

Catherine shook her head. "No, I'm afraid to drift off. Have you slept at all?"

"I've dozed a bit."

Catherine regarded him suspiciously. "How much is a bit?"

"Not much," he admitted.

Just as he lifted his hand to her hair again, they heard a great thump from the sitting room. Charles leapt off the bed, grabbed the pistol from the night table and made a dash for the door. He threw it open and stopped on the threshold, Catherine right behind him. Her heart all but stopped, then banged frantically in her chest as she peered around Charles. Her knees felt weak. Could it be? Was the murderer actually in her parlor?

The sitting room was dark save for the flickering candlelight from the bedchamber and a tiny gleam from a shuttered lantern. They squinted into the gloom for the source of the disturbance, Charles keeping the pistol steady.

"Nay then, m'lord! All's well." A sheepish James Benjamin knelt by a small, overturned table. He hastily righted it and retrieved the ornaments that had rested on it, avoiding Charles's eye. The candle that had been on the table had gone out as it fell.

Maidstone stood across the room with pistol ready. He uttered an oath as he lowered it. "Damnation, young 'un! I almost shot you. You scared me out of a year's growth."

Catherine sagged with relief against the doorjamb.

"What happened, James Benjamin?" Charles stepped into the sitting room.

"Eh, m'lord—" James Benjamin grimaced in disgust

"—I'm sorry. I was lying yonder." He indicated a rumpled blanket on the carpet. "I rolled over and fetched up against the table."

Charles heaved a sigh of relief. "Well, no harm done—except to Maidstone's longevity, and mine. Let us return to what rest we may get." After relighting the candle, he turned back to the bedroom, tucking an arm around Catherine's waist. Reaching the bed, they both sat on the edge of it.

"Were you quite frightened?" Charles pulled her close.

"Of course. I keep thinking about him—right here in our home, in my rooms." Catherine shuddered. "I feel that I'm not safe anywhere."

Charles nodded in understanding. "I would send you to London, but it is too cold for you to travel, and the trip is too long. You might develop an inflammation of the lungs." He placed a protective hand on her belly. "And with all the jolting, you might lose the child. I am doing all in my power to keep you both safe here."

Catherine rested her head on his shoulder. "I know that you are. I'm sure we will prevail eventually. It is just very difficult to be brave right now. I did not think I was so poor spirited."

"You are not. I have seen your courage. It is the waiting that is so difficult." Charles pointed to the dueling pistol on the bed table. "That is for you. I have its mate by the sofa. Use it if you need to. Don't hold back."

Catherine nodded. "I won't. After what he has done, I do not believe that I would hesitate a moment."

"Good." Charles pushed her back onto the pillows and kissed her. "Now. You need your rest."

The night had drifted into the small hours when Catherine dozed off. She was not sleeping soundly—she was far too tense for that—but little scraps of dreams chased across her consciousness, none of them pleasant. Fragments of screams choked off by remnants of laughter. Footsteps sounding behind her. She ran, only to wake with a start, swallowing a shriek. She could hear Charles's breathing on the sofa, but he did not seem to be sleeping. Would this night never end? Catherine turned impatiently onto her side.

Suddenly a great shout arose in the sitting room.

"Me lord! Me lord. He's here! I saw him. Damnation, young 'un! Where's the bloody candle got to?"

"I dunno, sir. Something blowed it out."

"Never mind! I got the lantern!"

The thud of booted feet sounded. Catherine shot to her own feet, fighting the bed curtains aside. Charles vaulted over the back of the sofa, pistol in hand. He paused but a second by the door. "Do not leave this room. Lock the door behind me, and keep the pistol in your hand. Cock it!"

Catherine ran to the door as he raced out. She had only a glimpse of the murky room beyond as she turned the key in the lock. Everything looked dark. What had happened to the candle in the sitting room, and to the others that had been left burning in the hallways?

She returned to the bed and picked up the pistol. Pulling the hammer back, she leaned against the tall bed, every nerve in her body screaming. Catherine could hear running and shouting, diminishing as the chase swept away down the hall toward the servants' stairs.

The room became quieter as the noise retreated. Catherine strained her ears to follow the direction of the pursuit, clinging to the last vestige of human presence. Never had she felt so alone. Outside the small circle of her night candle and the tiny fading glow of the banked fire, her room loomed large and obscure, with unseeable corners. Shadows shifted and crept over the wall. They seemed to move toward her. Catherine averted her eyes.

But this was foolish! She had only to light more candles. She picked up the candle holder and stood. A sudden gush of air whistled through the room.

The candle went out.

Oh, God! Catherine stood frozen in the dark, an unvoiced scream blocking her throat. She struggled for breath. Where had that draft come from? The drapes were pulled across the windows against the cold. No light or air at all seeped through.

Catherine urged her senses into the dark. Was something there? She saw nothing, heard nothing but the rush of blood in her ears. Setting the candle on the night table, she groped for the flint to relight it. She would have to set the pistol down to strike a light, or go to the fireplace. Did she dare…?

Someone else was in the room.

Suddenly Catherine knew it. She set the flint down and willed her eyes to adjust to the dark. Still she could see nothing. He might be coming toward her through the gloom. It was too dark to shoot. The killer might be on her before she could pull the trigger. She must move.

But which way should she go? Should she try for the door or one of the dressing rooms? Could she even find her way in such darkness? She might walk right into him. Oh, God! Catherine stood perfectly still, listening with every fiber of her being.

Then she smelled him. Not a strong smell, but sharp. An animal smell. Near the door to her dressing room. Sure now, Catherine glided toward the door to the parlor, commanding her bare feet not to whisper on the carpet.

Easing the door open, she darted through it, snatching at the key. Heavy footsteps charged after her. Something crashed, and she heard something like a snarl. Throwing her shoulder against the door, Catherine fumbled the key into the lock, turned it. A second later the handle moved, and the door rattled.

But the lock held.

He *was* there! He was in her bedroom! The intruder had only to run to Charles's room and come out by that door. The key to it was on the inside. She had to get out of the sitting room. Catherine fled in panic, crashing into furniture, knocking things about, the pistol still clutched in her hand. She made for a slightly darker rectangle across the room.

The door led into a corridor that ran the length of the wing. She slipped through it. A black tunnel met her eye. The terror almost undid her. Wanting only to sink to the floor and curl into a ball, Catherine pressed one fist against her mouth, forcing herself to calm, to think. *Breathe, breathe,* she chanted in her mind. *Quiet, quiet. Breathe. Think.*

Should she shout for help? No. Definitely not. Charles might well be too far away to hear, and she would reveal her position to the killer. She must be very quiet. Her best hope lay in following Charles and his party.

She must find them before the killer found her.

The men with Charles had run down the hall to her left. Shivering with cold and fear, Catherine turned in that direction, the thin, chill silk of her nightgown brushing against her legs. Sliding her left hand along the wall and gripping the pistol in her right, she inched forward several yards into the blackness. Abruptly her hand met nothing but air.

An open door. She extended her hand, groping. A wide

door. Now what? She had had little occasion to come this way before. She knew only that a number of parlors and bedchambers were located here. If she were not careful, she might veer off into an empty room, losing herself completely in the maze of connecting apartments. That would never do. The murderer knew the house better than she did.

Cautiously Catherine stepped away from the wall. One foot encountered the hall carpet runner. Good. If she kept one foot on the warm softness of the runner and the other on the cold of the bare wooden flooring, perhaps she could follow the hall to the servants' stairs. Oh, please let her find Charles and his men there!

Catherine peered over her shoulder into the darkness, searching for her pursuer. Where was he? She could perceive no movement in the gloom. Nor could she hear anything. Oh, God. Where *was* he? She began to hurry.

The emptiness of the house haunted her, mocked her, challenging her self-control. Every whisper of her breathing echoed off the walls like thunder. Or was it someone else's breathing? *His?*

Fear froze Catherine in place for a long moment. She held her breath. Silence. Resuming her cautious way down the corridor, she managed only a few steps before a puff of air sighed against her cheek. Her nightgown rippled icily along her body. She jerked back, stifling a shriek, every sense alert. What? What! His breath? She closed her eyes and gritted her teeth, willing herself to be reasonable. She could not indulge in fancy. Not now. She could *not* panic. She simply couldn't. Panic would destroy her. Catherine counted to ten. Better. That was better.

It was only a breeze. A cold breeze. A window must

be open somewhere. She leaned against the wall in relief, fighting the fear.

She must compose herself. The distraction of these false alarms might be her undoing. She must find Charles. Peering over her shoulder, she scanned the darkness. Nothing.

Suddenly, horribly, the eerie howling lanced through the night.

Catherine could no more have held back her answering scream than she could see in the dark. Her shriek joined the anguished wailing, reverberating through the hollow mansion. The baying sounded again. Catherine threw her free hand up to cover her ear. *Not again!* A third lament soared, trailing away into silence. Then, voices, hurrying footsteps. Thank God! Charles had heard her. He was coming. She took breath to call out to him.

And a brutal hand came from nowhere to seal her mouth.

The hand forced her shout back down her throat, choking her. With hideous strength a merciless arm jerked her back against a hard body. The pungent smell engulfed her. Hot, foul breath poured over her. Catherine kicked and twisted frantically, trying to turn so that she could get the pistol into his ribs. The crushing grip never faltered, paralyzing in its cruel power. She could not move. Could not cry out...

The voices grew louder now, footsteps racing up stairs. They were coming! Charles was coming. She must call to him. Let him know where to find her. But her captor clamped his hand tighter over her mouth, dragging her backward. He was taking her away!

Charles was coming, and the fiend was taking her away.

Desperate, Catherine tried to bite. Her attacker responded by gouging his fingers into her cheeks, the pain momentarily stunning her. He was pulling her farther and farther into the dark. Away from help. Away from Charles. She must shoot him. Somehow she must.

She bent her arm over her head, trying to point the pistol at his face. The man grabbed her arm, sliding his cruel grip toward the gun, forcing her arm upward, all the while hauling her backward into the dark. In the blink of an eye he would have it.

He would have her.

Catherine pulled the trigger. The blast deafened her. Chunks of plaster and dust rained down, striking them sharply. Emitting a grunt, her captor loosened his grasp for a split second. Catherine wrenched her head to one side and screamed with every ounce of breath at her command. As the gunshot died away, she heard footsteps sprinting toward them, Charles shouting her name. Her assailant hesitated but a breath. Then, with a growl, he flung her away and ran back into the dark. Catherine came up hard against a wall and crumpled to the floor, gasping for breath.

Suddenly she could see. Charles ran toward her. Maidstone followed close on his heels, carrying the lantern. Light pooled in the room. Charles knelt beside her where she lay trying to breathe, and gathered her into his arms, while James Benjamin raced by, following Maidstone past them into the next room. Bumps and thumps sounded as the runner and the groom moved through the adjoining chamber, searching in vain for their quarry.

Charles clasped Catherine to his chest, kissing her hair and murmuring over and over, ''Kate, Kate.''

She sobbed with relief against his shirt. Suddenly they heard Maidstone's shout.

''Bloody hell! He's gone!''

Catherine could not quit shaking. She sat in the chair that Charles had pulled near the bedroom fire, his blanket wrapped around her, and shook. Shook from the top of her head to the soles of her feet. She wondered idly if she would ever stop, and wondered if she cared. The cold, the fear and the strain of the grueling, blind flight through the echoing house had numbed her.

Listening to the steady blows of the hammer coming from her dressing room, she strained her ears to catch Charles's cool voice admonishing James Benjamin as the groom drove nails into the hidden door. She could hardly bear having Charles out of her sight. Her anxiety grew, and Catherine willed herself to be sensible. And still she shook.

Maidstone sat across from her, forearms on knees. At a knock on the door, he rose and admitted John David who bore a tray with hot wine. The whole household was astir. If the sound of Catherine's screams had not wakened everyone, the report of the pistol certainly had. Servants came boiling from every direction, many carrying whatever makeshift weapons came to hand, more cautious souls peeking around doors.

Charles, who had actually not left her side for more than a minute at a time, came back into the bedchamber and sat on the arm of her chair, his hand on her shoulder. Maidstone poured wine for Catherine and brandy for Charles and himself. At a gesture from Charles he leaned over and added a good dollop of the brandy to Catherine's glass. As they sipped without speaking, the hammering ceased, and James Benjamin came into the room.

"All done?" Charles signaled for Maidstone to pour a glass for the groom.

"Aye, m'lord. He won't come that road no more."

James Benjamin accepted his brandy with a nod of thanks and a sniff of appreciation.

"What galls me is we almost had him." Maidstone pounded a fist against his knee. "If it hadn't taken so long to find that door where he disappeared, we would have. Might never have found it if the young 'un here didn't have such sharp eyes."

James Benjamin nodded. "I knew there wasn't no road out. We could see all the room. There had to be a door hidden. Then I see the wardrobe was away from the wall a mite. It pulled right out when I tugged it."

Charles pulled Catherine closer to him. His presence was gradually calming and warming her, and she snuggled against his side, the trembling slowly diminishing. She listened drowsily as the men talked, feeling removed, as though she watched and listened from a great distance.

"We'll search that passage thoroughly tomorrow." Charles smoothed Catherine's hair, which tumbled around her face and shoulders in flaming disarray. She simply hadn't the strength to restrain it. "I wish we might do so tonight," Charles continued, "but it is not safe. We are exhausted. Of course, there will be no more light in there even in the day, but I want to be better prepared. That Lady Caldbeck knew he came from her dressing room allowed us to find the entrance, once we realized there was a hidden passage. The cupboard pulled out in much the same manner that the wardrobe did at the other end."

"And you never knew it was there?" Maidstone swirled his brandy in the glass.

"No, I did not, but I am not surprised. This house probably harbors many more secrets than that. It has been centuries in the building."

Catherine glanced up at Charles with another shudder. "Is it possible that there is another door into this suite?"

Charles looked down into her face, and for a moment Catherine shivered again at the deadly glitter in his eyes. But his voice was moderate when he spoke. "I doubt that very much. However, we will measure everything very carefully tomorrow. The reason we never suspected that the passage exists is that it lies between the walls where the cupboards in your dressing room and those in mine are built. The eye cannot discern the extra space." He looked back to Maidstone. "You are certain you saw Harry?"

"Oh, aye, me lord." The detective nodded. "At least, I saw a cove no more than four foot high and broad as he is tall. Powerful looking. Came up to the door of the sitting room, but soon as he set his ogles on us, he took to his heels. He must have opened that glaze out in the hall—to blow out the candles."

Charles frowned. "Might he have come in through the window?"

"I'd say nay. Ain't nothing but air for thirty foot down. We heard him go down them back stairs. What I can't rumble is how he got back round here so fast after we chased him down them."

"He didn't." At this unexpected contribution to the discussion the men all turned startled faces to Catherine. She went on. "The man who seized me was not a dwarf. He stood a bit taller than I do—not a great deal—but he was horridly strong. I was like a child in his hands."

The recollection brought on another shiver, and Charles tightened his arm around her shoulders. "You don't have to talk about it, Kate. You are overset."

"But I must." Catherine pulled the blanket more closely around herself and sat up straighter. "We must catch him, whoever it is. I know he was taller, because I could feel his chin and his breath against my hair. And he had a smell.'' She wrinkled her nose. ''Almost like an animal, but… Well, perhaps not an animal. Rather like the odor some people have when they are nervous, only it was very strong.''

''Hmm.'' Maidstone rubbed his chin, frowning. ''Then there's two culls in it. That ain't good. Not good at all.''

''I never thought Odd Harry would do naught like that.'' James Benjamin stared at his boots.

''Nor I.'' Charles stood and paced a turn around the room. ''Somehow this fiend has coerced him. That is the only answer.''

Maidstone regarded him skeptically. ''Could be, I suppose. But how? He looks stout enough.''

''Physically, yes. Formidable, in fact. But he is not so strong…'' Charles paused. ''*Mentally* is not the word I want. His mind is good, but he cannot deal with people. I do not believe he could resist threats well.''

''Well, be that as may be, he was here. We got to find him before he's much older.''

A blinding flash of insight swept over Catherine. She drew in a sharp breath, leaning forward in her chair.

''He *is* here.''

The three men looked at her as though her senses had flown. Charles reached for her. ''He is not here, now, Kate. He has run away. This has been a terrible experience for—''

She avoided his hand in irritation and glared at her protectors. ''No! Do not look at me that way. My mind is quite sound, thank you. I mean that he has been hiding within Wulfdale—in the house itself. That is why we can't find him.''

A stunned silence ensued. The men exchanged speculative glances.

"Don't you see?" Catherine was losing patience with them. "He stayed in the old part of the orphanage until we began to repair it. This house has an even bigger, older section. I have never even seen it, although—" she tossed Charles a miffed look "—I am told it is haunted."

Charles did not smile, but his eyes lost some of their icy gleam as he gazed at her.

"Hmm." Maidstone rubbed his neck. "Haunted by a dwarf."

James Benjamin narrowed his eyes. "Better than a boggart."

More than anything else, Charles felt astonishment. How could so many hidden passages exist in his home without his knowledge? When they cautiously entered the door secreted behind the wardrobe where the intruder had disappeared, a new world was revealed. They found not only the path back to Catherine's dressing room, but entrance after entrance into the system, most of the passages in the oldest part of the mansion, leading back to the pele tower and ancient hall. Two—one concealed in the wall of a cistern and one hidden by a chimney—led to the outside. They must all be blocked immediately. Charles shuddered at how vulnerable they had been.

Catherine had insisted on coming with them, partly, he thought, because she preferred to be in the middle of things and partly because she was afraid to have him leave her. He agreed because he did not want her out of his sight. The intrepid James Benjamin led the way, followed by Maidstone. Catherine came after the runner, and Charles brought up the rear so that she would constantly be under his eye. The men all carried pistols and lanterns.

"M'lord?" James Benjamin half turned in the narrow space. "Why did your grandfathers build this warren?"

"I would imagine that this is a testimony to the grim nature of the politics of the past—the further back, the grimmer. A lord never knew when his enemies would appear to carry him off to gaol—or to hang him."

"Maybe you should leave them open."

Charles raised an eyebrow. "I would like to think that I have no such dangerous enemies, James Benjamin."

"You got at least one." Maidstone held his lantern high, looking up a stone staircase. "Looks like this is part of the old tower."

Ascending the steps, they arrived at a battered wooden door. The groom cast an inquiring glance at Charles, and Charles nodded. "Open it carefully."

James Benjamin pushed the door back a few inches and peered through the crack. A foul smell leaked through. He opened it a little more and halted abruptly. Then he stepped back into the passage. "I'd say we found him, m'lord."

Maidstone pushed past James Benjamin with an angry exclamation. The groom followed him, and Charles moved around Catherine. "Stay here."

"Do not think, my lord, that I am staying in this wretched place alone." Catherine batted at a spiderweb and kept to his coattail as he cleared the door, coming into a windowless chamber concealed in the old tower wall.

Odd Harry lay dead, facedown in the center of the room.

Just outside a wide pool of blood, Maidstone and James Benjamin stood gazing soberly down at Harry's compact form. The wooden handle of a knife protruded from a shirt shredded with slashes and soaked with blood. The smells of death filled the hidden room. Catherine covered her mouth and nose with a handkerchief.

Finding a spot where he could reach the knife, Maidstone bent down and withdrew it from the body. Inching his boots away from the blood, he examined the blade. "Hmm." The detective glanced around the room. "Sharpened up like the one he sent her ladyship. And it looks like he was in a rage. Poor cully's cut to fish bait." He nudged James Benjamin. "Look round some, lad. See if there's another shiv."

All four of them searched the hidden room, but no other knives of any sort were found, although signs of habitation were everywhere. Food and dishes sat on a crude table, and a crumpled blanket covered a rough cot. Ashes filled the fireplace. Maidstone knelt and placed a hand near them. "Still barely warm. Nor that blood ain't all dried, neither. He done it last night—or rather early this morning, after we was done chasing him."

Catherine shook her head sadly. "The poor thing. You must be right, Charles. He was forced into this."

Charles knelt by the body, careful to keep his gray clothes clear of the bright blood. "Apparently Harry was sent to create a diversion last night. I would guess the killer became afraid that he was on the verge of telling someone. Harry may not have known what he was abetting until the abduction attempt."

"Aye, that's possible. He could have delivered the parcels without knowing. But then the cull wanted more— wanted to know the way in." Maidstone stood, dusting off his hands. "And he found it."

Chapter Twenty

Charles gave heartfelt thanks for the two quiet days that followed. He saw to having the entrances to all the concealed passages sealed, and stayed within earshot of Catherine virtually every moment. James Benjamin hovered in the background, and Maidstone moved from his lodging at the village inn to a room in Wulfdale. And still Charles felt tense and on edge.

He marveled at Catherine's resilience. She refused to be fussed over, going about her daily tasks with firm resolve. She insisted that he conduct her through the maze of rooms that opened on the corridor outside their suite, saying that she had no intention ever again of being lost in her own home.

Yet at times when she did not know he was watching, Charles glimpsed an anxious expression around her mouth, or found her staring out a window at nothing, a hand resting over her womb. Never, in all their planning for the welfare of their child, had he thought they would face such a danger. Even with Dr. Dalton's reassurances, Charles worried about her and the child, angry with himself and fate that he could not protect them from this ordeal.

His greatest concern centered around the inquest into Harry's death, which was to be held that afternoon. Both he and Maidstone were obliged to go and testify. Every precaution he could reasonably take for Catherine's safety seemed inadequate. Charles could not rest easy in his mind. Yet logic told him she would be safe surrounded by his staff and under James Benjamin's vigilant eye.

And Charles would see to it that she stayed surrounded by staff.

Early in the afternoon Catherine, her groom trailing behind her, walked with him to the library to meet Maidstone for their trip to the inquest. Just as they were getting up to leave, Hawes announced a caller. "Lord Lonsdale, my lord."

Charles covered his eyes for a moment and shook his head. Vincent was possibly the last person he wished to see. Unfortunately, young Lonsdale already stood in the doorway, his hat and riding crop clutched in his hands. And what did those white knuckles portend? Another tantrum? Charles did not have time to bring him to heel this afternoon. He drew a sustaining breath. "Good afternoon, Vincent. Come in. To what do we owe this pleasure?"

Vincent stepped into the room, but did not advance more than a few feet. "I am on my way to attend the inquest, so I will require only a moment of your time, my lord. I wish to convey my apologies to Lady Caldbeck." He turned toward Catherine, his face white around his compressed lips, and bowed. "Please accept my apologies, my lady, for any offense I may have given."

Any offense he *may* have given? Charles swallowed a sharp comment. At least it was a start—and far more than anyone had gotten out of Vincent in the past.

After a startled moment Catherine inclined her head graciously. "Of course, Vincent. Thank you."

The young lord turned back to Charles and Maidstone, his expression stonier than ever. "And you gentlemen… Perhaps…it is possible…" Vincent stared a moment at his boots, then with a half bow resolutely lifted his gaze to Charles. "I beg that you will also accept my apology."

Charles stood for a moment amazed. He had demanded no apology for himself nor Maidstone. Would wonders never cease? He looked closely at his nephew before answering with an infinitesimal nod. "Accepted."

Vincent glanced at Maidstone. The runner shrugged. "Aye."

"Thank you. I have already spoken to my stepmother and Lord Litton." He turned toward the door. "If you will excuse me?"

Something hopeful reared its head within Charles's breast. "We were just leaving for the inquest. Would you care to ride with us?"

Vincent hesitated, his face closed. "Thank you, no," he finally answered. "I have other errands on the way. Your servant, gentlemen. Lady Caldbeck." With this unprecedented courtesy, Lord Lonsdale took his leave.

"Well!" Catherine looked inquiringly at Charles. "It appears that your chastisement of Vincent has borne fruit."

Charles grunted assent. "Beyond my wildest expectations. Perhaps I may be saved the bruising I feared might accompany any further instruction of my wayward nephew."

"Don't speak too soon, me lord." The detective chuckled. "His lordship didn't look none too happy about it."

"No, that he didn't, but I am grateful for small gains."

Charles rubbed his chin. "I wonder why he is bothering with the inquest?"

"Perhaps he is taking some responsibility, at last, for his position in the community."

Charles gazed at his wife with one eyebrow elevated. "You cannot believe that."

The afternoon wore on dismally for Catherine. It was becoming more and more difficult to hold her fears at bay. No matter what she thought about, they nibbled at the fringes of her consciousness. As Charles had ordered, she stayed in her sitting room and tried to interest herself in her needlework, while James Benjamin sat uncomfortably on the edge of his chair, pistol beside him. Her own pistol lay on her worktable, a constant reminder of her peril.

Hardraw occupied himself in Charles's dressing room only a few feet away, and just outside the door to the corridor the whole force of footmen were busy polishing everything in the area that might conceivably be polished. Catherine sighed. Her husband was nothing if not thorough. If only he would come home.

In the course of the afternoon she and James Benjamin had exhausted every avenue of conversation either of them could think of—horses first, of course, followed by the weather, dietary preferences and Yorkshire customs. The lively groom had her laughing at his description of some of those, but by late afternoon the subject inevitably came around to the grim reality that held them in the room.

"James Benjamin, you have lived here all your life. Have you no idea who might be doing these awful things?"

Her bodyguard shrugged. "Nay, m'lady. I don't even see how anyone could do such a thing, never mind who."

"Did you know those women?"

"Oh, aye. Mrs. Ribble was right good to me and a toothsome cook. She give me pies now and now. Once you got used to… Well, I don't want to say nothing unkind. It was her eye, you know."

"Yes, I noticed her eye. It made it hard to follow her conversation at first."

"That it did—and the other one was the same—Mrs. Askrigg."

"Really? Her eye was…?"

"Nay, then, m'lady. It wasn't her eye. She was fair enough, but she had a great, dark, red mark on her face. I didn't like to stare."

"No, of course, you wouldn't. A birthmark, a portwine stain, someone said."

"Aye, that's what they called it."

"That's strange that both of them had something odd, and the Muker girl…"

"She was more than odd, ma'am. A right mooncalf, she was."

"Poor thing." Catherine stared into space for a few moments, a notion coalescing in her mind. "I wonder… Do you think that is why he chose them? The murderer, I mean. Because they were marred?"

"Who can say, m'lady? It *is* strange, but *you* don't have no oddity, and he's right set on you."

Catherine shuddered. "Don't say it! But maybe he sees something about me he considers a flaw. My hair or…"

James Benjamin looked unconvinced. "I'd say not."

The idea, however, was taking strong hold on Catherine. "Well, let us leave me out of it for now, then. All the others had an imperfection—and certainly I'm not perfect, come to that. Who else do you know who might attract his attention for that reason?''

The groom pursed his lips in thought. ''I don't know, m'lady—unless he sees the lass you brought from Skipton, the one with the bowed legs.''

''Laurie!'' The realization struck like a blow. ''My God! Why didn't I think of this sooner?'' Catherine leaped to her feet. ''She is in danger. We must—''

Before she could finish, the very air vibrated with the now familiar, but still horrible, howling. ''No! No, not again!'' Catherine slapped her hands over her ears as another bay wrenched her senses. No! Please, no. It was happening again. Another howling, another death... ''It's him! James Benjamin, we must do something. Now!''

''Nay, m'lady.'' The groom stood, grasping his pistol. ''He ain't here.''

''But it always happens! I hear the dog, and the next day someone is killed. We must do something!''

''Nay. It'll be me as is killed if his lordship finds I let you out of this room.''

''Nonsense!'' Actually, Catherine suspected that her husband would be highly displeased with both of them, but her intuition rode her, screamed at her that the girl's life hung in the balance. And she herself had brought Laurie here—into the danger. Catherine grabbed her pistol from the table, ran through her room to her dressing room and seized a cloak. As she sped back through the sitting room, she beckoned to James Benjamin where he stood mired in confusion. ''Come on!''

''M'lady! M'lady, come back!'' The bodyguard tore out of the room after her. Catherine never slowed. They raced past the footmen who, following them with bewildered stares, debated among themselves if they should follow. By the time they decided to do so, Catherine and

James Benjamin had gained the side door that led to the stables, the groom still calling pleas for her to stop.

In the stable yard James Benjamin finally managed to overtake Catherine's long stride and block her path. "M'lady! Where are you going? His lordship—"

"Move, James Benjamin." Catherine shoved him to one side and ran on. "We are going to the orphanage." He chased her into the stable. "Saddle my hunter! Hurry!"

James Benjamin perceived an advantage at last. He folded his arms across his chest. "Nay, m'lady. That I won't do."

"Very well! I will do it myself." Spotting a sidesaddle resting on a bale of hay, his mistress jammed the pistol into the pocket of her cloak and dragged the saddle to the ground. She drew it toward the stall housing her hunter.

"Nay, m'lady! You'll hurt yourself." James Benjamin made a grab for the saddle. Catherine pushed him away.

Regardless of his orders from his lord, James Benjamin clearly perceived that grappling with a countess constituted no part of a groom's duties. Not even a groom turned bodyguard. Cursing silently, he fell back. "M'lady! That's too heavy. You'll harm the wee one."

She did not answer, but continued doggedly pulling the saddle. Seeing that remonstrance was getting him nowhere, and fearing for his mistress's health, James Benjamin grasped the saddle and flung it over the mare's back. He'd be damned, though, if he'd do one thing more. He folded his arms again, leaning against the wall. His mistress struggled with the girth, finally managing to fasten it. She led the hunter from the stall to the mounting block. James Benjamin sprang after her.

"Nay, nay, m'lady. It ain't tight enough. You'll fall."

In desperation he adjusted the straps as Catherine climbed from the mounting block into the saddle.

"Come on, James Benjamin! We are losing time. Saddle a horse and come on. Hurry!" Avoiding her groom's lunge for the bridal, Lady Caldbeck kicked her mount into motion and galloped away into the gathering dusk.

Cursing aloud now, James Benjamin ran back into the stable. His lordship would roast him over a slow fire if anything happened to his lady. James Benjamin had no intention of wasting time on a saddle. He'd spent his life on horseback. He didn't need one. Running to the nearest stall, he led forth a protesting gray stallion. His lordship's newest acquisition, the mount was still nervous in the strange stable and definitely not in a good temper.

But he ran like a hart.

The groom grabbed a handful of the horse's mane and vaulted onto its back. Resentful of this cavalier treatment, the stallion reared before James Benjamin had secured his seat. The groom slid backward over the horse's croup, clinging tenaciously to the halter and further annoying the gray. It reared again, knocking James Benjamin against the stall. His head struck a post with a resounding crack. He slumped to the ground as the horse danced away.

"Spavined hack!" James Benjamin surged to his feet, only to have the earth come up to meet him as blackness closed around.

Where could he be? Catherine wondered as she glanced over her shoulder and scanned the road for James Benjamin. She had no doubt at all that he would follow her. Why couldn't she see him? Perhaps she rode a better mount, outdistancing him. But he could not be far behind. Catherine urged her mare to greater speed.

The valiant horse streaked through the twilight, hooves ringing against the hard-packed earth. Catherine strained her eyes, seeking the lights of the orphanage. There! At last she glimpsed a flicker of light in the hulking old building. A few minutes more and she drew rein before the gate to the courtyard. As she plummeted off the saddle and ran to open it, a very small voice caught her ear. Catherine stopped in her tracks.

"Me lady?"

"Yes?" Pausing, Catherine peered into the dim light, searching for the owner of the voice. "Where are you?" A tiny shadow separated itself from the larger shadow of the shrubbery, gliding silently toward her. She squinted into the gloom. "Why, Willy! What are you doing out here? And—" Catherine broke off in astonishment.

Willy had spoken!

A moment of joy filled her heart. How wonderful! The abused child *could* speak. At the moment, however, he was tugging at her cloak, pulling her toward the byre. She dug in her heels, bringing them both to a stop. "What is it, Willy? What do you want to tell me?"

The lad hung his head, whispering so softly that Catherine was forced to bend down and exert every sense to hear him. "The man took Laurie to the byre."

"To the byre?" Catherine turned to look toward the dark shadow of the barn. "What man, Willy? Willy...?" She turned back, only to see no sign of the boy. "Willy! Come back here!" Only silence answered her.

Catherine lifted her skirts and ran toward the byre. As she approached the door, caution again intervened. She tugged the pistol from the pocket of the cloak and crept forward quietly. The door stood open several inches. Catherine put her ear to the crack. Was that breathing she heard? Soft, very faint. She eased the door back a little farther and put her head through, wincing at the squeal of the hinges.

Darkness met her eyes. She pushed the door back enough to slip through, stopping just inside to listen. Yes, she did hear light breathing and…was that a whimper?

"Laurie?" Silence. Then a faint moan. Carefully Catherine moved toward the sound, feeling her way with her slippers. Her toe encountered something soft. Crouching, she felt for the object.

"Laurie?" Her hands found the softness of much-washed cotton, the firmness of young flesh. "Laurie!" Was she too late?

Suddenly lantern light flared around her. Hinges groaned. The door banged shut. A pungent scent assaulted her nostrils. Catherine whirled, bringing up the pistol.

He was on her. Before she could loose a shot, let alone aim, a heavy body struck her, knocking her backward into the hay. A great weight came down on top of her, an iron fist grasping her wrist, wrenching the pistol out of her grip and flinging it away. Hands clutched at her face. She opened her mouth to scream, and something rough was thrust into it, blocking the cry. The hands yanked her head forward, fumbling behind her, drawing knots tight as the gag cut into the corners of her mouth. Catherine choked on the smell surrounding her.

Her head fell back, and she looked up into the wild, staring blue eyes of Kirby Stalling.

"Whore! She-devil!" The words hissed through lips speckled with moisture. A few drops spattered her face. She tried to turn her head aside, but powerful hands clamped around it, digging into her hair. "I have you. At last, I have you. You will tempt men no more."

Catherine struggled for breath, Stalling's broad frame

crushing her into the hay, terror closing her throat. Frantic, she twisted and kicked, beating at him with her fists. He seemed not even to know that she had moved. His hoarse growl whispered around her. "I have seen you. Yes. I have watched. I saw you fall...saw your legs. White legs..."

He began to pant. Catherine shrunk away, but he seemed suddenly to have forgotten her, his eyes staring at nothing now, rolling up, the blue almost disappearing. Catherine lay very still, fascinated.

"White legs...just like the other one. Falling...legs white..."

The other one? What could he be talking about?

As though he read her mind, Stalling drew several deep breaths and pulled his mad eyes back to her face. "Yes, the other one—the one I took to wife. She tempted me, but I withstood. And then she fell." Again his gaze drifted away. "Fell with her white legs..."

Perhaps he had lowered his guard. Catherine cautiously brought her hands to his chest, hoping to push him away. A mistake. The movement jerked his attention back to her. He panted into her face. "But before I finished, she lay still. Never again..."

His disjointed thoughts floated away once more, but Catherine dared not move. Great heavens! His wife had died in a hunting accident. He must have killed his own wife! The fear grew until Catherine would be screaming if she could—screaming for Charles, for James Benjamin, anybody! She swallowed a sob. Kirby Stalling abruptly tightened his claws around her face.

"She wouldn't learn. She would not learn!" He pounded Catherine's head against the straw—once, twice. Her ears rang. "She would not be pure like my mother." Again the vacant stare, the absence of awareness. "My blessed mother..." Once again the return to Catherine, the clenching of the hands around her head.

"She bore the attacks of that beast with dignity—until she drove him away. And then..." Gone again, drifting. "She drove it out of me...drove the beast out of me...." And again he returned to Catherine. "You will not learn.... But I am strong now. I have found my power."

He rolled to his feet, lifting her with him like a rag doll, his strength unbelievable. Before she could find her footing, he slammed her against a support post, pinning her there with his weight. Catherine fought with every muscle in her body. Useless. Oh, God. Useless. As though her desperate struggles were nothing, he dragged her arms behind the post and fastened her wrists with cruel cords.

Finished, he stepped away. "Not yet. Time...time for the power, the fear to grow. But first I must cleanse the world of this abomination."

Panting again, he turned toward Laurie's half-conscious form, the filed point of a knife glinting in his hand.

Chapter Twenty-One

The inquest had been a completely useless waste of time. Riding home, Charles fretted that he could not put his horse to a gallop and leave Maidstone in the dust. The fear that all was not well grew in him until he cursed silently under every breath.

They rode into the stable yard just as the light of day was failing. Samuel Josiah, the groom, dismounted and took the bridles of the other two mounts, leading them into the stable. Charles and Maidstone had all but reached the door to the house when the groom came running toward them, shouting that James Benjamin was hurt.

Fear clawed at Charles's gut. If James Benjamin were in the stable, injured, then where was Catherine? He dashed into the lantern light to see Samuel supporting a groggy James Benjamin. The young groom kept shaking his head as if to clear his mind, while holding his hand to the back of it. When he saw Charles an agitated babble erupted from him.

''She rode off, m'lord. She rode off. I tried to stop her, but she wouldn't. The dog howled, and she said we had to go, that he'd kill Laurie, and I knew you wouldn't…

But she saddled the hunter. I didn't want to help her, m'lord, but she wouldn't stop, and—''

Charles seized his shoulders, gripping them with crushing intensity. ''Sneck up, James Benjamin! Make sense! Where did her ladyship go?''

''To the orphanage. Oh, m'lord! If she's hurt, I'll die meself.''

Charles was already springing back into his saddle. He turned to Maidstone. ''Come as best you can. I can't wait. Take care of him and get all the lads on horseback. Send them after me.'' He spurred out of the stable at a dead run.

It seemed forever before his lathered horse surged into the yard of the old manor. The house was quiet. Charles peered around him, searching for some clue as to what might be afoot. Instinct led his eyes to the old cow byre. Glimmers of light trickled out of the cracks in the weathered building. Why? Kettlewell should have finished his chores long ere now. Charles made a dash for the barn. Flinging caution aside, he threw the door open.

Never, as long as he might live, would he forget the sight.

Catherine, his love, the center of his world, stood bound to a pillar. Before her crouched Kirby Stalling, a knife in his hand and madness in his eyes.

''Stalling!''

At the sound of the shout, Stalling spun about, snarling, to face Charles. Charles charged into the byre. Stalling, who had just grasped the lantern to move it, hurled it at Charles's head. It sailed past him and crashed against the door, shattering. Streaks of fire dribbled down the wood and pooled on the dirt floor. Charles kept moving.

Raising his knife, Stalling met him in a lethal rush. Dodging the thrust, Charles lunged past him and turned, putting himself between Catherine and the crazed lord. Dancing backward, he cast about for a weapon. Out of the corner of his eye, he glimpsed a rake leaning against a stall. He reached for it, turning the handle in his hands like a singlestick.

For a moment no one moved. The sound of Stalling's harsh breathing filled the byre as he glared in rage at Charles. Balancing on the balls of his feet, Charles focused all his concentration on his adversary. A singlestick was easily a match for a blade, but he could not make a mistake—especially with an opponent too crazy to know fear. And he must keep the madman away from Catherine.

With a roar Stalling came at him, knife held before him. At exactly the precise second, Charles swung. The handle of the rake caught the knife hand with a sickening crunch. Stalling howled as the knife flew away. Still he did not slow his attack. Pressed, Charles skipped back, reversed the stick and swung at Stalling's head. The blow glanced off his shoulder and landed smartly against his ear. Stunned, Stalling collapsed to the floor.

A flash of light burst into the byre. In horror Charles looked up from the fallen man to see a wall of flames where the door had been. The light revealed Laurie coming groggily to her knees, a smear of blood across her forehead. He had to get them out of here! Charles dropped the rake and dived for Stalling's knife. Stalling didn't move.

Knife in hand, Charles raced to the post where Catherine was bound. He slashed at the cords holding her, one eye on his work and one on the fire. Was there another door? He didn't see one. If they didn't move quickly, they would be trapped. Perhaps they already were! He worked faster. Just as Catherine's hands came free, she uttered a muffled cry of warning, pointing behind him.

With a keening cry Stalling landed on Charles's back, throwing an arm around his throat. Charles gripped the arm and pulled with all his might. The arm tightened inexorably as the fire grew. God! The man's strength was monstrous. In a moment Charles's breath would be completely cut off. Already his vision was beginning to fade.

With the power of desperation he redoubled his effort, vaguely aware of Catherine with the rake in her hands. He saw her trying to get behind Stalling, but Stalling pulled him backward, leaving her no one but Charles for a target. Charles tried to reverse the situation, but his strength waned with his breath.

Abruptly, Stalling's arm fell away. A horrible scream of anguish filled the barn. Turning, Charles saw the man staggering backward toward the fire, the tines of a pitchfork protruding from his chest. Behind him Laurie still clung to the handle of the fork with a dogged grip, all her small weight thrown against it.

"Laurie! Come away." On hearing his voice, the girl dropped the weapon and ran toward him and Catherine. Catherine knelt and gathered her into her arms.

As they watched without breathing, Stalling stopped his backward progress and slowly turned toward the blaze. Opening his arms as if to embrace the flames, he crumpled to the earth, facedown in the fire.

As near to panic as he had ever been in his life, Charles vainly looked around for a way out.

"Me lord?" A little hand tugged at his coat.

Charles spared the girl a glance. "What, Laurie?"

"There's a wee door."

"A door! Where?"

Laurie took Catherine's hand and led the way back into

the byre. Charles followed, casting worried glances behind him. They had no more than a few minutes until the whole place became an inferno. Laurie pointed at a small hinged opening near the ground.

Catherine looked at Charles in consternation. "Can we get through that? What is it?"

"It's for the dogs," Laurie whispered. "The other children play here."

"We *have* to get through it." Charles began to kick at the door. Wood splintered as the door came off and the surrounding frame gave way. "There. That should be wide enough. Go, Laurie. Hurry!"

Laurie stepped back and shook her head sadly.

Charles's fear turned to exasperation. "What foolishness is this? Go!"

A tear slipped down the girl's face. "I can't crawl, me lord." She pointed silently at her bent legs. "You go."

Stricken, Charles stared at her. Catherine clutched his arm. "I'll go first, Charles. You push her, and I will pull."

She dropped to all fours and crept into the opening. Her dress snagged, but she went on, heedless of the ripping sound. Charles held his breath until she was through. Her arms reappeared in the opening.

"Now, Laurie." He unceremoniously tipped her off her feet and thrust her hands toward Catherine, holding her body off the ground and feeding it through the hole. The fire now blazed only a few feet away. Charles willed himself, in his haste, not to shove her into the splintered wood.

Catherine's voice sounded from outside. "I have her."

Charles dived through the tiny door. One broad shoulder jammed against the side, stopping him. He dug his boots into the ground and pushed with all the power of his muscular legs. Seconds passed.

Creaking in protest, the planks finally gave way. With the heat of the flames against the soles of his boots, Charles felt four slim hands grasping his shoulders, pulling. He rolled out of the byre into the welcoming dark, coming to his feet in the same motion.

"Run!" He grabbed for their hands and dragged them, stumbling and scrambling, away from the burning building. When he judged them safe, he stopped and looked back. Flames engulfed the whole structure, shooting high against the stars. Suddenly his knees gave way, and as if that were a signal, Catherine and Laurie tumbled to the ground beside him.

At what seemed a great distance, he could hear hoof-beats and voices. People from the house running and shouting, his men leaping from their horses to help. Catherine had a comforting arm around Laurie.

He reached for Catherine, pulling her into his arms. His efforts to speak clogged in his throat. He could only clasp her to him, holding tighter and tighter. At last he choked out a few words. "Are you hurt?"

He felt her head shake against him, but she, too, seemed beyond words. Alarmed, Charles lifted her face so that he could see it.

Catherine shook her head again. "I'm all right. Laurie?"

A murmur of assent answered her.

Charles looked down into his love's beautiful face and feelings welled up in his chest, hot and aching in their intensity. Something stuck in his throat again. He had to force the words of pain and relief around it.

"I thought I had lost you."

An odd dampness cooled his cheeks. Catherine wiped

it away with a gentle hand. Somehow she had moved. She was holding *him* now, her arms pressing his wet face against her breasts. A wrenching sob escaped him. Then another. And another. Catherine held him closer.

"It's all right, Charles. Weep all you wish."

Epilogue

Yorkshire, England, August 1811

The sun lifted its glowing face from behind the green summer hills and sent the first beam of light into the bedchamber. For the second time since he was eight years old, tears welled in Charles Randolph's eyes. They slid down through the black stubble of his unshaved beard and dripped onto the face of the black-haired baby boy sleeping in his arms. His son. His and Catherine's child. The greatest wonder of their wondrous life together.

He leaned across the baby to kiss his wife gently on the forehead. "You're certain all is well with you?"

Catherine reached up and wiped away his tears with a corner of the sheet, then blotted her own. She smiled. "I'm fine. Only a little tired. Do you like him?"

A smile warmed Charles's eyes. "I like him very well. I had thought to have a flame-haired daughter, but a son in my own image…" Tears shone again in his eyes. He brushed them away. "It is the greatest of gifts. Thank you."

"He is God's gift to both of us. Oh, Charles! I'm so happy." She reached for him, and they clung together for a long moment. When they parted, she added, "I hope he grows to be just like you."

Charles looked away into the middle distance while he thought about that. He wasn't sure he wanted that for his son. His strength, his logic—yes, he did want him to have that. But beyond that… "I would wish for him to be like me in many ways, but I hope he will learn from his mother the things that I have learned from her."

"Oh? And that is?"

Charles stroked his son's dark hair. "I want him to learn laughter and anger, the joy of smiling, of passion, and…yes…the joy of tears."

*   *   *   *   *

Your opinion is important to us!

Please take a few moments to share your thoughts with us about Mills & Boon® and Silhouette® books. Your comments will ensure that we continue to deliver books you love to read.

> To thank you for your input, everyone who replies will be entered into a prize draw to win a year's supply of their favourite series books*.

1. There are several different series under the Mills & Boon and Silhouette brands. Please tick the box that most accurately represents your reading habit for each series.

Series	Currently Read (have read within last three months)	Used to Read (but do not read currently)	Do Not Read
Mills & Boon			
Modern Romance™	❑	❑	❑
Sensual Romance™	❑	❑	❑
Blaze™	❑	❑	❑
Tender Romance™	❑	❑	❑
Medical Romance™	❑	❑	❑
Historical Romance™	❑	❑	❑
Silhouette			
Special Edition™	❑	❑	❑
Superromance™	❑	❑	❑
Desire™	❑	❑	❑
Sensation™	❑	❑	❑
Intrigue™	❑	❑	❑

2. Where did you buy this book?

From a supermarket ❑ Through our Reader Service™ ❑
From a bookshop ❑ If so please give us your Club Subscription no.
On the Internet ❑
Other _____ _____/_____

3. Please indicate by number which were the 3 most important factors that made you buy this book. (1 = most important).

The picture on the cover ___ I enjoy this series ___
The author ___ The price ___
The title ___ I borrowed/was given this book ___
The description on the back cover ___ Part of a mini-series ___

Other _____

4. How many Mills & Boon and /or Silhouette books do you buy at one time?

I buy ___ books at one time ❑
I rarely buy a book (less than once a year) ❑

5. How often do you shop for any Mills & Boon and/or Silhouette books?

One or more times a month ❑ A few times per year ❑
Once every 2-3 months ❑ Never ❑

6. How long have you been reading Mills & Boon® and/or Silhouette®?

_____ years

7. What other types of book do you enjoy reading?

Family sagas eg. Maeve Binchy ❑
Classics eg. Jane Austen ❑
Historical sagas eg. Josephine Cox ❑
Crime/Thrillers eg. John Grisham ❑
Romance eg. Danielle Steel ❑
Science Fiction/Fantasy eg. JRR Tolkien ❑
Contemporary Women's fiction eg. Marian Keyes ❑

8. Do you agree with the following statements about Mills & Boon? Please tick the appropriate boxes.

	Strongly agree	Tend to agree	Neither agree nor disagree	Tend to disagree	Strongly disagree
Mills & Boon offers great value for money.	❑	❑	❑	❑	❑
With Mills & Boon I can always find the right type of story to suit my mood.	❑	❑	❑	❑	❑
I read Mills & Boon books because they offer me an entertaining escape from everyday life.	❑	❑	❑	❑	❑
Mills & Boon stories have improved or stayed the same standard over the time I have been reading them.	❑	❑	❑	❑	❑

9. Which age bracket do you belong to? Your answers will remain confidential.

❑ 16-24 ❑ 25-34 ❑ 35-49 ❑ 50-64 ❑ 65+

THANK YOU for taking the time to tell us what you think! If you would like to be entered into the **FREE prize draw** to win a year's supply of your favourite series books, please enter your name and address below.

Name: _____

Address: _____

_____

Post Code: _____ Tel: _____

Please send your completed questionnaire to the address below:

READER SURVEY, PO Box 676, Richmond, Surrey, TW9 1WU.

* Prize is equivalent to 4 books a month, for twelve months, for your chosen series. No purchase necessary. To obtain a questionnaire and entry form, please write to the address above. Closing date 31st December 2004. Draw date no later than 15th January 2005. Full set of rules available upon request. Open to all residents of the UK and Eire, aged 18 years and over.

As a result of this application, you may receive offers from Harlequin Mills & Boon Ltd. If you do not wish to share in this opportunity please write to the data manager at the address shown above. ® and ™ are trademarks owned and used by the owner and/or its licensee.

0904/04

MILLS & BOON®

Live the emotion

Historical
romance™

ONE NIGHT OF SCANDAL
by Nicola Cornick

Deborah Stratton is a respectable widow – or so the inhabitants
of the Midwinter villages believe. But she hides a secret which
means she'll never marry again. Lord Richard Kestrel is
London's most notorious rake, a dangerous man to be around –
and he has shockingly offered to make Deborah his mistress…

PURITAN BRIDE by Anne O'Brien

Restoration England

Marcus, Viscount Marlbrooke, is a cynical observer at the
Restoration Court of King Charles. He doesn't believe love
can be found in matrimony, but he does need to secure his
claim to Winteringham Priory. Marriage to spirited Puritan
Katherine Harley is the key – and perhaps their marriage
needn't be as bleak as he fears…

MY LADY'S PLEASURE by Julia Justiss

Lady Valeria Arnold was shocked by the wanton impulses
that drew her to Teagan Fitzwilliams. He was nothing more
than a wastrel – surely not the kind of man to whom a virgin
widow should entrust her heart? Teagan despised the role
Society had forced upon him – but now his stolen moments
with the Lady Valeria made him feel his own worth…

Regency

On sale 1st October 2004

*Available at most branches of WHSmith, Tesco, ASDA, Martins,
Borders, Eason, Sainsbury's and all good paperback bookshops.*

When she was good,
she was very, very good.
And when she was bad, she was...

NAUGHTY MARIETTA

NAN RYAN

Published 17th September 2004

FREE!

2 Books
and a surprise gift!

We would like to take this opportunity to thank you for reading this Mills & Boon® book by offering you the chance to take TWO more specially selected titles from the Historical Romance™ series absolutely FREE! We're also making this offer to introduce you to the benefits of the Reader Service™—

- ★ **FREE home delivery**
- ★ **FREE gifts and competitions**
- ★ **FREE monthly Newsletter**
- ★ **Exclusive Reader Service offers**
- ★ **Books available before they're in the shops**

Accepting these FREE books and gift places you under no obligation to buy, you may cancel at any time, even after receiving your free shipment. Simply complete your details below and return the entire page to the address below. You don't even need a stamp!

YES! Please send me 2 free Historical Romance books and a surprise gift. I understand that unless you hear from me, I will receive 4 superb new titles every month for just £3.59 each, postage and packing free. I am under no obligation to purchase any books and may cancel my subscription at any time. The free books and gift will be mine to keep in any case.

H4ZEF

Ms/Mrs/Miss/Mr ....Initials..................
                                                              BLOCK CAPITALS PLEASE
Surname ....
Address..

....

....Postcode.............................

Send this whole page to:
UK: FREEPOST CN81, Croydon, CR9 3WZ